HIS CHRISTMAS ASSIGNMENT

BY
LISA CHILDS

All Rights Reserved including the right of reproduction in whole or in part in any form. This edition is published by arrangement with Harlequin Books S.A. The text of this publication or any part thereof may not be reproduced or transmitted in any form or by any means, electronic or mechanical, including photocopying, recording, storage in an information retrieval system, or otherwise, without the written permission of the publisher.

This book is sold subject to the condition that it shall not, by way of trade or otherwise, be lent, resold, hired out or otherwise circulated without the prior consent of the publisher in any form of binding or cover other than that in which it is published and without a similar condition including this condition being imposed on the subsequent purchaser.

Published in Great Britain 2015
By Mills & Boon, an imprint of HarperCollins Publishers Ltd
1 London Bridge Street, London, SE1 9GF

© 2015 Lisa Childs

ISBN: 978-0-263-91829-8

46-1215

Our policy is to use papers that are natural, renewable and recyclable products and made from wood grown in sustainable forests. The logging and manufacturing processes conform to the legal environmental regulations of the country of origin.

Printed and bound in Spain
by CPI, Barcelona

MILLS & BOON

Published in Great Britain 2015
by Mills & Boon, an imprint of Harlequin (UK) Limited,
Eton House, 18-24 Paradise Road, Richmond, Surrey, TW9 1SR

© 2015 Lisa Childs

ISBN: 978-0-263-91829-8

18-1215

Harlequin (UK) Limited's policy is to use papers that are natural, renewable and recyclable products and made from wood grown in sustainable forests. The logging and manufacturing processes conform to the legal environmental regulations of the country of origin.

Printed and bound in Spain
by CPI, Barcelona

Ever since **Lisa Childs** read her first romance novel (a Mills & Boon story, of course) at age eleven, all she ever wanted was to be a romance writer. With over forty novels published with Mills & Boon, Lisa is living her dream. She is an award-winning, bestselling romance author. Lisa loves to hear from readers, who can contact her on Facebook, through her website, www.lisachilds. com, or her snail-mail address, PO Box 139, Marne, MI 49435, USA.

Special thanks to Patience Bloom for bringing the bodyguards of the Payne Protection Agency to Harlequin Romantic Suspense!

Chapter 1

Voices rose in anger, penetrating the thin walls of Logan Payne's office. Garek Kozminski closed the outside door so softly that it made no sound. He probably could have slammed it and they wouldn't have heard him enter. But he was used to moving silently. In the past, his freedom and even his life had depended upon it.

Not much had changed...

He crossed the reception area and approached Logan's office—not to eavesdrop. Due to the volume of their argument, he could have heard them from the parking lot. Usually Logan didn't yell; as the CEO of Payne Protection, he didn't need to yell to be heard. The other voice was female and easily recognizable to Garek even though Candace Baker didn't usually deign to speak to him.

Apparently she had no problem talking *about* him.

"I can't believe you would consider offering this assignment to Garek Kozminski!"

He had figured Logan had called this meeting about a job. In the year that he'd been working for his brother-in-law he'd had many assignments. Had Candace protested every one?

"He's proven himself over and over again," Logan defended him. "He's a damn good bodyguard!"

"Garek Kozminski is a thief and a killer!" she yelled. "I can't believe you would trust him. I never will!"

Garek felt a twinge in his chest—one he refused to acknowledge as pain. Candace's low opinion wasn't exactly a surprise or unwarranted. And of course he had done nothing to change it; he'd actually done more to provoke it and her.

Logan's voice wasn't just loud but it had gone chillingly cold when he said, "He helped save my life and my brother's life—"

"Because of his criminal connections," she interrupted.

"That's enough," Logan told her. He didn't shout now; he sounded too weary to fight anymore. "Garek and Milek Kozminski are essential members of this team."

"They're your brothers-in-law…"

And maybe that was her real problem: Logan had married Stacy instead of her. She had obviously been in love with her boss for a long time; she'd left the River City Police Department when Logan did in order to join the fledging bodyguard business he'd started a few years before.

"Candace," Logan said, "if you can't work with them, maybe you can't work—"

"Hey!" Garek said as he pushed open the office door

before Logan could finish his ultimatum. He didn't want Candace fired. Sure, she hated Garek. But he didn't hate her.

He wanted her.

He had wanted her since the very first time he'd seen her. She was all long legs and sharp curves and sass. It sparkled in her blue eyes every time she looked at him. But she wouldn't look at him now. Instead she'd tilted her head down so that her jaw-length black hair skimmed across her face, hiding her eyes.

"I'm sorry I'm late," Garek said, although he'd had a good excuse. Someone else had called him about a job, an assignment he might not be able to refuse no matter how much he wanted to...

"It's probably a good thing you were," Logan remarked. "In fact you might want to give us a few more minutes..."

Candace lifted her chin and shook her head. "There's no need. I'm doing what I should have done a year ago..."

A year ago was when Garek had started at the Payne Protection Agency—after his sister had married Logan Payne. He doubted Candace's timing was a coincidence. She had probably wanted to resign then, but no doubt her pride had forced her to stay.

"I'm quitting," she finished.

Logan jumped up from the chair behind his desk and cursed. "Damn it—"

"You were just about to fire me," Candace pointed out. "This is for the best, and we both know it." She turned then and finally faced Garek. Her blue eyes had never been so cold as she stared at him.

Conversely, heat rushed through Garek as his temper ignited. But before he could say anything, Candace pushed past him. He reached out and grasped her arm.

She stared down at his hand. Her voice as cold as her gaze, she said, "Don't touch me. Don't *ever* touch me."

He would have teased her, as he had incessantly for the past year. But he sensed that her coldness was just a thin veneer for deeper emotions.

Candace Baker was strong. She was nearly as tall as he was, and she was all lean muscle. But there was also a vulnerability about her that she desperately tried to hide beneath a tough attitude. Just like the coldness, neither was who she really was.

"I didn't figure you for a quitter," he goaded her.

"You don't know me," she said as she jerked her arm free of his grasp. "And you never will…"

Before he could challenge her claim, she was gone. And he couldn't have that. He just couldn't have that…

"I'm a fool," Candace berated herself as she tossed clothes into the open suitcase on her bed. "I am such a fool…"

Not for quitting. Hell, she should have done that a year ago. She was a fool because she'd waited too long. And mostly because she had let *him* get to her.

How?

She knew what Garek Kozminski was. And unlike everyone else, she wasn't going to forget—because she couldn't let herself forget. In addition to being a killer and a criminal, he was also a flirt. Just a flirt…

That was why he kept teasing her. And looking at her…

She shivered even now thinking about how that silvery-gray gaze was always on her, touching her like a physical caress. He was just teasing her. He couldn't really want to touch her. He couldn't really want *her*.

She was always the *buddy*, the *gal-pal*—never the woman a man actually desired. So he was just messing with her for his own amusement. She was *not* amused. She was furious. And the more he flirted with her, the most frustrated she got. That was why she had lost her temper with her boss.

The doorbell rang, echoing throughout her bedroom from the wooden box on the dark blue painted wall. She doubted it was Logan paying her a visit. He had obviously been about to fire her before Garek had interrupted him.

After what he must have overheard her saying about him, why had Garek tried to stop Logan? Instead of insisting his brother-in-law terminate her on the spot, Garek had actually tried to talk her out of quitting.

But he didn't know her. And around him, she wasn't certain that she knew herself anymore.

The doorbell rang again, or rather incessantly, as if someone were pressing hard on the button. With a sigh she turned away from her bed and headed down the hall. But before she could even reach the front door, it opened. She knew that it had been locked; she always locked her door. And nobody else had a key to her place.

She reached for her holster only to realize she had left it—and her weapon—on her bed with the half-packed suitcase. But why would someone break into her place?

She had nothing of value. And while she had once brought a Payne Protection client to her apartment in order to guard the woman, she was alone now.

But then she was no longer alone as the intruder boldly sauntered into her apartment. He was incredibly tall with lean muscles and blond hair that nearly touched his shoulders. Her breath caught, but she shouldn't have been surprised. Who else would have so easily picked her high-tech lock but Garek Kozminski?

"What the hell do you think you're doing?" she demanded to know.

"I need to talk to you," he replied. But he was looking at her that way he always looked at her—like she was an ice cream cone he wanted to lick.

"So you picked my lock and let yourself inside?"

He shrugged as if breaking and entering was inconsequential. But surely he knew there were consequences for crimes; he had spent time in prison for at least one of the probably many offenses he had committed. "You didn't answer the doorbell."

"There are reasons people don't answer their doorbells," she pointed out. "I could have been gone." If she'd packed faster, she would have been gone. That urge she'd had to run intensified—probably because she had come face-to-face with the reason she wanted to run. That she *needed* to run...

His lips curving into a smug grin, he said, "But you're here."

"Not for long," she said as she spun around and headed back down the hall toward her bedroom. It wasn't too late. She could still escape.

But he followed her. "You're packing? Where the hell are you going?"

She paused as she was about to toss a sweater into the suitcase and realized that she had no idea. She had no plan. She'd only known she needed to leave—to get away for a while. Then she could decide if she wanted to come back. Ever.

"You don't know," he surmised.

"Anywhere you're not," she replied.

He clasped a hand to his heart. "Oh, that hurts—like a knife through the heart." Despite his playful tone, there was something in his gray gaze—something almost like real pain and regret. Did he actually care that she wanted to get away from him?

"Do you have a heart?" she wondered.

"Yes," he replied. "So much so that I convinced Logan you're a better man for this job than I am."

"Man?" Now she knew what he meant about the knife through the heart; a sharp pang in her chest felt as if he'd driven his blade deep.

"Yeah, that assignment you wanted—it's all yours," he magnanimously offered.

She shook her head. "I quit."

"Because you wanted that assignment," he said.

"No, I didn't." She hadn't wanted that assignment; playing bodyguard to some reality star turned B-movie actress held no appeal for her.

His gray eyes narrowed as he stared at her. "You just didn't want me to have it?"

"No, I didn't."

"Why not?" he asked. "What would I *steal* or who would I *kill* if I took this assignment?"

He had definitely overheard her argument with their boss. Her face heated with embarrassment—not over what he'd heard as much as having to explain why she hadn't wanted him guarding a woman who rarely wore clothes on camera, or according to the tabloids, off camera either. She wasn't certain she understood why herself.

She wasn't certain about anything anymore.

She shrugged. "It's a high-profile assignment—one that will raise the awareness of Payne Protection to the national level."

"Last year—all the attempts on Cooper's and Logan's and Parker's lives—raised the awareness of Payne Protection," he pointed out. "That's why an LA actress wants to employ one of our bodyguards. We're the best."

She wanted to argue the "we," but Logan had been right earlier. He and Parker probably wouldn't have survived if not for Garek's help.

"That assignment doesn't require the best," she said— since she suspected the entire need for a bodyguard was just the actress desperately trying to get some more minutes of fame.

"Then why didn't you want me to take it?" he asked.

She shrugged. She wasn't about to admit it had bothered her a *lot* to think of him with a scantily clad reality star. "It doesn't matter now."

"It mattered enough to you," he said, his voice deepening with confusion and concern, "that you quit the job you loved."

"*Loved* is right," she agreed. "Past tense. I don't love it anymore." But that was a lie; she knew it even as she said it. It wasn't that she didn't love her job anymore. It was that she was afraid she might fall in love with something—with *somebody*—else.

"Is that my fault?" he asked. "Or Logan's?"

That was why she couldn't risk falling again— because she had already made enough of a fool of herself over love before. "If this had anything to do with Logan, I would have quit when he married your sister."

"Maybe you were just waiting around for them to

fail," he said. "It's not like anyone really thought they'd last." He chuckled. "Least of all me."

"They have a child together," she said.

"Little Penny," he murmured, his grin widening with obvious love for his two-month-old niece.

Candace's breath caught in her lungs. Garek was so damn handsome it wasn't fair. "You shouldn't be here," she said. "You need to leave."

He glanced around as if just realizing where they were. "I've been wanting to get into your bedroom for a year now…" He stepped closer to the bed and ran his fingertips across the sheets. "Silk…"

She flinched with anger and embarrassment and lashed out, "Of course you'd be surprised a *man* like me would have silk sheets."

"Man?" he repeated, his brow furrowing with confusion. "What the hell are you talking about?"

"You just said I was the best man for the job—"

"I didn't mean it like that," he said.

"Why not?" she asked. "Everybody else thinks of me as just one of the guys."

He shook his head. "I have never thought of you that way." He stepped closer now and jerked her into his arms so quickly that she didn't have time to react. If she'd had time, she would have stopped him—she would have hurt him. Instead she just slammed up tightly against his chest, so that she felt his every breath, his every heartbeat…

"And I have thought of you," he said with an intensity in his gray gaze that had her heart racing with excitement, "every moment since I've met you…"

He lowered his mouth to hers but when their lips were

just a breath apart, he paused and murmured. "And I have thought of doing this…of kissing you…"

And then he did—he kissed her with that intensity she'd seen in his eyes. He kissed her with such passion that she had no doubt he didn't think of her as one of the guys. He thought of her the way she'd been thinking of him.

And she realized something else—it was too late to escape.

It was too late. No matter how hard he tried, Garek was unable to escape his old life. It just kept dragging him back in…

Back into a life lived on the edge, back into a life of danger…

Maybe it was a good thing that Candace had taken off the way she had, because at least he wasn't dragging her in with him. He didn't even know where she had gone— just that she'd finished packing her suitcases sometime that night and she'd left.

Her leaving had hurt more than the fist that slammed hard into his stomach. He coughed and doubled over in pain, but strong arms held him up so the fist could strike him again. Harder.

A curse slipped through his lips along with a slight trickle of blood. He didn't have any internal injuries; he'd just bitten his tongue. Purposely. He'd been beaten harder than this before; hell, his brother had beaten him harder than this before. Of course that had been years ago when they'd been just kids. But he groaned as if he were in agony. The truth was the old man didn't pack the wallop he had once had. But as the godfather of

River City, Michigan, Viktor Chekov commanded respect and fear.

And with good reason. The guy was a killer. And maybe it could finally be proven…

With a jerk of his silver-haired head, Viktor called off his goons so that they released Garek. He dropped to the ground with a groan and complained, "What the hell kind of greeting was that…?"

"How do you expect me to greet you?" Viktor asked. "You just walked away—"

"I didn't just walk away," Garek said. "I was taken off in handcuffs to prison."

A muscle twitched in Viktor's slightly sagging cheek. "That wasn't because of the work you did for me."

"No, it wasn't," Garek agreed. "But I might have avoided jail time if I'd given up what I did for you, or if I'd set you up…" Like he was setting him up now…

Viktor swung again—this time right at Garek's jaw. He could have ducked. But he took it on the chin. And this time he didn't bite his tongue on purpose. He spit out a trickle of blood and wiped his mouth.

"If you'd done that, you would already be dead," Viktor told him.

And this was why he hadn't given up or entrapped Chekov. The sentence he'd served out had been for something that hadn't actually been a crime.

"I never would have betrayed you." Then. But he was a different man now. He was actually a man now whereas when he'd worked for Viktor he'd been a desperate kid, living on the streets.

"You've been out of prison a long time, Garek," Viktor reminded him. "But until tonight you have never come back to the *family*."

Viktor and his organization had never been family. They had preyed on his desperation and utilized the skills he'd learned from his jewelry-thief father before Patek Kozminski had gone to prison.

"I made my sister a promise," he said. And while it had been a struggle at times, he had kept that promise—to never leave her again for either a jail cell or a grave. They had already lost their father—first to prison and then to death. "I vowed to her that I would stay on the straight and narrow."

"You've been working for her husband, that former detective, Logan Payne." Viktor had obviously been keeping track of him over the years.

"Still am," Garek said. Unlike Candace, he wasn't about to quit a job he loved—even for another job that had to be done.

"So why are you here?"

Garek wiped the blood that continued to trickle from the corner of his mouth. Maybe Viktor had hit him harder than he'd thought. "To offer my services."

Viktor glanced at his gargantuan goons and chuckled. "You think I need another bodyguard?"

"I think you need a good one," he said.

The two muscular guys glared at him.

Viktor shook his head. "I am perfectly safe."

"But the people close to you aren't," Garek said. "I heard you recently lost a member of your *family*." Not a blood relative but a very close associate.

That muscle twitched again in Viktor's sagging jaw. "It is too late for Alexander."

Polinsky had been murdered just days ago—shot in the head execution-style. The feds believed that Chekov had been the executioner.

"What about Tori?" Garek asked. "Aren't you concerned for her safety?"

Viktor's face flushed with color at the mention of his daughter's name, so Garek braced himself for another blow. But Viktor didn't swing his fist. Instead his shoulders slumped. "Tori is safe. Safer without you near her."

Garek nodded. "I thought that once, too." Actually he'd thought the opposite. *He* was safer if he was nowhere near her. Viktor loved his little princess so much that he would probably kill anyone who made her unhappy. And Garek hadn't ever seen the young woman happy.

"Why are you *really* here?" Viktor asked. He stared at him again, as if trying to see through him.

"You already checked me for a wire," Garek reminded him. He needed more than a recording with Viktor's admission of guilt. He needed evidence. And he had to get close in order to get his hands on it. "I want to make sure Tori is really safe," he said. "For old times' sake."

"What about that promise to your sister?" Viktor asked, his dark eyes still narrowed with suspicion.

Garek shrugged. "I haven't been happy with my sister for a while now."

"Then why work for her husband?"

"Logan didn't lie to me and Milek," he said. "Stacy's the one who kept secrets." That secret had affected and devastated Milek. While Garek had already forgiven her, he wasn't sure that their brother ever would.

Viktor nodded with understanding. He had obviously kept very apprised of not just Garek's life but Milek's and Stacy's, too. A shiver of unease chilled Garek's skin. He didn't care about himself but he cared that his past association might have put his siblings in danger.

"I think Tori would like it if I hire you," Viktor admitted. "Despite all the years that have passed, I don't think she ever quite got over you." He stepped closer, his hand reached out as if to shake, but he slapped Garek instead. "And if you hurt her again, I will hurt not just you," Viktor threatened, "but everyone close to you."

The unease turned into a shiver of dread and foreboding. It was good that Candace had left town; she would be out of danger. It was just everyone else that Garek had to worry about when he took down the godfather of River City.

Chapter 2

The lock rattled—just a couple of quick clicks—before the doorknob began to turn. Candace reached for her weapon, grasping it tightly in her hand as she approached the door to the condo she'd rented at a ski resort in northern Michigan.

Nobody knew where she was. And nobody here knew her at all. So who the hell was breaking into her unit?

Had Garek tracked her down—like he had that night at her apartment? Her heart rate accelerated, and her hand trembled slightly as memories of that night rushed through with a wave of heat.

Embarrassment—she called the heat. She was embarrassed for being such a fool. She couldn't be feeling desire. Not for Garek Kozminski.

Not again…

She lifted her weapon and pointed the barrel at the

person stepping through the door. Disappointment rushed through her now. Her intruder wasn't Garek.

She recognized the dark curls and eyes of the petite young woman who stepped through the door, her hands raised. "Don't shoot," Nikki Payne said, but her smile belied any fear.

"What the hell are you doing here?" Candace asked. "And why are you breaking in? Did Garek Kozminski teach you how to do that?"

"No, I picked the lock," another voice replied as the door opened farther to Stacy Kozminski-Payne. The woman dropped a packet of lock-picking tools into her purse.

"Doesn't anyone in your family wait for a person to open their door?" Candace asked.

Stacy shrugged. With tawny-colored hair and dark gray eyes, she didn't look that much like her brother Garek but for the quick, sly smile that crossed her face. "Why put you through the trouble of answering the door?"

Since the two women had already stepped inside, Candace closed the door. "See, look, no trouble."

But it was trouble that they were here. Neither of these women was her friend. Nikki had resented that her brothers had chained her to a desk at Payne Protection while they routinely assigned Candace dangerous field work. And Stacy...

Maybe that was more Candace's fault than Stacy's. She had disliked the female Kozminski even more than the males—because Stacy had posed such a threat. Candace had thought the woman had been a threat to Logan Payne's life, but she'd been a threat to his heart instead. Not that Candace had ever had a chance of winning his heart. He'd never been attracted to her the way he'd been to Stacy. The way he still was…

Candace couldn't blame him. Even though Stacy had given birth just a few months ago, she'd regained her petite figure with little effort. Candace wanted to hate her. But Stacy couldn't help that she was beautiful and lovable.

Candace turned away from her and focused on the youngest Payne. "You went to an awful lot of trouble to track me down." Since her brothers had strapped her to a desk, Nikki had become a computer expert.

Nikki shrugged her thin shoulders. "It was no trouble."

"I haven't been using my credit cards." When she'd taken off, she'd taken out enough cash to cover her expenses for months. She'd only been gone a couple of weeks.

"You ran a red light," Nikki reminded her.

Candace's face heated with embarrassment over her transgression. She'd been distracted—thanks to Garek Kozminski.

"I was driving a rental…" She had been so careful to cover her tracks, so that no one would find her. Or at least so she could convince herself that no one could find her. Then she wouldn't have been disappointed if no one had shown up.

Nikki snorted. "Ticket goes on your driving record but the registration is also listed for the vehicle you were driving at the time of the violation. And the rental has a GPS locator. So you were easy to find."

Despite her best efforts…

"Why?"

"The ticket," Nikki said. "The first one you've ever gotten, by the way."

Like Candace didn't know that. "I meant *why* did you track me down?" She was pretty sure it hadn't been her idea. "Who asked you to?"

Garek? But then why hadn't he come himself?

"I did," Stacy replied.

"You asked her to track me down?" she asked. "Why? To make sure I stay gone?"

Stacy laughed. "I can understand why you might think that…"

Candace wouldn't have blamed Stacy if she had asked Logan to fire her. She—and everyone else—knew that Candace had been in love with her boss. What wife would be okay with a woman working with her husband when the woman was in love with him? A woman who was very secure in his love.

Stacy confirmed this when she continued, "But I actually wanted to find you to bring you back."

Panic, at the thought of facing everyone again, pressed on Candace's chest. And she shook her head. "No, I should have quit a year ago."

"But you didn't," Stacy said.

"I should have," she repeated. Not because of the embarrassment over everyone knowing how she'd felt about Logan. She'd endured worse things than embarrassment.

Before joining the River City PD, she'd been an army reservist who'd done a tour in Iraq. And in the River City PD, she'd done a stint in vice—dressing up like a prostitute. That hadn't lasted long, though, because few johns had tried picking her up. It had been quite the joke in the department. She had been the joke. But she hadn't left the River City Police Department until Logan had.

No, there were worse things than embarrassment—like heartbreak.

She should have left because of Garek.

But if she had left…

Her face heated again and this time it wasn't with embarrassment. Her entire body flushed as she remembered that kiss and what had followed…

She shook her head, as much to dislodge those memories as in refusal of Stacy's invitation to return. "I can't go back," she told her. "Logan must have told you…" She doubted he kept anything from the woman he loved. "If I hadn't quit, he was going to fire me."

"You don't have to work for Logan," Nikki said.

Candace laughed. "He's the boss." And not just because he was the oldest Payne sibling but also because it had been his idea to start the protection agency. It was his business.

"He's the CEO but he's franchising the business," Stacy explained. "After all the publicity last year, Logan felt as if he needed to expand to keep up with the demand for Payne Protection."

"Cooper and Parker will each have their own franchise now," Nikki said. "I'm going to work for Cooper. You could, too. He's bringing in his own team of former marines."

Candace hadn't been a marine. But she had served.

"Or with Parker," Nikki continued, her voice lilting with enthusiasm. "He's recruiting former cops. You'd fit in there, too."

"Logan would like you to come back to work for him," Stacy said.

Candace shook her head again. If that were true, he would have come himself; he wouldn't have sent his

wife and sister to find her. He might not even know that
they'd been looking for her. So it was just curiosity that
had her asking, "What's his team going to be?"

"Family," Stacy replied.

"I'm not family," she said. "And that was made very
clear to me."

"Is that why you left?" Nikki asked. "Because you
thought there was too much nepotism—with me and
Parker and Cooper?"

"It wasn't the Paynes that were the problem," Stacy
said, answering for her before Candace had had the
chance. "It was the Kozminskis. *We* were why she quit."

Candace flinched at how petty she sounded. She
wished that had been the reason she'd quit: pettiness.
But fear was what had compelled her to quit. She hadn't
realized it at the time—because she had never acknowledged fear before. She wouldn't have become a soldier or
a cop if she had. So because she'd never acknowledged
it before, she hadn't recognized it.

"Not all of you," Candace said. "I have no problem
with Milek. I actually feel sorry for him."

Stacy flinched now and quietly admitted, "I made
a mistake."

Nikki glanced at her sister-in-law, and while there was
affection, there was also disapproval in her dark eyes.
"You kept a *secret*—a really *big* secret—from him." The
youngest Payne hated secrets and didn't understand that
there were reasons to keep them. To Nikki, there was
only black and white.

Candace understood gray. She had kept more than her
share of other people's secrets; that was another reason
that she was always the buddy—the friend. She knew

too much but she kept her mouth shut. "It wasn't Stacy's secret to tell."

A soft gasp of surprise slipped through Stacy's lips. "I'm glad Nikki tracked you down."

Candace shrugged. "It doesn't matter that you did. I'm not going back." Not to Payne Protection. Maybe not even to River City.

"Why not?" Nikki asked the question.

Candace suspected Stacy knew. The woman's dark gray gaze was focused on her as she studied her intensely. What had Garek told her?

She fought the urge to blush. Surely, he wouldn't have told his sister...

But what if he'd told anyone else or everyone else? Despite her best efforts, her face flushed again. So she turned away from them to gaze out the window. Snow drifted softly to the ground but melted as soon as it hit the grass. The weather was unseasonably warm for December—which had caused the ski resort to be unusually quiet. "I like it here."

It was quiet. It was safe. Due to the weather leaving the slopes more green than white, it was nearly deserted. So it was boring as hell.

"Why?" Nikki asked the question again, her voice full of confusion. She wanted excitement—had been fighting Logan for years to put her in the field. She didn't understand that sometimes boredom was good.

"It's pretty here," Stacy answered for her as she stepped closer to the window and Candace and watched the big fluffy flakes fall onto the grass. "And it's peaceful. I can see its appeal."

Candace turned back toward them. Even if she ignored them, they weren't going away. She might as well hear them out.

Unconvinced, Nikki shook her head. "I can't. You need to come back, Candace. The agency is taking off right now. We're busy as hell. We need you."

Stacy said nothing—to Candace. Instead she turned to her sister-in-law and asked, "Will you give us a few minutes alone?"

Nikki nodded and headed toward the door. "Hope your pitch works better than mine did."

Candace waited until the door closed behind Nikki then asked, "Why would you give me a pitch? Why would you care whether or not I came back?"

"Because I care about my brother."

Candace had never had a problem recognizing fear in others. She heard it now in Stacy's voice. "What are you talking about?"

And what had Garek told her?

"I'm losing him."

"Milek?" That was who they were talking about? Candace had never had a problem with the younger Kozminski brother, but she'd never had a relationship with him either. Not that she had a relationship with Garek either. She'd had just that one, unforgettable night...

Stacy's breath escaped in a shaky little sigh. "I think I already lost Milek. And now I'm losing Garek, too."

"Have they quit, too?"

Stacy shook her head. "No. They both get along with Logan."

Candace couldn't suppress a smile. Men were so simple. They could go from being archenemies one minute to best friends the next. Maybe that was why she'd always gotten along better with them than women. "Then

I don't understand what you want me to do. If Logan can't help you mend fences with your brothers, I certainly can't."

"I don't want you to help me mend fences," Stacy said.

Her patience worn thin, she asked, "Then what *do* you want?"

Stacy's dark gray eyes glistened as tears welled in them. "I want you to help me stop Garek from getting himself killed."

While she hated to admit it, she found herself leaping to his defense. "He's handled himself well in a lot of dangerous situations. He'll be fine."

"Not this time," Stacy insisted. "Not with *these* people."

"Did he take that assignment with the starlet?" That was another reason she'd gone off the grid and rented a place with no TV and no internet. She hadn't wanted anyone or anything to find her—to disturb her peace. If only she'd really found peace…

Stacy shook her head. "No. Logan sent Milek. Garek had already taken another assignment—one he sought out on his own. He's going back to his old life, Candace. He's working for Viktor Chekov."

Candace should have felt vindicated. It was what she'd been saying about him all along—that he hadn't changed. But over the past year she had watched him closely, nearly as closely as he'd watched her, and she'd never seen any evidence that he was still a thief. He'd worked hard—nearly as hard as he'd teased and flirted with her.

Had she actually been right about him?

Her legs weakened, and she felt the need to sit down. So she dropped onto the edge of the rental's lumpy couch. Of course he'd always had that effect on her—that ability to make her knees weak—no matter how much she had fought her attraction to him. She should have kept fighting.

"What does any of that have to do with me?" she wondered.

"He didn't take that assignment until you left," Stacy said, and now there was anger and resentment along with tears in her eyes. "You drove him back to his old life."

She laughed at his sister's outrageous claim. "That's ridiculous." Garek would have actually had to care about her for her leaving to affect him. And it just wasn't possible that he did.

"I know my brother," Stacy said. "I know he really liked you. But you never gave him a chance."

He definitely hadn't told his sister anything about that night.

"So he's gone back to his old life," Stacy continued. "To Viktor Chekov. Those people are dangerous, Candace."

She didn't need to tell her. As a former cop, Candace knew exactly how dangerous Chekov was. While he'd never been convicted, he had committed every crime on the books. The last news she'd heard as she'd driven out of the city had been a report that Chekov's right-hand man had been executed. While the reporter hadn't dared to speculate, it was clear that everyone thought Chekov was the killer.

"They're really dangerous," Stacy said, her voice shaking with fear. "Garek's in trouble."

Garek was in trouble—more trouble than he could have even imagined. He couldn't get Candace out of his mind. And he couldn't afford the distraction right now—not with the dangerous game he was playing.

What if he'd been followed to this meeting? He'd watched the rearview mirror and hadn't noticed anyone tailing him. But instead of the road behind him, he'd kept seeing Candace: her blue eyes wide with shock as she'd stared up at him, her lips red and slightly swollen from his kiss.

What if he'd missed a tail? He reached beneath his jacket and closed his hand around his weapon as he stepped out of the SUV. Nobody was going to get the jump on him. But he still could have been followed. And if someone saw him with the person he was meeting…

From an alley between two buildings, beams of light flashed. On and off. On and off.

Garek glanced around the deserted industrial area. Had anyone else seen the signal?

He could detect no movement but the December wind tossing snowflakes around the night sky. Maybe he hadn't been followed. But he still had that uneasy feeling, that tingling between his shoulder blades that made him feel as if he was being watched.

The lights flashed again. Of course he was being watched by the person who waited for him inside the other SUV. Garek glanced around once more before heading toward the alley. He moved, as he always did, quickly and silently—keeping to the shadows.

Slipping between the SUV and the building beside it, he pulled open the passenger's door. No dome light flashed; the person he was meeting knew all the tricks of maintaining his anonymity. In his line of work, he wouldn't have lived long if he hadn't.

FBI agent Nicholas Rus had done a lot of undercover work in his career with the Bureau. Before Garek had agreed to work with the man, he'd checked out his background. He didn't care that Rus was related to the Paynes—that with his black hair and blue eyes, he looked eerily like the twins Logan and Parker. The FBI agent hadn't been raised with them, by Penny Payne, so Garek questioned his integrity. He didn't know too many people who were beyond corruption—besides the Paynes.

"Why you acting so nervous?" Rus asked as Garek slid into the passenger's seat. "I didn't notice any tail coming in behind you. Did you see a suspicious vehicle?"

"No." But that didn't mean that he hadn't been followed. He peered through the tinted windshield, trying to see beyond the alley.

The snow had thickened, now, from flurries to sheets of white. The mild winter was over; the cold and snow coming in earnest now. He couldn't see anything out there anymore. But whoever was watching him wouldn't be able to see either.

Rus sighed and murmured, "Guess you'd be an idiot if you weren't nervous…"

"I was an idiot to let you talk me into this," Garek said.

"You're the only one who could do this," Rus said. "Viktor Chekov wouldn't have let anyone else inside, and there's no time. We have to recover the murder weapon before he ditches it."

"If he hasn't already," Garek said. "He'd be a fool if he hasn't." And Viktor Chekov was nobody's fool.

Rus shrugged. "The witness says he hasn't."

"The witness could be lying." Especially if the witness was who Garek suspected it was. Viktor would not have killed in front of her.

Rus shrugged again. "That's why we need the murder weapon."

"We need more," Garek said. "We need an admission of guilt." Because that witness would never testify—for a few reasons.

Rus laughed. "If you think Viktor Chekov is going to confess, you actually might be an idiot."

"He won't confess to authorities," Garek agreed.

"You think you can get him to confess to you?"

"Confess?" Garek shook his head. "Threaten? Brag?" He nodded. "Yeah, I can get him to do one of those."

A muscle twitched along Rus's jaw he clenched it so tightly. He hadn't been raised with his half brothers but yet he shared some of their tells when it came to stress.

The special agent asked, "Is he still having his guys check you for a wire every time you show up for a protection duty shift?"

Garek nodded. As he'd said, the man was nobody's fool; he knew not to trust Garek.

Rus's irritation escaped in a ragged sigh. "He'll kill you if he catches you wearing one."

Garek nodded again. But *his* life was the least of his concerns. He was more concerned about his family.

At least Candace was gone. He didn't have to worry about her. He only had to worry about getting her off his mind so that he wouldn't get so careless that he'd wind up dead.

Rus gripped the SUV steering wheel so tightly that his knuckles turned white. "I want this guy. I *really* want this guy. But if your family knew that you were risking your life to help me…"

"They're your family, too," Garek reminded him. Actually they were more Rus's family since he was a blood relative albeit not a legitimate one. Garek was only related through marriage, and his sister's at that.

Rus shook his head. "They don't feel that way—at least not all of them."

Garek knew the Paynes well enough to know who had welcomed Rus and who hadn't. Nikki hadn't. But of all of the Paynes, Penny had welcomed him the most—despite his being the evidence of her late husband's betrayal.

But that was the kind of woman Penny was—the kind who'd taken an interest in the kids of the man who'd confessed to killing her husband. She had welcomed the Kozminskis as warmly as she had Nicholas Rus.

"Give them time," he said. While Penny had accepted Garek and his siblings, it had taken the other Paynes more time.

"If something happens to you while you're carrying out this assignment for me…" Rus shook his head.

Garek wanted to assure the FBI agent that nothing would happen to him, but he knew Viktor Chekov too well to make any promises. "I'll let you know when I get the evidence you need…"

If I'm alive…

Rus must have had the same thought because he reached out and squeezed Garek's shoulder. "I appreciate your doing this."

Garek shrugged off his gratitude and his hand. "It's like you said. Nobody else could do it."

"But that doesn't mean you had to agree. You could have refused."

He could have. He might have…if Candace hadn't

taken off on him the way she had. But she was gone and with her any excuse he might have had to not finally do the right thing—what he should have done fifteen years ago. Take down Viktor Chekov.

He pushed open the passenger door and stepped out into the snow and the cold. "I have nothing to lose."

"Just your life…"

He softly shut the door and hurried away from the alley. He moved quickly now, not so he wasn't noticed, but so that he didn't freeze off his ass. Christmas was only a few weeks away. Hopefully he would wrap up this assignment before then, so that he could spend an honest holiday with his family.

And Candace?

Where was she?

Other than on his mind? She was always on his mind, staring up at him with such confusion and desire. Her pupils had dilated so only a thin rim of blue circled them. She'd wanted him, too. But then why had she left?

Dimly he heard the SUV pull out of the alley and drive away. But he didn't glance back as he hurried toward his vehicle. He didn't look back until it was too late—until he'd finally heard the footsteps rushing across the asphalt behind him.

He had been followed. He had been watched—just like he'd feared.

Before he could turn around, a body connected with his and slammed him into the side of his SUV. His head struck metal, and like the snowflakes, spots danced across his field of vision—momentarily blinding him. He had no idea who had attacked him and no idea if he would survive the attack.

Chapter 3

Candace was home. In River City again, at least. Raised an army brat, she'd never had a real home. But she had lived in this city longer than any others. So it was probably as close to home as she had ever come.

She had already done what she'd had to do. Not what she'd wanted to do. She wasn't sure what she actually wanted anymore.

Her hand trembled as she slid the key in the lock and turned the knob. But Candace hesitated before pushing open her apartment door.

He was gone.

She knew that. After all, two weeks had passed and she knew what he'd been doing during that time. Sort of. As much as anyone ever knew what Garek Kozminski was doing. He wasn't still in her apartment. But he'd been there the last time she had been.

So she stepped carefully inside, but she didn't stop in the living room. She carried her suitcase directly down the hall to the bedroom.

Some of the clothes she hadn't packed had fallen to the floor around the bed. And on the bed the silk sheets were as tangled and twisted as she—as *they*—had left them. Her face heated with embarrassment. What had she done? And why the hell had she come back here? To the scene of the crime. The scene of her stupidity.

The scene of the most exciting night of her life. And Candace, as a soldier and a police officer, had lived an exciting life.

Her breath shuddered out in a ragged sigh—like it had that night he'd kissed her. She should have stopped him then. She'd pulled back. But then he'd looked at her—like no one else had ever looked at her—with such hunger and desire. And instead of shoving him away, she had looped her arms around his neck and pulled his head down for another kiss.

She had been a fool that night. And she'd been an even bigger fool to come back. Garek Kozminski had gotten what he'd wanted from her. He wanted nothing else—or he would have been the one who'd tracked her down. Not his sister.

She shouldn't have let Stacy get to her. She should have just stayed away. Not that she doubted what his sister had told her. She believed that Garek had gone back to his life. What was the saying—once a thief always a thief?

But she had found no evidence that he'd been stealing anything since he'd been a teenager. Was he just so good that he had never gotten caught?

Or that lucky?

If he was working for Chekov again, his luck would probably run out. Like Stacy had said, he was in danger. Candace just didn't believe there was anything she could do to stop him. Or to protect him.

By coming back, she had only put herself in danger—her heart and maybe even her life.

"What the hell are you doing?" Garek asked when his vision cleared and he recognized his brother as the one who'd knocked him into the side of his SUV.

"What the hell are *you* doing?" Milek asked, his voice raised and sharp with anger.

Garek blinked again—making sure he was really seeing his brother. Milek didn't get angry; he didn't lose his temper anymore—not even when he had every right. "What's wrong with you?"

Milek shoved him back, knocking him against the SUV again. "What's wrong with you?"

"I don't know what you're talking about," Garek answered honestly. His brother wasn't making a whole lot of sense. "And how the hell did you find me here? Did you follow me?"

He had suspected someone might have, but he hadn't seen anyone behind him. He'd been distracted, though. But…

"Did you follow me?" he asked again.

Milek snorted. "How else would I have found you? Of course I followed you. You're not as good as you think are."

His brother must have been right—about Garek's not detecting a tail. But maybe that wasn't the only thing Garek wasn't as good at as he'd thought he was. Candace had left that night—after they'd finally given in to the attraction that had burned between them for a year.

At least he'd felt it.

"*I* taught you everything you know about following someone," Garek reminded him. That was why Milek was so good. "And I may have noticed you were behind me, if I'd known you were back already."

Milek had taken the assignment Candace hadn't wanted him to take—protecting the reality star. Why hadn't she wanted him to take it?

She had never explained her real reason. Jealousy?

But if she'd cared, she wouldn't have run away—like she had sometime in the night. She wouldn't have left him if she'd really wanted him.

"The girl wasn't in any danger," Milek said. "It was just a publicity ploy."

Which was what Candace had suspected. The woman was so astute. How had she never realized how he'd felt about her—how he'd felt about her for nearly a year?

"It took you two weeks to figure out it was all a publicity stunt?" Garek teased.

Milek shook his head. "It only took me two minutes."

"So you milked the assignment to enjoy the weather in California?" Garek gestured at the snow. "I don't blame you." He would have razzed him about staying for the starlet. But it was too soon to tease Milek about women.

"I might have stayed longer," Milek admitted, "if Stacy hadn't called me."

Garek shook his head, both frustrated with and sympathetic to his sister. "I told her to back off and give you time."

"She didn't call me about *that*," Milek said.

That was the single most devastating thing that had ever happened to his brother. So it was no wonder he didn't want to talk about it; he probably couldn't.

Garek had tried a couple of times to get him to talk, and Milek had asked him to move out of the warehouse apartment they'd once shared. He'd moved into an apartment while he'd looked for something more permanent.

Milek continued, "She called me to talk about you."

Garek chuckled. "Sounds like she was just looking for any excuse to reach out to you." And he couldn't blame Stacy for trying. He wanted to try again, but he was worried his brother would cut him completely out of his life then.

Milek shook his head. "It wasn't an excuse to talk to me. She didn't want to call me. So she hesitated—maybe too long. How deep are you in?"

Garek sucked in a breath and then choked on the cold air. "I—I don't know what you're talking about."

Milek shoved him again. But Garek was already backed up as far as he could go against the SUV. "You're working for Viktor Chekov again."

"Not like I used to," Garek assured him. And he felt a flash of pain that his sister and brother had assumed he had. Didn't they know him better than that? He could understand other people thinking the worst of him; he'd done nothing to correct misconceptions of him. In fact with Candace, he had enjoyed playing the bad boy with her—to tease her and irritate her. But he hadn't been a boy for a long while—if ever. "It's an assignment—a protection job."

Milek cursed him. "You brought Viktor to Payne Protection as a client. You sought out this assignment. I'm going to ask you again—what the hell are you up to?"

Garek opened his mouth, ready to spin the situation the way he had to Logan, so the CEO of Payne Protection had agreed to take on the Chekov family as a client. But Milek knew Garek hadn't been in love with Tori—like he had professed to Logan. His brother would immediately know he was lying.

So he admitted, "I'm not supposed to tell anyone what I'm really up to."

"Is that what whoever you just met in the alley has been telling you?"

Milek hadn't seen Rus. To keep the FBI agent out of it, Garek could lie about whom he'd just met. He hesitated as he considered it.

And Milek asked, "Don't you think I've had enough secrets kept from me?"

That question struck Garek harder than Milek had when he'd knocked him into his vehicle. He nodded in agreement. "But it's hard to be totally open and honest when you're working undercover."

The tension eased from Milek's shoulders and he breathed a sigh of relief. "That was Special Agent Nicholas Rus who you met in the SUV in the alley."

"Nobody can know."

Milek tensed again. "You're trying to take down Viktor Chekov?" The anger was back in his voice as he asked, "Are you crazy?"

"Maybe…"

But a man had been murdered. Recently. Before that there had been others. Lives Garek could have saved had he taken Chekov down fifteen years ago. He hadn't been brave enough then; he'd been a scared kid who'd given in to threats. But now he was a man, and he knew if Chekov wasn't stopped, there would be more lives lost.

"But it needs to be done," Garek said. "He has to be stopped, or he's just going to keep killing. He should have been stopped a long time ago."

"Killing…" Milek murmured.

Garek wanted to bite his tongue again—that he'd brought up a subject too close to his brother's wounded heart. "I'm sorry…"

Milek raised his voice again, which shook with anger. "Garek, this is too dangerous."

In the spirit of being honest, he had to admit, "And it's not dangerous just for me. He threatened if my assignment is more about betraying him than protecting Tori, he won't just hurt me. He'll hurt my family, too. He'll hurt everyone I care about."

Garek shuddered but not because of the cold; he shuddered because he remembered the coldness with which Viktor had so casually uttered that threat. But he knew it hadn't been idle.

"If you want to do this or you feel you have to, don't worry about me," Milek said. "I can take care of myself."

His brother always had.

"And Logan will protect Stacy just like he did before," Garek said. He was trying to assure himself that he hadn't put everyone he loved in danger. "You'll all be fine…"

But then Milek warned him, "I'm not the only one Stacy reached out to…"

Garek raised his brows. "Who else is there?"

Since their father had gone to prison, it had been just the three of them. Their mother didn't count; she had never been there for them and then she'd turned on them. He wouldn't have gone to prison and Milek juvenile detention if she hadn't testified against them. They had an aunt and uncle, too, but they had only wanted to exploit them—like Viktor Chekov had.

"Candace," Milek said. "Stacy was going to track her down and bring her back to River City."

"Damn her." He loved Stacy, but she had interfered in their lives too much. Her interference had cost Milek everything that mattered to him. What would it cost Garek?

Candace?

Logan couldn't stop staring at his wife—with his usual awe at her beauty. But he was also in awe of her powers of persuasion.

"How did you do it?" he asked.

She paused with her fingertips on buttons at the front of her blouse. "You did this," she said. "You threw me down on your desk the minute I stepped inside your office."

He grinned unabashedly. "That is true," he admitted. Then he leaned down and gently skimmed his mouth across hers; her lips were slightly swollen from his previous kisses. "But that's because you're irresistible. And beautiful and amazing…"

Beneath his, her lips curved into a smile. "I love you."

"And I love you," he said. He pulled back and leaned his forehead against hers. "I missed you."

"I guess." She gestured at the papers and pens strewn across his floor. He'd swept them off when he'd pulled her down onto the mahogany surface with him. "Nikki and I were only gone a couple of days."

"That's a couple too many," he said.

She nodded in agreement. "It was." Disappointment darkened her already dark gray eyes. She stepped back from him and uttered a heavy sigh. "And it was for nothing. I couldn't convince Candace to come home."

He skimmed his fingers along her bottom lip and tilted it back up. "You were so successful she actually beat you home."

"Really?" Stacy's eyes brightened, and her whole face lit up with a smile. He hoped their daughter took after her beautiful mother. "She must have packed right up and headed back. Nikki and I only stopped at an outlet mall for some early Christmas shopping."

"Nikki, of course…"

Stacy arched a brow. "You wondered how I found Candace on my own?"

"I don't doubt you could have done it," he said. His wife was as brilliant as she was beautiful.

"I didn't have any time to lose, though, so I asked for Nikki's help."

His sister was as brilliant as his wife. If only she could be happy doing what she did best—instead of nagging for dangerous field work.

Then Stacy's words sank in and he asked, "What's the urgency in bringing Candace back? I know I've been griping about not having her on my team, but…"

She smiled and kissed his cheek. "You think I did this for you. That's sweet."

He grinned at her teasing. "And obviously off base. Then why did you want Candace back so desperately that you and Nikki tracked her down and convinced her to come ask for her job back?"

Stacy cupped his cheek now in her soft palm and gave him a pitying smile. "Men are so oblivious."

He was used to his wife giving him a hard time; they'd been going at each other since they'd been teenagers. If only he'd realized sooner most of that resentment and anger had been attraction and passion...

"What am I missing?" he asked.

"Candace didn't come back for her job."

He tilted his head. "Then why did she ask me for it?" Even though he had been able to tell that it had been really difficult for her to bury her pride and ask...

Stacy shrugged. "I guess she needs the job. But it's not what she really wants."

Logan tensed with dread. He had been oblivious once before, totally unaware the woman he had considered a friend and only a friend had had a crush on him. "What are you up to?"

Stacy patted his cheek and laughed. "Sweetheart, once again—not about you. Candace has been over you for a long time. Not that I think her feelings even ran that deep or she wouldn't have been able to continue working for you after you fell for me. Nobody's that much of a masochist."

That was what he'd thought, too. That everyone had exaggerated what might have been Candace having a small crush on the boss.

"No, Candace came back for Garek."

He cursed as his dread rushed back.

Stacy's smile faltered, and she insisted, "That's a good thing."

Logan shook his head. "No, no, it's not."

Now hurt flashed in her dark gray eyes. "Do you think she's too good for my brother?"

He cursed. "That's not it at all. You know I love your brothers." Which hadn't always been the case. But they'd helped save his and his brothers' lives.

Then he'd gotten to know them and had learned how

hard they'd worked to build new lives for themselves. They'd also brought him a ton of business—better business than Chekov. But because Garek had brought him so many clients, he hadn't been able to refuse to take on Chekov when his brother-in-law had asked—especially once he'd explained to him why—which was also why Logan hoped that Candace hadn't come back for Garek.

"She's the only one who will be able to get through to him," Stacy insisted, "to get him away from Viktor Chekov." She shuddered—with revulsion and fear—as she uttered the mobster's name.

"What makes you think that?"

"Because she's the reason he went back to that life," Stacy said. "When she quit Payne Protection and left town, he was devastated."

Logan snorted. "He's Garek. Nothing devastates Garek." He'd never known a more resilient human being. The guy had been through hell and back and never lost his sense of humor.

"She did."

He shook his head. "You're wrong."

"He was crazy about her," Stacy insisted.

"Garek flirts with every female," Logan said. "He's even flirted with my mom."

"Penny's a hottie," Stacy said with a giggle. "But Candace was different. He tried to be a better man for her. For the past year he hadn't even dated another woman. That's why, when she took off, he was devastated—so devastated he went back to his former life."

Logan needed to find a way for her to make up with her brothers. She was so estranged from them that she didn't even know them anymore.

"No," he told her. "That's not why he went back to his old life."

"It's not?" She furrowed her brow and studied him as if he had been holding out on her. "What do you know?"

"Only what Garek told me," he said. "He had a reason for asking for this assignment with the Chekovs." One that had convinced Logan to take on a mobster as a client. "He wanted this assignment so he could protect Tori Chekov."

Stacy shrugged. "Why?"

"Because he's in love with her."

He heard a gasp, but it hadn't slipped through his wife's lips. He turned to the open door of his office. Had they forgotten to shut it? He'd wanted his wife so badly he hadn't even noticed. His desire for her only seemed to intensify the longer they were together.

Candace Baker stood in the doorway, and all the color drained from her face, leaving it stark with shock. And he realized his wife had been at least half right. Candace had come back for Garek.

Now, having overheard what she had, would she quit again? The news had obviously affected her.

While he didn't want to lose her as a team member again, he didn't want to lose her as a friend either. They had been friends for years. So he was worried about her—worried about her safety if she were to stay. It would probably be the wisest and the safest thing for her to leave again.

If Tori Chekov thought Candace could potentially be a threat to her relationship with Garek, she might have her father take care of the female bodyguard.

Permanently…

Chapter 4

At that ski cabin in Northern Michigan, Candace had gotten her quota of quiet. She might have needed it then—the boring to outweigh the excitement she'd had and left. Now she needed noise, and it had to be loud enough to drown out the voice in her head that kept calling her an idiot.

She had found it at the downtown club. The music was so loud that it wasn't heard; it was felt. It throbbed low in her body, beating as hard as her heart. But her heart hadn't started beating that hard—that frantically—until she'd seen *him*.

On some level, she'd probably known Garek would be here—since Viktor Chekov owned the club. It was probably why she'd gone home and changed after she'd awkwardly stumbled into the middle of that conversation at the Payne Protection Agency. She'd told herself that she'd just wanted to look her best to make herself feel better.

But she'd wanted to make him feel bad.

As if Garek would care…

He hadn't sought her out. And now she knew why. He'd reunited with the girl he'd loved since they'd been teenagers. Or so Logan thought. Stacy had denied her husband's claim even though it was apparently what Garek had confided in him.

Logan had broken that confidence because he hadn't wanted her wasting her time or her heart again—like she'd wasted it on him.

Yet here she was, wasting her time some more—coming down to a club to torture herself with the sight of Garek and his girlfriend. At least her martini was good. Over the rim of the glass, Candace studied them. They were a distance away since they sat at some raised-up, roped-off table near the dance floor and she sat at the crowded bar.

She'd been lucky someone had given up his seat to her. He'd even bought her martini. He stood near her now, his mouth near her ear as he tried talking to her. She couldn't hear anything, and it had nothing to do with the music. It had everything to do with that voice in her head—the one that continued calling her names.

Tori Chekov was as beautiful as Candace had suspected she'd be. Petite. Curvy. With long curly blond hair. No one would treat this woman like one of the guys—or a buddy.

But Garek…

He wasn't flirting and joking as he usually did. Instead he seemed tense, on edge—more cognizant of his surroundings than of the woman who sat beside him. He acted as if he was on a job—not a date.

But he looked like he could be dressed for a date. In a black shirt and pants, he looked dangerously sexy. His blond hair gleamed like gold under the strobe lights from the dance floor.

In Candace's mind flashed the image of how she'd seen him last, lying naked in her bed, moonlight gleaming off his bare skin. He was almost too beautiful to be a man, but he was masculine, too—all toned muscle and chiseled edges.

How had she left him lying there alone? How had she just walked away?

But she hadn't just walked. She'd grabbed her half-packed suitcase, and she'd run.

Garek continued his visual surveillance of the club—his attention on everything but the woman beside him. She knew he was assessing the entire building for possible threats like the vigilant bodyguard he was. In that assessment, he turned and his gaze met hers.

The air between them vibrated like the bass of the music. There was an electricity—a connection so overwhelming that she had that urge to run again.

And this time she needed to keep running.

"Damn it!" the words slipped involuntarily through Garek's lips as he leaped to his feet.

One of Chekov's goons reached beneath his jacket for his weapon. "Is there a problem? A threat?"

Tori reached out and grasped his arm. "What's wrong, Garek?"

He shook his head and lied, "No problem..."

But he had a problem. She sat at the bar, her legs endlessly long and sexy beneath the short hem of her strapless dress. It was red and tight and so damn sexy that it was drawing every man in the club to her.

One of those men placed his hand on her bare shoulder, and Garek ground his teeth together as jealousy and rage coursed through him. He wanted to break every finger in that man's hand for having the audacity to touch *his* woman.

Candace was *his*.

But he couldn't stake his claim—not without risking her life when Garek put Viktor Chekov behind bars. Because even from behind bars Viktor would be dangerous—maybe even more dangerous because he would be out for vengeance.

And if he wanted to hurt Garek…

He was already hurting, every muscle tense with desire and fear for Candace. He had never wanted any woman the way he wanted her. And making love with her once had only increased the intensity of that desire to madness. His body throbbed with the need to be with her again—to be inside her—because now he knew how amazing it was. How amazing they were together…

"You want me to get rid of her?" a voice in his ear asked.

He touched his fingers, which shook slightly, to his earpiece.

"What?" he asked, fear gripping his heart in a tight fist.

"I can get rid of her," the man offered.

Because the danger was real, he thought immediately she would be gotten rid of for good—forever. But then he remembered the man talking to him wasn't one of Chekov's hired goons. It was his brother's voice in his ear, offering to help—not hurt.

Not that Candace wouldn't get hurt. Hell, knowing Candace, Milek might get hurt, too, if he tried to get rid of her. The woman wouldn't go anywhere unless she wanted to. She was stubborn and strong.

So why had she left him that night?

He wanted to know. Had to know...

"I'll handle her," Garek said, although he doubted he was any more capable than Milek of getting Candace to go anywhere she didn't want to. As a former soldier and cop, the woman had skills. "I need you to watch Tori."

Her hand tightened on his arm. "Nobody needs to watch me," she said, her tone as waspish as it had been since he'd taken over as her bodyguard.

She hadn't welcomed him back into her life. In fact he wasn't sure from whom he had more to fear: her or her father. Viktor had accepted his explanation for why he'd stayed away after he'd been paroled. Tori wouldn't even let him explain. She had barely spoken to him over the past two weeks—which was probably fortunate for him, given how nasty she sounded when she did speak to him.

"It's for your protection," Garek reminded her.

She pulled her hand away from his arm and sat back in her chair. He didn't know why she'd wanted to come here. She didn't dance. She didn't drink. She didn't even seem to enjoy the music. Hell, she didn't seem to enjoy anything anymore. But then, had she ever?

He wasn't sure if he ever remembered Tori Chekov being happy—even when they'd been younger. He hadn't had the chance to be a kid; his father and uncle had recruited him into the family business at a young age. And then when his father had gone to prison, he'd gone to work for Tori's father. She hadn't had to work, though. Ever.

Her father made sure she had everything she wanted. So why wasn't she happy?

But then Milek—finally—approached the table, and she actually smiled. "It's great to see you. Come sit with me," she implored him.

Milek slid past Garek to take the chair he'd vacated, and his brow was furrowed in bewilderment. Maybe Tori's warm greeting had confused him since she'd never been that friendly to him before. Or maybe he was worried that Garek intended to speak to Candace.

He wanted to do more than speak to her. He wanted to do everything he'd done to her that night—over and over again. But she'd run from him.

She wasn't running now—which was good, since it had taken Milek too long to take over for him on protection duty. And the club was crowded, so crowded he had to push his way through a crush of bodies to reach the bar.

For a moment he thought she'd slipped away, but then a man moved and he saw her sitting on that stool, her long legs crossed. She had painted her lips as red as her dress, and they were curved into a smile as she looked up at the man standing over her.

Garek's blood heated with jealousy and anger. He'd arrogantly thought she had come to the club to see him. But what if she'd actually come here for a date?

He wouldn't have brought her to a place like this. It was too loud. He would have taken her someplace quiet and intimate—like her bedroom.

He wanted to take her there now. He pushed forward and wedged the other man aside with his shoulder. His maneuver brought his thigh flush against hers. His body tightened with desire.

"Hey!" the guy protested.

Garek turned to him and for once he dropped the mask of humor and let his true feelings show. He also lifted his arm just enough to reveal the holster strapped beneath it.

The guy lifted his hands and backed up. "I had no idea she was yours. Sorry, man."

"I am not his," Candace called after the man.

But either he didn't hear her or he didn't believe her because he hurriedly disappeared into the crowd. Before turning toward her, Garek summoned the grin and the cocky attitude he had always shown her. "I just found out a few hours ago you were back," he said casually, as if his heart wasn't pounding erratically with each breath he took.

He stood so close to her that he could feel it when she breathed in; her breast swelled and pressed against his arm. "I wouldn't have figured this for your first place to hit."

She turned back to her drink, running her fingertip around the rim of the martini glass. "You don't know me," she said. "So how would you know what kind of places I frequent? Maybe I'm a regular here."

In her sexy red dress, with her black hair fluffed up and her lips painted—she looked like the other female club patrons. But she wasn't any more comfortable than he was in his undercover assignment. She visibly fought the discomfort though, lifting her chin as if she was ready to take a blow, and her brilliant blue eyes glared at him.

"I could be a regular," she insisted.

He laughed. He couldn't help it. He loved her prickliness. That was probably why he'd spent the past year provoking her—trying to get a reaction from her. Trying to get her attention. He had missed her. He'd missed her so damn bad.

"I know you," he said. He'd made a point of learning everything about her—while being careful to reveal very little of himself to her.

She shook her head in denial. "No, you don't. But I know you."

She had to talk loud—because of the music. But there was still the danger that someone else might overhear her. It was better if no one knew how close they were. Or had been…

Nobody could know what she really meant to him. Not even her. So he lost the grin, and he drew on another mask—one of coldness. "If you actually knew me," he said, "you would have known better than to show up here."

"I didn't show up here for you," she said, her tone so disparaging he almost believed her.

He glanced toward the crowd into which the guy had disappeared. "That loser wasn't your date, was he?"

She lifted her martini glass. "He bought me this."

"So you're just here to pick up guys?"

She shrugged her naked shoulders. "Why not?"

Because she belonged with him.

"So that's why you came back to River City?" he asked. "To pick up strange men in bars?"

She glared at him again, her eyes narrowed. "You say that like you doubt I can."

He hadn't meant to challenge her. He knew she could pick up any man she wanted. Even him…

And he had no business letting her affect him. But his

body ached with wanting hers. "I say that like I wonder why you'd want to," he clarified.

"I think it's safer picking up strangers than taking a chance on a man I know." She sighed. "The men I know always disappoint me."

He opened his mouth to argue, to point out she hadn't given him a chance. For a year she had ignored him or fought with him. When he had finally gotten close to her, she had run from him.

"Maybe you didn't really know them," he said.

She met his gaze and held it for a long moment before nodding in agreement. "Maybe not…" She wriggled down from the stool, and her body pushed against his.

He remembered that night—remembered how close they'd been, nothing between them as skin had slid over skin. His breath caught in his lungs. He couldn't breathe, couldn't speak. But he could hear the warning Milek uttered in his earpiece. "You have a problem."

He'd already known that. But he glanced up and noticed Viktor had stepped from his back office into the heart of the club. If he saw Candace…

She leaned closer, her lips brushing his ear and murmured, "Or maybe I've known them too well…"

He shook his head. "If that were true, you wouldn't have come back. You would have kept running."

Anger flashed in her blue eyes. She didn't deny, though, she had run.

He stepped aside, so that she could get past him. And he advised her, "Run, Candace, run…"

She called him a name no lady should even know. But she was Candace. She'd fought in a foreign country. She'd fought in her own country. She was the toughest woman he knew. But when she walked past him, he noticed the faint sheen in her eyes. He had hurt her, and he hated himself for hurting her. But instead of reaching for her, he curled his fingers into his hands and resisted the urge.

He had to let her go.

And go she did. Her head held high, her chin up, Candace walked past him as if she didn't know him. As if she didn't care...

Had she cared? Had whatever Stacy had said to her compelled her to come back? To try to help save him from himself, or from Chekov?

And had he just thrown away whatever chance he might have had with her?

Like he'd resisted reaching for her, he resisted watching her walk away. Instead he lifted his head and met Viktor Chekov's gaze. The man had avoided prison for so many years because he didn't miss anything. He knew how to find and exploit the weaknesses of his enemies.

Had he just discovered Garek's greatest weakness?

Candace's eyes stung. But it wasn't with tears. It was the cold that was getting to her. While she'd retrieved her long jacket and winter boots from coat check, she still wasn't warm enough. The winter breeze penetrated her jacket and chilled her to the bone.

She should have used the valet parking. But she'd wanted easy access to her vehicle in case she'd needed it. Two blocks and an alley away wasn't easy access, though. She shivered and blinked. But it wasn't against tears. She was blinking away snowflakes.

They fell heavily, wetting her hair and dampening her jacket—chilling her even more. But maybe it was Garek's words and his attitude that had chilled her most.

He hadn't wanted her to come back.

She'd tried to pretend that night had never happened. She hadn't realized that he would want to pretend the same thing—until she'd looked into his face and seen no memory of their encounter in his eyes. He had looked at her as if he'd never seen her naked.

As if that night had never really happened…

Had it?

Or had she dreamed it all?

Garek Kozminski had her doubting herself all over again. She'd thought she'd known him so well. But maybe she did. Maybe that was why he'd pushed her away like he had. He didn't want her too close.

Not because of Tori Chekov. Just like she hadn't seen any memory of their night on his face, she hadn't seen any love for that woman on his face. He had lied to Logan about his reason for working for Viktor Chekov again.

Why? What was he really doing for the gangster?

For the past year she'd been claiming he hadn't changed—that he was still the criminal he'd once been. Of course she'd had no evidence to back up her suspicion. She wasn't even sure why she'd been so desperate to believe the worst of him. Because he'd irritated and frustrated her? Because she hadn't wanted to acknowledge or give in to the attraction she'd felt for him?

But maybe she had been right about him after all. Had he gone back to his old life in every way?

She stepped off the sidewalk to pass through the alley to where her car was parked on the other side—on another street. The snow was deeper between the buildings as were the shadows. Her boots slipped on the snow-covered asphalt, but she regained her balance, catching herself before she fell.

She uttered a little gasp of surprise and relief, grateful she hadn't fallen. Despite her jacket and boots, she wasn't dressed warmly enough to take a tumble in the snow. So she slowed her steps, moving more carefully as she continued into the alley.

Maybe the person behind her was moving just as carefully or maybe the snow had cushioned his footsteps— because she didn't hear him until his shadow fell across her. She barely had a moment to reach for her purse, to fumble for her gun, before he attacked.

Her purse fell from her shoulder, dropping—with the gun still inside—into the snow. She couldn't use it to protect herself. And with her limbs numb from the cold, she wasn't certain she could move quickly enough to fight off her attacker. He was big, his hands strong— as they wrapped around her neck. She couldn't see his face, though. He wore a ski mask, but it wasn't in deference to the cold. It was as a disguise. So she couldn't identify him.

Why had he bothered? It was apparent he had no intention of letting her live.

Chapter 5

Fear clutched his heart in a tight vice, making the pressure on his chest unbearable. That pressure had begun to build the minute Garek had seen that sheen of tears in Candace's eyes. She acted so tough and was so strong physically, but emotionally she was vulnerable. And he'd hurt her.

He hated himself for hurting her and just letting her walk away. But then another feeling had come over him, chilling his skin and his blood even in the crowded, heated club. Fear.

He wasn't worried about just her emotional state anymore. He was worried about her physical state, too. So he'd ignored Viktor gesturing him over to his private table. And he'd pushed through the throng of club patrons to the exit.

He asked the valets in the club foyer, "Did you bring a car around for a beautiful woman—"

"Lots of beautiful women come and go from Mr. Chekov's club," one of the valets sarcastically remarked.

"This one is really beautiful," Garek said. "She's tall with black hair and—"

The cocky kid clicked his fingers together. "Oh, yeah, that one…"

The other kid uttered a lustful sigh. "She has legs that went on forever…"

His buddy bumped his arm with his fist. "You'd know, you lucky bastard. She leaned against you to change from her heels to her boots."

At least she'd put on boots. "So did you bring her car around for her?"

The kid shook his head. "No, she didn't check it with us. She walked."

That fear clenched his heart harder. "Which way did she go?"

One of the kids pointed toward the left.

"Are you sure?" he asked. "There aren't any parking lots that way."

The valet shrugged thin shoulders. "She must've parked along the street."

She couldn't have parked close to the club then. Those spots were always already taken—no matter what time of day. Even when the club was closed, Viktor did *business* here. It may have been where his right-hand man had been killed.

That crime scene hadn't been discovered—just the man's body in a Dumpster. A Dumpster that had been near the club…

Garek pushed through the doors and rushed out of the foyer. "Mr. Koz," one of the kids called after him. "You don't have a coat."

He didn't care about the cold. He cared only about finding Candace before she wound up in a Dumpster, too. Footprints led away from the front of the club— going off in different directions. More than one set led off the way the valets had indicated she'd gone.

Had she been walking with someone? Or had someone followed her?

He tracked those footprints. None of them stopped at the curb but continued down the street and around the block. But the wind picked up with a mighty gust that obliterated the rest of the footprints—the rest of the trail.

Where the hell had she gone? Had her car been parked near here and she'd left already?

That chill had gone deeper than his skin, though—to his blood and bone, and it wasn't from the cold. It was from that odd premonition he'd had about her safety. The worry and unease hadn't left him yet.

She wasn't safe.

Then he heard it. Something striking metal—like a Dumpster. The noise ricocheted off the brick walls, as if coming from an alley.

He saw it a little farther down the block, the opening between two tall buildings. Uncaring if he stepped in front of traffic or not, he jumped off the curb, squeezed between two cars and ran across the street to the alley.

"Candace?" he called out as he ran. His shoes slipped on the snow, and he nearly fell. But he caught the wall, brick stinging his palm as he hurried around the corner into the alley. With his other hand, he drew his weapon.

Between the tall buildings, the alley was dark. He could see nothing until his eyes adjusted—too slowly. Somebody ran out the other end of the alley, but all

Garek saw was a huge shadow—a bulk of muscle and height.

That wasn't Candace.

He had to find her—had to make sure she was all right. Maybe she hadn't even been in the alley. But then his eyes adjusted, and he noticed the body lying in the snow—beside the Dumpster.

"Candace!"

He dropped to his knees beside her. Snowflakes fell on her face, melting against her silky skin and running down her cheeks like tears. "Candace!"

Her long lashes, thick with snowflakes, too, fluttered and opened. While he felt a moment of relief, she obviously didn't—her eyes widened with fear.

"It *was* you!" she said, her tone full of accusation.

"What was me?" he asked, as he leaned closer to her.

She shrank back in the snow. "You attacked me."

A pang struck his heart. Obviously her opinion of him hadn't changed any. No wonder she'd left that night. "No, I didn't. I just found you."

She stared up at him through narrowed eyes, her suspicions not appeased yet.

He studied her face, checking for blood—for injuries. "Are you okay?" She'd been out for at least a moment. Had she hit her head? He reached for her, but she flinched and lifted her hands to fend him off.

There was blood on her fingers. He caught her wrist. "You're bleeding."

"That's not my blood." She sat up and now she studied him as intently as he had been studying her. "Where are you bleeding?"

"I'm not."

She touched his neck, and her fingers were like ice against his skin. "You're not…"

"Where are your gloves?" he asked. But then he noticed them lying in the snow beside her. She must have taken them off to fight her attacker.

Her fingers stroked along his throat now, and concern replaced the suspicion in her beautiful blue eyes. "Where is your coat?" she asked.

"I didn't take the time to grab it." And while snow was falling, he barely noticed the cold. Her touch heated his blood. He lifted her from the snow, wrapping her tightly in his arms. "You must be freezing."

She shook her head, but her teeth clicked together with a slight chatter. Snow covered her, clinging to her coat and her skin. "I'm fine…"

"You're not," he said, calling her on her obvious bluff. Candace hated admitting to any vulnerability—either emotional or physical. "You've been attacked. Are you sure you're not hurt?"

She shook her head again, but then her head lulled back against his shoulder—as if she'd nearly passed out.

"I'm taking you to the emergency room," he decided. He couldn't risk that she wasn't seriously injured.

She struggled in his arms, but her struggle was far weaker than what she was usually capable of. He easily held her.

"Where's your car?" he asked. She must have been walking toward it when she'd been attacked, so he suspected it was closer than his.

She gestured toward the other end of the alley. So she'd only been cutting through on her way to her vehicle. But that was also the way her attacker had gone. Was he waiting for them at her vehicle?

"Who the hell was it?" he asked. "Who assaulted you?"

Viktor had just stepped out of his office. He wouldn't have had time to send someone after her...unless he'd noticed her on the security cameras in his office. But he wouldn't know who she was—or what she meant to Garek that quickly.

"I thought it was you," she murmured.

Her admission struck him like a blow. Pain clenched his heart over the fact she could think so little of him yet—that she could think he could hurt her. But then he remembered her tears and acknowledged he had hurt her.

But then a physical blow struck him, catching him off guard. It hadn't come from the direction her attacker had gone. It had come from behind him. Had the man circled back?

With Candace clasped tightly in his arms, he couldn't reach for his weapon. He couldn't draw his gun in time to protect her. All he could do was use his body to shield her the best he could from another attack.

Candace's hand shook so badly that she couldn't get the key into her lock. A hand covered hers, steered the key inside and turned the knob for her. The hand was strong, the man to whom it belonged tall, blond and handsome.

But her skin didn't tingle. Her heart didn't race. How could two men look so alike and affect her so differently?

As Milek escorted her inside her apartment, he murmured, "Garek is going to kill me..."

He would have—in the alley—if he hadn't turned around to discover the man who'd struck him in the back was his brother. She shivered as she recalled that intense look in his silvery eyes. He'd been so...

Protective. She shivered again. Nobody had ever been protective of Candace. They hadn't had to be; she took care of herself. Would she have been able to fight off her attacker, though, without Garek arriving when he had?

She'd clawed at the man's throat and kneed him in the groin. And when he'd been doubled over in pain, she had shoved his head against the Dumpster. But it hadn't fazed him in the least. And the look in his eyes, which were all she'd been able to see through that mask, had been more intense than Garek's. It had been murderous.

He would have killed her.

She shivered again.

"Garek was right," Milek said. "I should have taken you to the emergency room."

"I'm fine," she assured him. Or she would be. She stripped off her wet coat and grabbed up a thick, fake fur blanket from the couch and wrapped it around herself. Before she'd left that night, she'd turned up the thermostat. Heat blew from the registers, but it didn't dissipate her chill yet.

"You were attacked," Milek said.

She turned to him now and studied him with suspicion. How had he known she'd been attacked? Garek could have been carrying her because she'd fallen in the snow. Milek was tall and broad-shouldered like his brother and like the man who had attacked her. With his coat collar raised and a scarf wrapped around his neck, she couldn't tell if he had any scratches.

"How did you know that?" she asked.

He tensed and asked, "Know what?"

"That I was attacked." It was warm in her apartment,

but realizing she was alone with Milek, she shivered again. And she had always considered him the nicest of the Kozminski siblings.

He shrugged. "I just assumed…"

"Why?"

"That's a rough neighborhood." That was no lie. A lot of River City was rough, though. "A woman walking alone in that area is always at risk of being attacked."

An average woman. But Candace wasn't an average woman. As a bodyguard she protected others. And she always protected herself.

Well, usually…

But the memory of that night with Garek flashed through her mind, and heat flashed through her body—finally warming her cold skin. She had definitely not protected herself *that* night. She'd left herself vulnerable to all kinds of pain and humiliation.

"I'm not sure it was a random attack," she said.

Milek sighed. "Maybe it wasn't…"

She remembered how he'd struck his brother from behind. "You thought Garek had attacked me. You suspected your own brother."

He shook his head. "No…"

"I did, too," she admitted. "It was obvious from the way he acted in the club that he wanted to get rid of me."

Instead of arguing with her, Milek admonished her, "You shouldn't have gone there."

She couldn't really argue with him either, but she tried. "I can have a drink wherever I want."

"You knew Garek would be there," he said, as if that knowledge was an accusation.

She could be as evasive as he had been. "How would I know that?"

"Stacy told you," he said.

She shook her head. "Stacy didn't tell me to go to the club."

"Maybe not," he agreed, but his voice was gruff with doubt. She suspected it was more his sister he didn't trust than her. "She convinced you to come home because she's worried Garek has gone back to his old life."

"Has he?" she asked. If anyone knew, it'd be Milek—because he probably would have gone along with him. Until tonight—until he'd struck Garek—she'd thought he'd idolized his older brother. "Have *you*?"

He only addressed her first question when he asked a question of his own. "What exactly do you think Garek has gone back to?"

"Tori Chekov?" That was what he'd obviously wanted Logan to believe. But she agreed with Stacy. Garek hadn't looked like a man in love at the club. He'd looked like a bodyguard on an assignment.

Milek tilted his head as if about to nod.

And she snorted. "I don't believe that any more than you do."

"You don't know what I believe," he said.

Which was true. Despite or maybe because of his usual mild manner, Milek was hard to read.

"No," she admitted. "But I can tell he's not in love with her."

He arched a brow. "That sounds like what *you* want to believe."

Garek hadn't told Stacy about the night they'd shared. Had he told his brother?

"Are you going to try to convince me that he does love her?" she asked, nearly choking on the words as the thought struck her harder than she'd hit the asphalt in the alley. At least the snow had broken her fall there. "I thought you'd be the last person to lie to me. You know what it feels like to be lied to."

"My situation is a little different," he pointed out.

And shame gave her heart a twinge of regret that she'd presumed to compare their situations. He had been denied so much because of secrets.

"You're right," she agreed. "Maybe he does love her…" Again the words choked her. She struggled to swallow before adding, "But I don't believe that's why he's back working for Viktor Chekov."

"Garek works for Logan," Milek said, and for once his voice was hard with defensiveness. "He works for Payne Protection."

She snorted again. "He's working for Chekov. And I want to know why. Has he returned to his old life? Is he stealing again? Or…"

"Or what?" Milek asked.

"He went to jail for murder," she reminded him and herself. How had she forgotten for a moment who Garek Kozminski was? She'd kept bringing up his past to remind herself. But then that night had happened…

And she'd hoped he really had changed like everyone else had claimed. Of course he hadn't made any such assurances. He'd let her believe whatever she wanted while everyone else had sung his praises, saying what a good man he was. What a loyal brother. What a hard worker. She wished he really was reformed.

A grimace crossed Milek's face.

And she regretted bringing up bad memories for him. He and his family had been through a lot. But there had been different versions of exactly what had gone down. Most people said Garek had deserved a medal for killing his stepfather instead of a five-year sentence for manslaughter. He had only served six months, though—due to good behavior and probably Mrs. Payne's influence on one of the judges she'd known.

"Should he have gone to jail?" she asked.

Milek shook his head.

Maybe it was a reply. Maybe it was a refusal to answer.

"Why do you care?" he asked. "You've made it clear what you think about Garek. The worst."

She couldn't deny she had once thought the worst of him. Now she wanted to prove herself wrong. She wanted to be wrong so badly.

Milek was torn. He hesitated with his hand on the door of Candace's apartment building lobby. Outside snow fell heavily, lightening the night sky. But it wasn't the cold weather causing him to hesitate.

Should he have told Candace the truth? Garek had sworn him to keep quiet. But Garek didn't always know what was best for him.

Candace was best for him.

And that was why Milek had needed to hold his silence. But it wasn't just Garek's undercover assignment that Milek was keeping quiet about. He'd been holding his silence for years—too many years.

But it probably was better Candace continued to think the worst of Garek. Then maybe she would stay away from him and stay safe.

Milek tightened his scarf around his neck before pushing open the door and stepping out into the cold. The wind took away his breath for a moment, burning in his lungs.

What a god-awful night…

The street was so deserted there weren't even tracks in the snow. His and Candace's had already blown over on the sidewalk. And the street was snow covered, as well.

He'd parked at the curb just outside her apartment building. He'd been grateful then to find a spot so close—because he'd been concerned about Candace. Now he was happy for himself.

He hadn't been inside her apartment long, but an inch or so covered his vehicle. He clicked the lock and pulled his snow brush from the backseat. As he cleared off the SUV, he noticed movement across the street. A man stood in the shadows of the dark building.

Milek narrowed his eyes and peered through the snow. The guy was dressed too nicely to be homeless. Even huddled over inside his jacket, the guy was big— like Chekov's hired goons.

Could this be who had attacked Candace?

Had he followed them back to her place?

Milek cursed beneath his breath. His brother had pounded it into his head to always check his rearview and side mirrors, so much so it was a natural instinct for Milek. He wouldn't have missed a tail.

Or had he?

Clasping the brush tightly in one hand, he headed across the street. In addition to the brush, he always had his gun—holstered beneath his jacket. He'd use them both if necessary. But the man noticed him, turned and ran.

He was bigger than Milek, though, and slower— maybe because he'd been standing in the cold. Milek caught up to him and reached out, grasping his shoulder.

The guy swung around and smashed his fist into Milek's face. His vision wavered, blurring the man's face. He noticed nothing of his features. The only thing he registered was the claw marks on the man's throat. Then he dropped to his knees in the snow as oblivion threatened to claim him.

If this man was Candace's attacker, how the hell had she survived? And if this was the man, then he must have followed her to finish the job he'd failed earlier.

Milek had to protect her. Or Garek would kill him. If this guy didn't beat him to it…

Chapter 6

He shouldn't have trusted Milek. Hell, he shouldn't have trusted *anyone else* with Candace's safety.

If he hadn't followed her out…

Garek shuddered as he considered what might have happened to her. He might have lost her longer than two weeks. He might have lost her forever.

"Who is she?"

He glanced up from the fire burning in the hearth in Viktor's den. Tori was the one who asked the question. When he'd seen Viktor a little while earlier, the man hadn't asked him about Candace.

Because he already knew?

He actually hadn't asked him anything. He'd only glared at Garek when he'd arrived at the house.

"I'm sorry," Garek had said. That was why Milek had tracked him down in the alley—because Viktor had been leaving with Tori and his entourage. And Garek was supposed to be part of that entourage.

Viktor's glare had become even fiercer. "Some bodyguard," he'd muttered before leaving Garek alone in the study.

He could have defended himself. He could have justified his disappearance because he'd been checking out a threat. But he didn't want Viktor thinking Candace posed a threat to his daughter. No, Candace was the one who'd been threatened.

Who had been attacked…

Was she really okay? Had Milek taken her to the emergency room as Garek had ordered him?

He didn't doubt that Milek would have obeyed him—had Candace allowed him. Had she agreed to get checked out?

"Who is she?" Tori asked again as she stepped closer to the fire and him.

Garek had been standing there for a while, but the chill hadn't left his body yet. It had gone far deeper than his skin. "I don't know who you're talking about…"

"The woman at the bar," Tori said, "the one with the dark hair…"

He shrugged.

"C'mon, Garek, you noticed her the moment she walked in," Tori said. "Don't try to bluff me. I know you too well. I also saw how jealous you looked when that man talked to her. I've never seen you look like that. She obviously means something to you."

Everything…

The realization staggered him. But he shook off the romantic notion. He didn't believe in happily-ever-after. He only believed in taking his happiness where he could find it.

With Candace…

He had been very happy that night in her bed—until he'd awakened alone.

He forced a laugh. "C'mon, Tori, you know me. When has anyone or anything ever meant anything to me?"

"Your family."

He couldn't—and *wouldn't*—deny that. "She's not family." At least not blood. But Payne Protection had become an extension of his family—an extension of him.

"Who is she then?" Tori asked, her voice going sharp as it rose on a whine. "And don't try to tell me that you don't know her."

"I know her," Garek admitted. There was no use trying to deny what must have been written on his face the moment Candace had walked into the club. "But you don't need to know who she is."

Tori's face twisted into the usual petulant frown she wore. "You're not very good at this."

"This?" Relationships? He'd never had one—not with Tori anyway. They'd hung out as teenagers, but that was a lifetime ago.

She nodded. "This undercover thing."

He tensed and glanced around the den. He wouldn't put it past Viktor to have it wired. He looked more closely, but microphones were tiny now and could be hidden anywhere. If it was wired and Viktor kept the recordings…

Maybe that would be the extra evidence Agent Rus needed to finally put Viktor Chekov away. Where would Chekov keep the tapes? With the gun—if he'd kept it. In a safe? Garek would be able to crack it; he'd never met one he hadn't. He just had to find where Viktor had hidden it. In his home? Or the office in his club?

"I'm a bodyguard," he reminded her. "Just a bodyguard…"

She flashed him a snide smile. "Yeah, right…"

He laughed. "I'm an ex-con," he said.

He had never had to remind Candace of that. She'd never let him forget—his former career as a thief or the stint he'd done in prison for manslaughter. He had been crazy to think he would ever get her to change her mind about him. But then he'd never tried explaining what had really happened either. Maybe he should have…

Maybe he would have if he'd awakened with her beside him, in his arms…

That night…he'd caught her at a vulnerable moment, her usual prickly defenses down for once. But she must have been so horrified over what she'd done, since she'd run off in the middle of the night.

Why had she come back? And why had she come to the club?

He wanted to ask her. Most of all he wanted to make certain she was all right.

He also had to make certain she stayed safe from now on, and the only way he could do that was to make sure nobody in the Chekov family gave her another thought.

"How does an ex-con become an undercover agent?" he asked sarcastically. "Like that would ever happen…"

"Surely you've heard of police informants," she said. "They're usually criminals."

He narrowed his eyes and studied her. "Usually," he agreed. "But sometimes they're just someone close, someone who's seen something…"

She shivered and stepped closer to the fire. "Something they wish they could *unsee*…"

He sucked in a breath. He'd suspected she was Rus's eyewitness. Now he knew for certain. "Tori…"

She shrugged. "It's not like I didn't know what he was."

"Was?" Did she not even consider Chekov her father anymore—after what she'd seen him do? She must have been so disillusioned to discover the man she'd always idolized was really the monster everybody said he was.

"Is," she corrected herself.

"You did the right thing," he assured her. But he doubted she would follow through and testify. She adored her father and was too much of a daddy's girl to ever cross him.

"What about you?" she asked. "Are you going to do the right thing?"

He sighed. "I'm trying…"

If only he could find that damn gun…

But Viktor had had plenty of time to dispose of it. Without the gun, it wouldn't matter if Tori testified— not if she had no evidence to support that testimony.

"Then you need to let that woman—*whoever she is*—go."

He had let her go. But then he'd been compelled to follow her.

"I don't know what you're talking about," Garek said. "She doesn't mean anything to me." The lie nearly stuck in his throat.

"That's good," Tori said. "Maybe she'll be okay then."

Did Tori know something about the attack on Candace? He opened his mouth to ask.

But then she continued, "Because you and I are too much alike, Garek."

She wasn't proposing they rekindle a teenage romance? He'd worried about that—when he'd taken the position as her bodyguard—she might misconstrue his reasons. Apparently she knew them better than he'd realized—since she'd suspected he was working undercover as an informant on her father.

"When we care about someone," she continued, "they wind up getting hurt."

That was why she'd gone to the police—why she'd been willing to testify. The man that had died had meant something to her—maybe everything.

He couldn't imagine what she must have gone through—watching that man die. And he never wanted to go through that with Candace. He had to keep her safe.

Stacy gripped the top rail of the crib as she leaned over it and watched her baby sleep. Little Penny was all Payne with her dark curls; they lay damply against her head. Despite the cold outside, the baby was warm. Her blue eyes—so like her father's and her uncles'—were closed as she slept peacefully.

Stacy could find no peace tonight. She had only been gone two days to track down Candace, but as Logan had already said, it had felt longer. She had missed him and their baby. She'd missed her family.

But even though she was back home—back in Logan's arms and had had her baby back in her arms, she still missed her family.

Milek and Garek were gone yet.

She had lost them.

"Why are you awake?" a gruff voice asked.

She turned to where her husband leaned against the doorjamb, his chest bare but for a dusting of dark hair. He was so damn good-looking…

And she was so lucky he had fallen in love with her. He had saved her life—literally and figuratively. Because if she didn't have him and little Penny now…

He uttered a sympathetic sigh and stepped forward to wrap his arms around her. She leaned into his embrace, accepting his comfort—even though she didn't deserve it. She didn't deserve him. She didn't deserve this happiness.

"You have to give Milek time," Logan advised her.

Since her brother had listened to her about Garek, she'd gotten her hopes up. He'd come home to help, too. But he obviously only intended to help Garek. Not her. Because now he was ignoring her calls again, sending them straight to voice mail.

"He's not the only one not answering my calls now," she admitted. And that bothered her even more. Milek had a reason to be angry with her. But Garek…

She'd only been trying to help him.

"Da…" Logan caught himself midcuss and amended it to, "Darn it…"

She smiled, amused he was already correcting himself in front of their baby even though she was too young to talk. And she wasn't even awake.

"But you had to know he wasn't going to be happy you interfered with his life."

She leaned fully against him, confident he could support her weight. That he would support her. She wanted the same for her brothers. She wanted them to find someone strong enough to love them no matter what.

Candace was that woman for Garek. Couldn't he see

it? Hopefully he would realize it before it was too late. Before he lost Candace or his freedom or his life…

Because if he didn't get away from Viktor Chekov, he was in danger of losing all three.

After two weeks away, Candace should have been eager to sleep in her own bed again. But she had avoided it and the memories it held. Even though it was unlikely after all this time, she'd worried the sheets might have smelled like Garek—like that curiously spicy, musky male scent she could smell even now. On her.

Of course he had picked her up in the alley; he'd held her easily, effortlessly. And Candace wasn't petite and delicate like the mobster's daughter. She was tall and firmly muscled. But he hadn't dropped her, not even when Milek had struck him from behind.

Milek. He'd left a while ago. And he'd left her unsettled with his evasiveness. Had both he and Garek returned to their old lives?

What were they doing for Viktor Chekov? Were they stealing again? They had been little more than toddlers when their father had taught them how to break and enter—homes, safes, museums…

Was there some particular target Chekov wanted hit? Was that why Garek had gone back to work for him?

Or was it because of what Stacy had said? Because he'd tried to be good for her—for Candace—and she'd never given him a chance?

She had that one night—for a few hours. Muscles tightened low inside her belly as desire for him returned. It didn't matter that she'd avoided the bed; she couldn't avoid the memories. She'd curled up instead on her couch, with that heavy blanket wrapped around her, but she couldn't sleep. Maybe that was because of residual adrenaline from fighting off her attacker.

She preferred to blame that than desire for a man like Garek, a man she couldn't trust. While he hadn't been the one who'd attacked her in the alley, he could have had something to do with it. He hadn't wanted her anywhere near that club. But if he knew her at all, he would know an attack wouldn't frighten her away.

She had never feared physical pain. It was the fear of emotional pain that had had her running away that night…

And she had been right to run. She had been right about Garek all along. Hadn't she been?

Despite the blanket and the heat blasting out of the registers, she shivered. No. It wasn't desire keeping her awake. And it wasn't fear.

It was anger. Anger over the attack. And anger over the fact that her attacker had gotten away. She needed to track him down, needed to find out who he was and why he'd meant her harm—or worse.

But if it hadn't been a random attack and he'd really wanted to hurt her, then she wouldn't have to track him down. He would try for her again.

The thought had no more crossed her mind than she noticed, in the faint light streaming in from the street, the doorknob turn.

She had locked it—after she'd shown Milek out. She'd made certain of that. But the door hadn't rattled as if someone had been picking the lock. The knob turned easily, as if it hadn't been locked. Or as if somebody had a key.

She reached beneath the pillow on which her head lay. And she closed her hand around the Glock she'd put there before she'd settled onto the couch.

She had never given out a key to her apartment. She'd never been close enough to anyone—not even Logan— to give them a key to her place.

The knob didn't even click before the door began to open, spilling light from the hall into the living room. Candace shut her eyes just as it illuminated her face. But then the door closed, plunging the room into darkness again.

She opened her eyes, which gradually adjusted to that faint light coming through the window. She could make out the shadow of her intruder. He was tall and broad-shouldered—like the masked man in the alley.

He hesitated for a moment before stepping away from the door and starting—slowly—toward her. She tightened her grasp on her weapon, ready to draw it. She had no compulsion against using it.

She had fired her weapon before. But she waited— wanting to identify her intruder before she shot him. She had no doubt he meant her harm, though, or he wouldn't have broken in during the night.

Or the wee hours of the morning. She had no idea how long she'd been lying there...not sleeping. Thinking about Garek...

She couldn't remember a time when he hadn't been on her mind. Even now...

She could still smell him, but not like she had earlier. His scent was stronger now. The spice, the musk...

Her skin tingled and finally heat chased away the last of her chill.

The shadow loomed larger, as the man neared the

couch. He chased away the light and cast her in total darkness. But she instinctively knew when he reached for her.

And she was ready.

Chapter 7

He was ready for her. So when she grabbed his arm and tried to flip him over the back of the couch, he caught himself, so he didn't land on the floor. He landed on top of her. Her breath whooshed out, warmly caressing his throat. She wriggled beneath him, but her arms were pinned between their bodies. When she lifted her knee, he caught it with his thighs—before she did any damage.

"It's me," he said. "It's Garek…"

"I know." But she continued to struggle, bucking beneath him. Her breasts pushed against his chest, and her hips against his.

He groaned as his body reacted. "Candace…"

And finally she went still beneath him except for the frantic beat of her heart. He could feel it beating in her breast—feel it beating in sync with his—like it had that night when they'd made love.

"Why are you fighting me?" he asked.

She began to wriggle again. "You broke in!"

He chuckled. "I didn't break in."

She stilled again and said, "No, you didn't. How did you get in?"

"I took a key," he admitted. "When I let myself out the morning after…"

That night. That incredible night.

His body tensed, every muscle taut with desire for her. He had been attracted to her since the first moment he'd seen her—looking so strong and beautiful and irritated. But he hadn't realized the depth of the desire he could feel for her or the pleasure he could feel *with* her.

Until that night…

"You had no right to take a key," Candace said. She was tense, too, but probably with anger.

"Maybe you should have stuck around then," he said, "instead of running off the minute I fell asleep." He regretted that—regretted closing his eyes for a moment that night. But it had felt so right making love with her, being with her; he had achieved a level of peace he'd never known before. Until that night there had been very little peace in Garek's chaotic life.

"That night never should have happened," she said. And even in the dim light coming through the window, he could tell how deeply her face flushed with embarrassment. "It was a mistake."

He wanted to argue with her. But she was right. It would have been easier for him had they never made love. Then he wouldn't know how incredible they were together. He wouldn't think about her constantly. He wouldn't want her as much as he wanted her again.

"Ah hell," he murmured as he lowered his head to

hers. This was no tentative kiss. No brushing of lips over lips. He took her mouth, like he'd taken her body that night. He kissed her passionately, parting her lips, so he could taste her. He slid his tongue over hers, deepening the kiss.

She nipped at his lower lip, catching it between her teeth. She could have bitten him hard—could have stopped the kiss. But she kissed him back instead. And her hands moved between them, touching his chest and his stomach.

He wished his clothes were gone, wished hers gone. He wanted nothing between them. Like that night, he wanted skin to skin. But when he reached for the blanket covering her, she shivered.

And he remembered what she'd been through and why he'd come to her place. To check on her…

To make sure she wasn't hurt or in danger.

He dragged his mouth from hers. Panting for breath, he leaned his forehead against hers. Staring into her eyes—her beautiful eyes—he asked, "Are you all right?"

Her forehead moved against his as she shook her head. Then she moved again. Catching him by surprise, she flipped him onto the floor.

His back struck the hardwood, his head just missing the coffee table. Like hers had earlier, his breath whooshed out. "You seem just fine to me."

"I am fine," she said.

"Is that what the ER doctor said?"

"I didn't go to the ER," she replied.

Concern and irritation struck him harder than he'd struck the floor, and he sat up. "I told Milek to take you to the emergency room."

She sat up, too, on the couch. But she kept the blanket wrapped around her. The chill must not have left her body. "And I didn't want to go to the ER."

So why hadn't Milek been answering his phone? Garek had thought that his brother must have shut off his cell while he'd been in the hospital and he'd just forgotten to turn it back on.

"Where's Milek?" he asked.

She shrugged. "I don't know. He left a while ago."

Milek shouldn't have left her—unprotected after someone had attacked her. What the hell had he been thinking?

"He should have stayed," Garek murmured.

"Why?" Candace asked.

"You were attacked," he reminded her. "You're in danger."

"You don't think it was just some random attack?" she asked.

He bit his lip—harder than she had and wished he could take back the words. He didn't need to rouse her suspicions any more than Stacy already had. He shrugged. "I don't know what it was."

"I intend to find out," she said.

Panic clutched his heart. "No, Candace, you need to let this go."

"Someone attacked me, and I'm supposed to forget about it?" she asked.

Hell, no. He wouldn't forget either. He wanted that person to pay. Painfully.

"I didn't need to go to the ER," she repeated. "I needed to go to the police department and report the attack."

"No," he instinctively replied. If the police started snooping around the club, asking questions, asking for security footage to see who might have followed Candace out, then Viktor would dispose of that gun for certain.

"Why not?" she asked. Her hand slid beneath the pillow on the couch.

And Garek caught the glint of metal. She'd been sleeping with a gun beneath her head.

He was lucky she hadn't used that on him. But she shouldn't have had to be armed. Milek should have been standing guard—if not inside her apartment, then outside—to protect her.

"Why shouldn't I go to the police?" she asked again, her eyes narrowed as she stared down at him. It was times like this he could see the former cop in her; she had probably been a fearsome interrogator.

He hesitated, uncertain what to tell her.

"Who are you protecting?" she asked.

"You," he replied. "I want to protect you." That was why he'd wanted her to leave the club. That was why he should have stayed away from her.

But when Milek hadn't answered his phone, he'd worried she'd been hurt worse than he'd thought. And he'd needed to check on her. However, even if Milek had answered his phone, Garek might have needed to see for himself that she was all right.

She tilted her head. "Then shouldn't you want me to find out who attacked me?"

"I'll find out," he said. And he would make sure that person never hurt her again.

She shook her head. "I think you already know…"

"If I knew, I wouldn't be here," he said.

"You shouldn't be here." She held out her hand. "Give me back my key."

He pulled it from his pocket and, rising up on his knees, leaned over the couch and dropped it into her palm. Then he moved even closer, so his mouth nearly touched hers and asked, "Do you think it matters I don't have a key? Do you think you can keep me out?"

She pulled the gun from beneath the pillow and pointed it at him. "Yes, I do."

He laughed. "Why didn't you pull that gun on me when I first walked in here?"

She must have known it was him. And even though she obviously didn't trust him, she had kissed him back. The attraction wasn't all one-sided anymore. She wanted him, too, and if he hadn't remembered what she'd been through earlier that night, they might have made love again.

But like the first time, that would have been a mistake— it would only strengthen the connection between them. And if he intended to keep her safe, he had to break that connection. He had to keep her away from him.

"I wasn't sure who you were when you first came in," she said. But he saw the lie in her eyes—in her inability to meet his gaze.

He eased back—not because of the gun—but because the temptation to kiss her again overwhelmed him. "Next time," he advised her, "pull the gun."

"There won't be a next time," she said as she closed her hand around the key.

They both knew not having a key wouldn't keep him out. But he wouldn't break in again. He had to stay away.

He was worried that wouldn't be enough to keep her safe, though—she was still in danger. And where the hell was Milek? Why hadn't he stayed close to protect her?

He intended to find out. But he was reluctant to leave

her. Then another thought occurred to him. Maybe something had happened to Milek.

Maybe Garek had put his brother in danger, too. No, it was best he leave Candace and stay far, far away from her. Because maybe Tori Chekov was right, the people they cared about always got hurt.

The noise of the police department washed over Candace. The beeping phones, the drone of voices…

Then FBI Special Agent Nicholas Rus closed the door to his office and muted the noise. A year ago he had been assigned to investigate corruption in the River City Police Department. It had been far more extensive than anyone had realized—which was probably why he was still here.

At least career-wise. But he had another reason to stay in River City. His family.

With his chiseled features and dark hair, his resemblance to Logan and Parker was uncanny. It was as if they were triplets instead of twins. But his mother wasn't Penny Payne, which was his loss on more than one count. Penny was amazing. And her children resented Nicholas for being evidence of their late father's betrayal of their mother's love and loyalty.

While Candace had once wanted to be part of the Payne family herself, she didn't envy Nicholas Rus. And it didn't matter to Penny that Candace didn't have any Payne blood; she'd included her as family. Like she had the Kozminskis…

Special Agent Rus settled into the chair behind the desk while gesturing for her to take one in front of it. "Why didn't you report this last night?"

"I don't know…" She'd been cold and dazed and

Garek had rushed her off with Milek. "Everything happened so quickly. And the Kozminskis were there."

"Did you think they'd called?"

She nearly laughed at the thought. "That's unlikely…"

"Why?"

"You know their history."

"It's history," Rus repeated.

She knew that. But for some reason she hadn't been able to let it go. She could believe Milek had changed. But she hadn't been willing to believe Garek had. And apparently with good reason; he hadn't.

"You're in law enforcement," Candace said. "You know how often offenders repeat."

"So you're saying the Kozminskis attacked you?" he asked, and he picked up a pen as if ready to take down notes. He hadn't taken any earlier—when she'd given him the time and location of her attack.

It was almost as if he'd already known when and where it had happened. Maybe Garek or Milek had called it in. But then why had no one contacted her? She'd been the victim. Not that she'd seen enough of her attacker to make a positive identification.

She shook her head. "No, the Kozminskis didn't attack me. But Garek's working for Viktor Chekov again. Even his sister's convinced he's gone back to his old life."

His brow furrowed with obvious confusion. "What does any of that have to do with you?"

Candace wasn't certain either. But Stacy had thought it had everything to do with her. That he'd returned to his criminal ways because Candace hadn't given him a chance. But that was ridiculous…

"Really," Rus persisted. "Why would any of them— the Kozminskis or Viktor Chekov—want to hurt you?"

She considered the question for a moment before she answered honestly, "I don't know."

She was certain Garek didn't want her around, though. Or she'd been certain at the club. Then he had shown up—with her key—at her apartment the night before. Or early this morning. And he'd kissed her, like he'd kissed her that night two weeks ago. So she wasn't sure what he wanted with her.

But he'd definitely *wanted* her for a moment. She'd felt his erection against her belly. Her pulse quickened remembering his body lying heavily on hers and then his mouth on hers. She'd wanted him, too.

If he hadn't pulled away...

Rus was speaking again. "Isn't it more likely someone saw you in the club—someone you arrested while you were with River City PD—and that person followed you to attack you out of vengeance?"

That did make more sense. But the way Garek had treated her in the club—as if he wanted her nowhere near it—had roused her suspicions. He didn't want her around because he didn't want her discovering whatever he was up to. What crime had he committed or was about to commit for Viktor Chekov?

"Did you recognize anyone in the club?" he asked.

She shrugged. "Sure, faces looked familiar. That kind of place attracts criminals. More drugs and sex are sold there than alcohol."

"Allegedly," Rus said.

Alleged because no one had ever been able to arrest Viktor Chekov for any of his numerous crimes.

"But nobody was looking at me like they recognized me." Hell, she'd had someone hitting on her. That wouldn't have happened, had he or anyone else known she'd once been a cop. "And I don't remember arresting any of them either."

"Do you remember everyone you've ever arrested?" Rus asked. "Because I don't. But I'm pretty damn sure they all remember me."

"Sure," she admitted. "I've had my share of threats while I was on the force. But I haven't been with River City PD for years."

Rus nodded. "Exactly. So it's more likely some of the perps you arrested would be out on parole now."

Her head had begun to pound, maybe from lack of sleep, maybe from frustration. "You sound convinced that this attack was about me." Or he was trying really hard to convince her of that.

"It could have been random," he acknowledged. "That's a rough neighborhood."

"That's what Milek said," she admitted.

"I'll work both those angles," he assured her.

Goose bumps lifted on her skin with a shiver of unease. Was Nicholas Rus the right agent to investigate corruption in River City? "But not Viktor Chekov?"

His brow furrowed as if the question confused him. "Why?" he asked. "Has he threatened you?"

"I've never met him."

"Then why would he send someone after you?"

He probably wouldn't have. So who had? Garek? Had he been trying to scare her away? A physical threat wouldn't do that—only an emotional threat would. He should already know that, though.

"Forget it," Candace said. "You don't need to look into this at all. I'll investigate on my own."

"You're not on the force anymore," he reminded her. "You're a bodyguard."

She nodded. "Yes, I am." And the body she was protecting now was her own. But it wasn't really her body she needed to protect; it was her heart. "And you're an FBI agent. This little assault is beneath your pay grade. I shouldn't have bothered you with it."

"I'm glad you did," he said. "But why did you?"

She could have reported it to someone else. She still knew some officers on the force—the ones that had survived Rus's corruption arrests.

"If the Kozminskis are involved with Chekov, it'll reflect badly on Payne Protection just as Logan is getting ready to franchise," she said. "So it needs to be handled with discretion."

"What does?" Rus asked. "It sounds to me like Garek saved you and Milek helped you home. How would that reflect badly on Payne Protection?"

From that perspective she should have thanked Garek and his brother. But even their sister thought Garek had gone back to his criminal ways. Since Agent Rus wouldn't investigate, she would.

As if he'd read her mind, Rus said, "I'll handle the investigation. I'll check into recent paroles, other assaults in that area—see what we can turn up on security cameras."

For some reason, she doubted he would turn up any suspects. But she stood up and said, "Thank you." Then she headed toward the door.

He was there, opening it for her. Penny Payne may not have raised him, but he had the manners she'd ingrained in her children. But then he gave her a strange look, and in a deep and ominous tone advised, "Be careful, Candace."

Instead of sounding like concern, his comment

sounded like a threat. The chill rushed back over her, lifting those goose bumps on her skin again. Was there anyone she could trust?

"I trusted you to protect her," Garek said as he slammed the door to Milek's place. It was a converted warehouse space with high metal ceilings, and bare concrete floors so every sound was magnified.

Milek groaned as the crash reverberated in his already pounding head. He reached for the pharmacy bag on his kitchen counter, grateful now he'd filled the prescription he'd considered refusing. He was already in so much pain he hadn't thought his injuries would bother him at all—once he'd had his broken ribs wrapped.

"What the hell happened to you?" Garek asked.

"Protecting Candace," he murmured through his swollen lips. "You're welcome."

"Why didn't you call me?" Garek asked.

He pulled his phone from his pocket and held up the smashed screen. "It took a beating, too."

Garek uttered a stream of curses followed by a heartfelt apology. "I'm sorry. I'm so damn sorry for dragging you into all of this."

"Nicholas Rus dragged you first," Milek said. "But even then I'm surprised you'd go back—surprised you'd risk it."

Garek shrugged. "I need to do this. I could have taken Chekov out years ago—could have given him up to the authorities and gotten myself out of jail time."

"And he would have killed us all."

His brother lightly touched his swollen face, but Milek flinched at even slight pressure on his bruises. Yeah, he was glad he'd filled that prescription.

Garek warned him, "He still might kill us."

"We're not scared kids anymore," Milek reminded him. "We can handle Chekov. We can protect ourselves."

Garek raised a brow. "Really?"

"Hey, you should see the other guy."

Garek breathed a sigh of relief. "You got him? You took care of him."

"Not me," Milek admitted. "You should see what Candace did to him, though. She clawed the hell out of his neck. We'll be able to track him down easily enough if he's one of Chekov's men."

Garek shook his head. "Damn that woman. If the guy hadn't wanted to kill her before, he's going to want to now for sure."

"Candace can take care of herself." Milek tore open the pharmacy bag. "Hell, she can take care of herself better than I can. You don't need to worry about her."

"That man is still out there," Garek said. "I'm going to worry about her until we find him."

Milek shrugged. "It doesn't matter if we find him. If Chekov's behind it, he'll just send someone else." He hadn't agreed to help Garek just because he was his brother. He knew Chekov had gotten away with his crimes for too long. "We have to stop him."

Garek nodded. "I just hope we can stop him before Candace gets hurt again."

Or worse…

Chapter 8

While Garek loved his brother, it was Candace that he didn't want taking a beating because of him—like she nearly had in the alley.

He had to keep her safe. He had to stay the hell away from her—which wouldn't be easy since he was pretty damn sure she was following him. He peered into his rearview mirror but couldn't catch another glimpse of her car.

She was good. But he knew she was back there. He'd noticed her as he was leaving Milek's place for the second time that day. Of course she would have tracked him down there; she'd known he was worried about his brother.

He picked up his cell and punched in the number for the phone he'd brought back to Milek's after tracking him down the first time. He'd returned the second time to bring him the replacement phone and some food.

"That was quick," Milek answered. His voice was clear.

"You didn't take the drugs yet?" he asked.

Milek sighed. "I thought I should eat first. Thanks for the soup."

"How bad you hurting?" He wished back the question the minute he uttered it. He knew Milek was hurting badly. The man had lost everything before he'd even realized it was his.

All stubborn pride, Milek stoically replied, "I'm fine."

"Fine enough to take my bodyguard shift with Tori?"

Milek sighed. "The girl isn't in danger of anything but breaking a nail texting."

"No, she isn't in any danger," Garek agreed. "But her protection duty is what's getting me close to Viktor. And I need to get close to him if he's ever going to get caught."

But he didn't want Candace close to the mobster. He didn't want Candace anywhere near Viktor Chekov. So he couldn't lead her back there.

"Since you need to be close to Viktor, shouldn't you work your own shift?" Milek asked—speaking slowly as if Garek were the one who'd taken the beating and was confused.

"Candace is following me."

"And you figured out she was tailing you?" Milek asked. Then he uttered what sounded like a victory cry. Or maybe given his injuries it was just a cry. "You didn't realize I was tailing you that night I caught you meeting with Rus."

Garek smiled. Since they were kids, Milek had been trying to get one over on him. He definitely had that night, so Garek expected to hear about it often.

"No, I didn't make you," he admitted. That had been Candace's fault, however. She continued to distract him.

"I'll take your shift," Milek agreed. "What are you going to do about her?"

"Lead her as far from Chekov as I can…"

He wanted to lead her back to his place—not to his apartment but to the home he'd bought before Rus had pulled him into the undercover assignment. He hadn't moved into it yet because he couldn't risk Chekov finding out Garek had bought a house in the 'burbs. The mobster would know for certain there was nothing left of the corruptible kid Garek had once been. And he would never let down his guard enough to reveal anything incriminating. Hell, he'd probably fire him—at the least. Kill him at the most.

So he kept driving and acting as if he had no idea she was back there. While he didn't see her again, he knew he hadn't lost her.

"Where the hell is he going?" Candace murmured to herself. Fortunately she had a full tank of gas because he had led her all over the city for most of the afternoon. Night was nearly about to fall now.

What was he doing? Casing places for Chekov? He never went inside any building, never did more than pull his SUV to the curb outside of a building.

Did he know she was following him?

She shook her head. There was no way. She was too good. But he was good, too. She remembered how he'd easily followed Logan and Parker. And they were the ones who'd taught her how to spot and lose a tail.

But Garek wasn't following her. And he was too arrogant to consider she might be able to follow him. No, he hadn't spotted her. She was sure of it.

Each time he stopped, she picked up her phone and took a photo of the building. If something got robbed in it, she would have dated and time-stamped proof he'd been there. That had to be what he was doing for Chekov—something involving his breaking and entering and safecracking skills. He certainly wasn't protecting the man's daughter.

And despite what he'd told Logan, he wasn't in love with Tori Chekov either. If he was, he wouldn't have kissed Candace like he had the night before. His body wouldn't have reacted so physically and passionately to the closeness of hers.

Her body reacted now, flushing with heat, as she could almost feel the weight of him on top of her. But the image that flashed through her mind was from weeks ago—his naked body moving over hers, moving inside hers.

A soft moan slipped through her lips. She had never felt what he'd made her feel. So much…

Passion.

Desperation.

So much pleasure.

It had overwhelmed her. *He* had overwhelmed her.

The slamming of a car door jerked her from those intimate memories. He'd actually gotten out of his vehicle this time. She glanced around, trying to determine where they were. It was an industrial area of the city.

No jewelry stores or museums here. But maybe someone warehoused their art collection in one of these buildings. Maybe that was Chekov's target. She needed to investigate; she needed evidence to prove Garek had returned to his old life.

She wasn't certain she would share that evidence with Special Agent Rus. But she needed the evidence for herself—so she would stop wanting Garek.

She opened her door and stepped onto the street. Snow had begun to fall. But the flakes were huge and sparse. They floated softly from the sky with no breeze to blow them about, and it was warm enough again that the snow which had fallen the night before had melted from the asphalt and the concrete sidewalks. This wasn't the revitalized part of the city, but someone had decorated a few of the straggly trees along the sidewalk, stringing twinkle lights over the bare branches.

So she couldn't use his footprints to track him; she had to keep him in her sight. But he moved quickly, as if concerned someone might have followed him.

Had he noticed her tailing him? But Garek always moved with the speed and silence of a thief—either because it was in his genetics or he'd learned it so young from his father.

So she hastened her step, too. But he turned a corner and disappeared from her sight.

"Damn it…"

Had he gone inside one of those buildings? She needed to determine which one and why. She hustled up to where he'd turned. But he hadn't gone inside a building. He'd gone into an alley.

Night had already fallen between the buildings, casting the alley in darkness. She couldn't see inside—couldn't see if he'd slipped into some back entrance of a building. Or if he'd simply walked through it on his way to another street.

She drew in a deep breath and stepped into the shadows. But she'd only gone a few steps when strong arms wrapped tightly around her. She lifted her elbow, intending to drive it into his ribs.

But those arms spun her around, as if they were doing some kind of strange, fast-paced dance. She didn't need to figure out any steps, though, because he lifted her from her feet and propelled her back.

Pressed against the wall, she couldn't back away from him. And she couldn't move forward, either, because his body was there. His chest pressed against hers, his hips pushed against hers—like when he'd fallen on top of her on her couch.

"Didn't you learn your lesson last night?" Garek asked.

She'd learned the closeness of his body ignited a fire inside her. Desire overwhelmed her, claiming her common sense. She knew he wasn't good for her—he would only break her heart. She couldn't fall for him.

"You could have been attacked again," he continued. His body was tense against hers. Maybe with anger. It was in his silvery eyes as he stared down at her. But then his pupils dilated, leaving just a thin rim of silver outlining the black. And he wasn't angry anymore.

"You're not going to attack me," she murmured.

He leaned closer, pushing her more firmly against the brick wall. It might have been cold and hard against her back, but she noticed nothing of that. She felt only the heat burning between them, felt his body as it hardened and pushed against hers.

He groaned. "I wouldn't be so sure about that…"

"Why?" she asked.

"I think you know…" He leaned in, pressing his erection more firmly against her belly. And a moan slipped involuntarily through her lips.

She'd never wanted anyone the way she wanted him. If only she thought they could have a future...

"Why did you go to work for Chekov?" she asked. "Why would you back to that life?" Was it her fault— like Stacy believed? Had he really been trying to be a better man for her?

"It's just an assignment," he said.

At least he hadn't claimed to her what he had to Logan—that he loved Chekov's daughter. But which of them was he lying to?

Logan.

Or her?

Maybe she was fooling herself—or making a fool of herself again. But she didn't believe he could love one woman and want another woman like he obviously wanted her.

But then she'd always known he was a playboy, that he flirted with every woman he encountered. Even Penny Payne...

But in the year he'd been working for Payne Protection, she'd only seen him flirt. She'd never heard about him hooking up with anyone else. She'd never even heard about his dating.

"What am I?" she asked him. And she moved against him, arching her hips to rub against his erection.

He groaned again. "Trouble..."

"I'm trouble?" She smiled. No one had ever called her *that* before. She was the buddy. The friend. The person a man could rely on—not one who caused him trouble. To her it was a compliment.

But then she lost her smile because he kissed it away,

his lips moving over hers. He must have released her arms because she was able to lift them, to lock them around his neck, as she kissed him back. She parted her lips, inviting him to deepen the kiss.

He accepted her invitation. He nipped at her bottom lip, then slid his tongue over it and inside her mouth. She sucked on it before sliding her tongue over it.

Her heart pounded frantically, in rhythm with his. Even through their coats and clothes, she could feel the beat of his heart. Could feel the heat of his body...

He groaned and drove his tongue deeper inside her mouth. And she shuddered as desire overwhelmed her.

How could just his kiss drive her so crazy she didn't care they were in an alley? She wanted him like she'd had him that night of their first kiss. They hadn't been able to stop at a kiss then either. The attraction between them was too much—too explosive.

He pulled back, panting for breath. "I know trouble," he said. "And you're trouble, Candace, more trouble than I've ever gotten into before..."

That night she hadn't believed she'd affected him like he had her. She'd thought she was falling alone. That he'd only gotten what he'd been after—one night. That she'd been a challenge he'd won, a conquest.

Now she wasn't so certain. He clearly wanted her again. She arched into him, desperate to feel him inside her—as she had that night. She'd missed him—missed what she'd never imagined she would have. Passion. Crazy, desperate passion...

"You're the one who's trouble," she said. "I knew it the first moment I met you."

Unlike her, he didn't smile. He obviously didn't consider it the compliment she had. "I wasn't trouble *then*," he murmured. "But I am now…"

Because of what he'd done—or was doing—for Chekov.

"Quit the assignment," she urged him. "Let Logan give it to someone else. Or, better yet, have him drop Viktor Chekov as a client."

He stared down at her, his gray eyes going stormy with conflict. His jaw went taut as tension filled him. He wanted to—she knew it.

Or maybe she only wished it.

"Please," she implored him. And she rose up the scant inches that separated them and pressed her lips to his. "Please…"

She had never begged before. Not even Logan when she'd wanted him to fall in love with her instead of Stacy Kozminski. But then she had never wanted Logan the way she did Garek. What she'd felt for Logan had been just a silly schoolgirl crush. What she felt for Garek was…

Madness.

She kissed him again, sliding her lips over his.

A groan rumbled in his throat before his lips parted. She deepened the kiss, sliding her tongue inside his mouth. The passion ignited between them.

She wanted him so much, but she wanted all of him. She wanted his body and his soul. She didn't want him selling it out to someone like Chekov.

But most of all she wanted his heart.

"Garek…"

He leaned his forehead against hers, panting for breath, and shook his head. "I can't quit this job. I'm in too deep, Candace. I have to see this through."

"What do you have to see through?" she asked. "What are you doing for Viktor Chekov?"

But he wouldn't answer her. He only shook his head again.

Before she could press him for more information, she heard the rev of a car engine—which was odd. She hadn't noticed any other traffic passing the alley.

But then she'd been distracted, overwhelmed with her desire for Garek Kozminski.

"What the hell..." Garek murmured, as he heard it, too.

Then the car was there, roaring into the alley. With them both standing against the brick wall, they had no place to go—no way to escape.

The vehicle was certain to crush them...

Chapter 9

Logan hadn't been this angry in a while—probably not since he'd nearly fired Candace. He stared across his desk at her and his brother-in-law and threatened, "I should fire you both."

"For nearly getting killed?" Candace asked.

"Exactly."

Garek snorted. "That makes no sense."

So Logan pointed out what should have been obvious to the two of them. "Who the hell is going to trust a bodyguard to protect them that someone else is already trying to kill?"

"No one's trying to kill me," Garek replied.

But Candace shot him a glance that could have done the job. There was more than anger in her gaze, though. Stacy had obviously been right about the female bodyguard's feelings for her oldest brother.

"I wasn't the only one that car nearly ran over," she reminded him. "You were there, too."

"Lucky for you," Garek said.

Color flushed Candace's face, which was good since she'd been so pale when he had first summoned them to his office. They had had a close call. Even though he hadn't been there, Logan knew—because nothing usually fazed Candace.

She was tough.

Now she was embarrassed. But she ruefully admitted, "You did save my life."

Garek shrugged off her gratitude and turned away from her. But Logan caught his grimace of guilt.

Garek may have claimed the driver hadn't been trying to run him down, but he felt responsible for the attempt. Why? What the hell was really going on?

Apparently Stacy had also been right to worry about her brother. Logan made a mental note to never again doubt his wife. "Lucky for me that you both survived," Logan said. "With franchising the agency, I can't afford to lose any of my team. We're busy as hell right now."

"And don't need the bad publicity," Candace said with a resentful glance at Garek—her gratitude gone.

"There were no reporters there," Garek said. "And it's unlikely any would care about a car that could have just had a stuck gas pedal or something…"

"Or something…" Candace murmured.

Logan sighed. Had he and Stacy acted like that? Bickered like children? They had certainly fought a lot before they'd given in to their feelings for each other.

"We need to get back to work," Logan said. He had meetings with his brothers about the franchise. He had to focus on Payne Protection, but without his bodyguards, there would be no Payne Protection.

But these two weren't just bodyguards; they were family, too.

"You're right," Candace agreed. "You hired me back, but you haven't given me a job yet."

He nodded. "I'll find you something."

But first he wanted to talk to his half brother and learn what Nicholas knew about the attempts on Candace's life. Had they been random? Or was she really in danger?

"You don't have to look for anything," she told me. "I already know what job I'm perfect for."

Garek tensed and began to shake his head—as if he already knew what she was going to say.

Candace leaned forward and implored Logan, "Give *me* the assignment protecting Chekov's daughter…"

Logan rubbed his jaw as he considered her request.

Logan was actually considering it. Garek's heart rate had finally slowed back to normal—or at least as normal as it ever was around Candace—but now it started racing again. Like that car had raced toward them.

He didn't know if it had been instinct or his late father acting as his guardian angel that had had him diving out of the way with Candace wrapped up tightly in his arms. He had saved her that time, but if she took away his assignment, he wouldn't be there to protect her next time.

And he was pretty damn certain there would be a next time. Why?

Had Viktor figured out what Garek was up to? Had Tori warned him? She never stayed angry with her father; she idolized him too much. So was Viktor going after Candace as a warning to Garek?

"Don't even think about it," Garek advised his boss. "I brought you this client. This is my assignment."

"Why?" Candace asked. "We all know it's better if a female bodyguard protects a female subject. This should be my assignment."

Garek shook his head. "Viktor would never agree to an outsider protecting his daughter. He doesn't trust easily."

And Garek needed the mobster to trust him again if he was ever going to find wherever he'd hidden the murder weapon. His safe?

But if Tori had ratted him out, he would have disposed of the gun already. So Garek would have to find other evidence, or somehow compel Chekov to confess.

"I can understand why it's hard to trust some people," Candace said, and she turned and glared at him. All her desire for him was gone now. Maybe almost getting killed had brought her to her senses again—like it had brought him.

He had nearly told her everything in that alley. He'd nearly confessed his assignment wasn't for Viktor Chekov or Payne Protection. His assignment was for the FBI. But if he'd told her the truth, she would insist on sticking beside him. And being too close to him had nearly gotten her killed more than once. He couldn't risk her life—even if it cost him his chance of ever earning her love.

He wasn't above doing whatever necessary to keep her safe. So he asked, "And really—should she be protecting anyone if someone's after her?"

Candace gasped. "Nobody was after me until I went

to Chekov's club. Those attempts have everything to do with him and you."

He couldn't disagree with her. Chekov had to be responsible. "All the more reason you can't have anything to do with this assignment."

Logan had his thumb pressed to his temple. "Okay, enough arguing. You two are giving me a headache."

Better a headache than the heart attack Garek nearly had when that car had come rushing toward them in the alley. He still wasn't certain how they had survived. He must have a guardian angel, which was kind of fitting during the Christmas season. He would have doubted it would be his father, though—except Stacy had claimed the man had been repentant before he'd died. Maybe, in the afterlife, he was trying to make amends for being a lousy father.

"She never even got checked out after that first assault," Garek persisted. "She refused to let Milek take her to the ER. She could have a concussion."

"*I* don't have a headache," she said.

Logan sighed. "He's right. You should have gotten checked out." He pressed the intercom button on his phone. "Nikki, I need you to do something."

"You have an assignment for me?" his sister hopefully asked.

Garek wasn't worried Nikki was getting the job with Chekov. Her brother would never risk *her* safety.

"I need you to take Candace to the ER to get checked out."

"Of course I will," she said. But Garek heard the disappointment in her voice.

"But I'm fine," Candace argued.

Logan pointed at her. "If you want an assignment, you need to be cleared medically first. Go."

Candace jumped up from her chair, glared at Garek again, and then walked out of the office. She slammed the door behind her with such force Logan flinched and Garek jumped. He was on edge now and had been since she had walked into Chekov's club.

"Nikki won't be in danger taking her to the ER?" Logan asked, as if reconsidering the assignment he'd given his sister. "You think someone's really after Candace?"

"Two random attacks?" Garek asked. He shrugged. "Hell, anything's possible in River City." Rus had a long way to go before he cleaned up all the corruption and crime. That was why he needed Garek's help.

"So it is possible someone's after her?" Logan asked. He narrowed his eyes and glared at Garek now. "Is it your fault?"

He sighed. "I honestly don't know. I don't see how…"

How the hell could Chekov have figured out his feelings for Candace when he wasn't even certain of them himself? Sure, he wanted her. He wanted her more than he'd ever wanted any other woman. That desire bordered on desperation. If that car hadn't sped into the alley, he might have taken her there—against the brick wall in the cold.

"I can't give her an assignment if she's in danger," Logan said.

"You have to," Garek said, as it presented the perfect solution. "You have to give her an assignment that's far away from River City." And far away from him.

Logan nodded in agreement. "The only problem will

be getting her to take the assignment without quitting again."

"You have to convince her," Garek said. It was the only way to keep her safe.

"I'm supposed to bring you to the ER," Nikki protested as she pulled her Payne Protection Agency SUV to the curb beside the string of Christmas lights strewn over those bare branches. The lights twinkled even brighter since night had fallen completely now. "Not here."

"I don't need to go to the ER," Candace said. "I'm fine. All I need is my car." And she'd left it here because Garek had insisted on her riding with him back to the Payne Protection office. As if he'd been worried someone might try running her off the road.

She could handle herself. Sure, she hadn't reacted as quickly as he had in the alley. But she would have reacted. She was a bodyguard. She was trained to protect others and herself. She hadn't needed Garek to save her.

But she *had* needed Garek. Physically. Passionately. What the hell was the matter with her? She'd never been one of those silly women who went for the bad boy. She'd always thought those women were ridiculous. Who wanted that kind of trouble in her life? That potential for pain?

Bad boys didn't change. They didn't grow into good men. She never should have been tempted by Garek Kozminski, let alone have given in to that temptation.

"Are you sure you're okay?" Nikki asked, her brown eyes full of concern. She looked like her mother, whereas Candace actually looked more like Nikki's brothers—at least in coloring. Maybe that was why they coddled Nikki and treated Candace like one of the guys.

Garek didn't treat her like that, though. He treated her like she was a woman—a desirable woman. She shook her head, trying to get him out of her mind.

Nikki reached for the SUV shifter. "I'll take you to the emergency room."

"No," Candace said. "Physically, I'm fine."

Nikki turned to her, studying her across the console. "So someone's trying to kill you—that affects even someone like you?"

Candace smiled. "Someone like me?"

"You're like Wonder Woman or something," Nikki replied. "You're tough."

The younger woman's admiration warmed Candace's heart. But it was unwarranted.

"Physically, I'm tough," Candace clarified. Then she sighed and added, "It's not the attempts on my life that have shaken me up."

Nikki wiggled a dark brow and asked, "Garek Kozminski?"

She wasn't too proud to admit it. "Yeah…"

"You agree with Stacy then?" Nikki asked. "He's gone back to his old life?"

He had all but admitted it to her when he'd said he was in too deep with Chekov. Did he gamble? How was he in too deep? And should she even try to help him out?

Yet her lips tingled from their passionate kisses. And she knew she would try. But first she had to find out exactly how he was in too deep.

"I don't know for certain," she said. But she intended to find out.

"But you're worried he has?"

She nodded.

Nikki sighed. "I don't think any man is worth the potential heartache. How can you ever trust one?"

Especially a man like Garek, who'd had a colorful past and was keeping secrets again. Candace would be crazy to trust him.

But then she saw where Nikki's attention had gone. FBI Special Agent Nicholas Rus had pulled in front of them and alighted from his Bureau SUV.

Nikki blinked. "Even my father…"

Poor Nikki. She would never get over her father's betrayal even though her mother had made peace with it long ago—before Nikki had been conceived.

Candace had no words of wisdom to offer Nikki. She was hardly an expert where trust was concerned. She opened the passenger's door and stepped onto the sidewalk. "Thanks for bringing me back to my car."

Nikki nodded and then drove off once Candace closed the door. She had rarely said more than a couple of words to the brother she hadn't known she had.

"Hope she didn't rush off my account," Rus said as he watched the SUV drive away.

"I'm sorry," Candace said. It wasn't his fault he was too painful a reminder to his half sister.

He shrugged. "She'll get over it…" He sighed and added, "Never."

"Yeah, probably not," she agreed. "I'm surprised you showed up here. An attempted hit-and-run isn't much of a crime for an FBI special agent to investigate."

"You brought your complaint to me earlier today," he reminded her.

"I shouldn't have wasted your time with it either," she said.

He gestured toward the crime scene tape across the

alley. "There was another attempt, so it obviously wasn't a waste of time. Did you see the driver?"

She shook her head. "He was wearing a mask—like the guy was wearing the night before."

"So you're pretty sure it's the same guy?"

She shook her head. "Not at all. It could have been a similar mask and a different guy."

Chekov had a lot of muscle working for him. So why had he needed Garek as a bodyguard? He wouldn't have needed him for protection. Nobody had ever been able to touch Chekov—physically or legally.

Agent Rus drew a folder out of the inside of his overcoat and flipped it open to some mug shots. "Could it have been any of these guys?"

All guys with big heads and no necks. "It could have been all of them. Who are they?"

"Guys you arrested who've been recently let out on parole. They all potentially have an ax to grind with you."

She laughed at his hypocrisy. "You don't think they were reformed in jail like everyone—including you—believes Garek Kozminski was?"

"This has nothing to do with Garek Kozminski."

"This has everything to do with Garek Kozminski," she said. Until she'd gotten involved with him, nobody had ever tried to kill her—at least not outside of a war zone or in order to get to the subject she was protecting.

"Here's a whole gallery of suspects," Rus said. "Why is it so hard for you to believe one of them would come after you?"

"This has nothing to do with me," she insisted. Or someone would have tried to kill her before. "This has everything to do with Viktor Chekov."

Rus glanced around—almost as if he was afraid someone might have overheard her accusation. "You have to be careful, Candace," he warned her again. "Chekov isn't someone you want to go after without evidence…"

She would find the evidence—even if she had to do it alone.

Then he added, "Or an army."

She'd been part of an army before. But most of the time it had taken only one soldier to take out the enemy. She was no sniper but she was smart. Viktor Chekov would not take her out before she was able to take him down.

Chapter 10

Garek clicked off his cell phone and sighed. He hadn't needed Agent Rus's warning to know Candace wasn't about to give up and stop interfering. After having her life threatened—not once but twice—someone else might have taken the warning and backed off.

But not Candace.

Didn't she have any idea how much danger she was in? That car could have killed them both and probably would have had he not been able to move as quickly as he had. And if he hadn't gone after her when she'd left the club the night before...

He shuddered to think what might have happened to her. Sure, she was tough. But anyone could be taken by surprise—as she had been that night.

He drew in a steadying breath before pushing open the door to Viktor's office at the club. But that breath whooshed out when a fist slammed into his stomach. He doubled over in pain. "What the hell…"

When the big man swung again, Garek was ready—catapulting himself at him and knocking him to the floor. The first thing he looked for were the marks Candace had put on her attacker. But this man's neck bore no scratches—just stubble. The guy bucked him off just as two other men grabbed him. Another fist slugged him—this one belonged to Viktor.

It didn't hurt as badly as the first blow had. But he doubled over again and tugged free of the men who held him. Neither of those two had marks on their necks either. These were Viktor's usual guys—the closest of his *family* since the man killed Tori's boyfriend. If Viktor had sent someone after Candace, it would have been one of them.

Or himself…

"What the hell's wrong with you?" Garek asked. "You already put me through this gang beat down weeks ago." He must have discovered Garek was working for Rus. But if Chekov had, he probably would have done more than beat him.

Viktor laughed. "Gang? You call my *family* a gang?"

It was certainly no family Garek would want to be part of. He shrugged off his comment. "I was just trying to be funny."

"Oh, yeah, you're a funny guy," Viktor agreed. "You ask me for this job—to hire your brother-in-law's business to protect my daughter. You promise me that you're the only one who can protect her—then you pawn her protection off on your brother. What the hell's wrong with *you*?"

Garek cursed. "I trust my brother. I can't say the same for you or any of your *men*."

"What do you mean?"

"Your right-hand man was killed," Garek said—as if Chekov would have needed the reminder. "That's why I worried about Tori. Anyone gets close to you, they wind up dead."

Probably at Viktor's hand—because he'd seen something they'd done—maybe an involvement with his daughter—as a betrayal.

"Then I get close to you," he continued, "and suddenly someone's trying to kill *me*."

Viktor laughed. "This was hardly a beating. You've gotten soft, Garek."

"Someone tried running me down earlier today," he said. Of course he probably hadn't been the target—unless Viktor already believed he'd betrayed him. "And did you see my brother today? Someone really roughed him up last night."

"You and your brother both?" The color left Viktor's face. Was he shocked the attacks had happened or shocked they had survived them?

"Yeah." And Candace. But he didn't want to bring her to Viktor's attention—if she already wasn't. Could Rus be right? Could that attack in the alley have been some guy she arrested years ago?

Maybe even today—the car—that could have been someone else, too. What the hell was really going on?

And if Candace was in danger on her own—he needed to be with her, not putting her in even more danger with his involvement with Chekov. His heart wrenched as if torn in two. He didn't want to be the one who'd put her in danger; he wanted to be the one to protect her.

"Why would someone go after you and your brother?" Viktor asked. "Are the two of you into something—have you crossed someone?"

They had crossed a lot of someones when they'd helped protect the Paynes a year ago. But most of those someones hadn't survived the firefights. Or they were in such high-security prisons they wouldn't be able to get so much as a postcard to the outside.

"I don't think it's about us," Garek replied. "I think it's about you."

"Why?" Viktor scoffed. "You're not close to me."

"We're close to Tori—we've been protecting her," he pointed out. "Someone could be trying to get me and Milek out of the way, so they can get to Tori."

Now color flushed Viktor's face a mottled red, and rage burned in his dark eyes. "Nobody better hurt her," he threatened. "Or I'll tear them apart."

Garek didn't doubt him.

Then Viktor swung his arm around, encompassing all the men in the room. "And I'll tear apart anyone who lets her get hurt."

Garek restrained an involuntary shudder. He didn't believe Tori was in danger—probably even if Viktor discovered she was the one who'd gone to the FBI about his killing Alexander Polinsky. But Garek still intended to make damn certain she stayed safe. He didn't want to incur Viktor's wrath.

But what about Viktor? How could he be so worried about someone else hurting her after he already had? He was the man who'd hurt her most when he'd killed her lover. Shouldn't he at least confess to killing Polinsky in order to make amends to her? Or explain why he'd done it?

He'd heard that Alexander had been a bit of a playboy. Maybe he'd cheated on Tori, and Victor had killed him because of that betrayal.

Garek had an opening now to get Viktor to talk. And while they'd beat the hell out of him when he'd walked into the office, for the first time they hadn't checked him for a wire. There was the risk they might next time—when he was actually wearing one. But even if he found the murder weapon, it didn't put the gun in Viktor's hand that night.

Only Viktor could do that.

He had to get him to talk and soon—before anyone else got hurt.

Candace hadn't intended to return to the club. But it was where it had begun; it was from here someone had followed and attacked her.

Why?

She walked in with the intention of talking to Viktor Chekov himself—of asking him for his security footage from the night before. But, even this near closing time, the club was crowded. Nobody at the bar would ask for more than her drink order. When she demanded to speak to the owner, they walked away from her.

So she moved instead toward the roped-off table where Tori Chekov sat. She didn't watch the crowd or move with the music. Her only interest appeared to be in her phone until she glanced up and saw Candace. Recognition flashed in her dark eyes.

Milek stood up. His face was swollen and bruised. Concern filled her. "What happened to you?"

"I got involved in something that was none of my business," he told her, and his voice was colder than she'd ever heard it—than she'd thought Milek capable of being. "You need to leave, Candace."

"I want to talk to Chekov," she said.

"That's not possible," another man answered. He was big—bigger than Milek—and obviously armed, his gun too big for his holster.

She glanced at his neck, but he had no scratches. This wasn't the man who'd attacked her. What about Chekov's other men? It could have been any of them, and she suspected he had several in his employ.

"Where's Garek?" she asked.

The woman snorted—something Candace wouldn't have thought such a princess type capable of doing.

She turned toward her. "What?"

"Chasing after him like you are is very unattractive," the woman told her.

No one had ever called Candace beautiful—except Garek. He had kept saying it that night—as he'd undressed her, as he'd made love to her. And after as he'd held her...until he'd fallen asleep. Then she'd slipped away from him—because she hadn't been able to believe him. To believe in what had happened between them.

But then she'd been right to leave—since he had proved to still be the man she'd been afraid he was.

But what if she hadn't left that night? Would he be working for Chekov? Was this all her fault?

Candace shrugged. She could have told the woman Garek was the one who'd been chasing after her—that he had chased her for a year before finally catching her. That even last night he'd let himself into her apartment...

But she suspected while Garek wasn't in love with

Chekov's daughter, the same might not be true of Tori. Being around him again might have rekindled her teenage crush on him. Because she was acting almost proprietary.

Candace recognized the woman's attitude because she felt that way herself—possessive of Garek Kozminski. It was crazy. Garek Kozminski wasn't the kind of man that any woman would ever possess. He would belong to no one. The most a woman would get from him was a night like Candace had had—a magical, wondrous night of unsurpassed pleasure.

That was another reason she had slipped out that night—so she wouldn't expect more from him than he was willing or able to give. No. Nothing would have changed if she'd stayed.

"I need to talk to him," Candace persisted. If anyone could get Chekov to turn over the security footage, he could. She needed to see it—to see if any of his men had followed her out. Or maybe Rus was right and one of those mug shots he'd shown her had followed her.

As if thoroughly disgusted with her, Tori snorted again. Then she said, "You're embarrassing yourself."

"Probably," Candace acknowledged. "But it won't be the first time. Fortunately no one's ever died of humiliation."

"Maybe not but plenty of them have died of stupidity," a deep voice murmured.

Her skin tingled in reaction to Garek's closeness. But then he was grasping her arm and tugging her through the crowd.

"What are you doing?" she asked, as she tried to wriggle free of him.

"What the hell are you doing?" he asked. "Are you *trying* to get yourself killed?"

She tried to dig her heels into the floor. But it was concrete, so she caught no traction. She wasn't able to slow him down as he effortlessly pulled her along behind him.

"No," she replied. "I'm trying to find out who's trying to kill me. I need the security footage from last night."

"Do you have a search warrant?" he asked. "Oh, that's right. You're not a cop anymore. Seems like you've forgotten."

"I haven't forgotten how to investigate a crime," she said, "which is what I intend to do."

"This isn't your case," Garek said. "It's Rus's. Let him handle the investigation."

So he knew she'd gone to the FBI agent. How? Had Rus questioned him or colluded with him?

"Do you think he'll be able to get a search warrant for the security footage?" she asked.

She was surprised when he answered honestly, "No."

"Then let me see it," she said. "If Chekov has nothing to hide…"

He let out a bitter chuckle and flinched. His hand skimmed over his stomach, and she realized he'd been hit. Milek wasn't the only one who'd been roughed up. What the hell were the Kozminskis involved in?

"Chekov doesn't have anything to hide about *you*," he said. "He doesn't even know you exist."

She doubted that—since his daughter seemed to know and pity her. And since she was pretty sure the man who'd followed her from the club and attacked her in the alley probably worked for Chekov. But then most of the criminals in River City worked for him.

"And we're going to keep it that way," Garek said as he continued tugging her through the crowd toward the exit.

"You can't throw me out of here," she said. "I haven't done anything wrong."

"We reserve the right to refuse anyone's business," he said, and he pointed to the sign in the lobby proclaiming exactly that.

She tugged free of his grasp before he could toss her onto the street. The two valets in the lobby stared at them—until Garek glared back. Then they quickly stepped outside into the cold.

"*We,*" she repeated what he'd said. "You are working for Chekov."

"I'm on assignment," he said.

"You admitted to me that you're in too deep," she reminded him.

He shrugged. "And that surprises you? You're the one who kept warning Logan that I hadn't changed—that I was a criminal and a killer." He flinched again, but she suspected it had nothing to do with whatever injuries he had and everything to do with what she used to say about him.

She reached out to him instinctively, wanting to soothe his pain—his physical ones and whatever emotional ones she might have inflicted. It had been wrong and out of character for her to act like she had with him. She was never judgmental and unforgiving—until him.

But he caught the hand she reached toward him before she could touch him. "You were right about me," he said. "Doesn't that make you happy?"

It made her sick with disappointment. And it confused her—because if he truly was the man she'd worried he was, she doubted he would have admitted it. Was he lying to her like he'd lied to Logan about loving Tori Chekov?

Why?

"But that night…" That night had changed everything, had made her want to believe in him, to trust him.

"It was a mistake," he said. "We both know that."

Tears stung her eyes, but she blinked them back and lifted her chin. She could take a hit, too. She certainly had over the years.

He continued, "And your coming here was a mistake. You need to leave and never come back."

"But I need to find out who attacked me."

"Leave that investigation to Rus," he said. "And leave me alone." He released her hand then and opened the door.

A blast of cold air slapped her in the face and brought her to her senses. She had made a fool of herself— letting herself believe Stacy was right, that he had cared about her.

"I'll leave you alone," she promised. "But you need to stay the hell away from me, too."

"I will," he said.

As she passed by him to step out the door, she heard him murmur, "I have to…"

She stopped in front of him and met his gaze. His gray eyes were dark with emotions, but she could read none of them. She couldn't read him. She could only feel her own attraction to him, in her quickening pulse, in the tingling in her body. Her breath escaped in a gasp, but all she said was, "Goodbye." Then she walked away.

This time she was ready when she left, though—her

hand on her gun. If anyone tried to attack her again, she would protect herself. Physically.

She hadn't been able to protect herself emotionally though. Garek Kozminski had gotten to her—had broken her heart before she'd even realized he had stolen it. She had been right about him; he was a thief.

Milek swallowed hard as he stared down the barrel of the gun. Last night he'd been beaten nearly to death. Tonight he nearly got shot.

"What the hell are you doing following me?" Candace asked. Even though she'd identified him, she hadn't put away her weapon. She held it on him as they stood near where she'd parked her car.

It was a couple blocks down the street from the club but nowhere near the alley where she'd been attacked. She'd been fortunate enough to find a space near the more populated area of the city, where Christmas lights and wreaths decorated the lampposts.

He knew she had never trusted Garek, but she hadn't given him the hard time she'd given his brother. "What do you think I'm doing?" he asked.

"I don't know," she said. "Do you work for Chekov, too?"

Milek wanted nothing to do with the mobster. But he wasn't going to let his brother get himself killed either.

"I'm helping Garek," he said. "He asked me to protect you." He'd also yelled at him for letting her talk to Tori. But Milek had pointed out how hard it was to stop Candace from doing what she wanted.

"By following me?"

"By making sure nobody hurts you again."

Her lashes fluttered as she blinked. She wasn't flirting, though. She wouldn't even look at him now. And he realized he was too late. Somebody had already hurt her. Garek.

"What is he doing?" she asked. "Why would he get involved with Chekov again?"

Even though he knew, Milek only shrugged. But the sight of her—so close to tears—got to him, and he added, "Everything isn't always what it seems."

Especially when it came to his brother. Garek acted as if nothing bothered him and as if he cared about nobody and nothing. But he had and would sacrifice everything for those he loved. Milek suspected Garek loved Candace, or he wouldn't be so worried about her. But he was worried because of Viktor's threat. If the mobster figured out Garek was trying to get evidence against him, he would go after everyone Garek loved. Maybe he was already going after Candace as a warning for Garek to not betray him.

But if he really wanted to make sure Garek wouldn't betray him, he might just eliminate the threat. He might kill Garek before he ever got the chance to discover the evidence he needed to put Chekov away.

"You're worried," Candace said, and finally she holstered her weapon.

Milek nodded. "He's playing a dangerous game with dangerous people."

She blinked again, but the hint of tears she fought wasn't for herself. These were for his brother. "Protect *him*," she said. "I can protect myself."

He would have argued Garek could protect himself, too. But with this assignment, he wasn't so certain. It was just too dangerous…

Chapter 11

Anger coursed through Garek. That damn woman was so stubborn—she was going to get herself killed for certain. He was furious she'd shown up at the club again. And he was even more furious she'd caught Milek following her and sent him away.

She needed protection. She needed *him*.

But Garek had vowed to stay away from her. So after seeing Tori back to her father's heavily protected estate, he'd headed right home—to the apartment he'd begun to resent. It was all white trim and beige walls—colorless and impersonal. He wanted to move into the house he'd bought with its richly painted walls and ornate trim. He wanted to move on with his life.

But he couldn't do that until he wrapped up this assignment—until he put Chekov away. Even after that was done, he doubted he would get another chance with

Candace. He never should have told her that night had been a mistake. He'd hurt her. Then he'd convinced her that she'd been right about him, so she would never trust him now. She would certainly never love him.

Distracted, as always, by thoughts of her, he nearly missed it when he slid the key in the lock. Usually he would have noticed the gouges right away—the telltale sign someone had picked his lock. He shook his head and murmured, "Amateur…"

Before he'd turned double digits, Garek had been able to pick a lock without leaving a single mark on it. What the hell had this person used? An ax? Patek Kozminski would have been horrified. But then his father hadn't tolerated incompetence—at least not in his sons. He had treated Stacy like a princess while Milek and Garek had been his lackeys—thieves in training.

No wonder Candace hadn't believed he could change—not when he'd been raised a thief. After his release from jail, he'd kept his skills honed breaking into museums and businesses. But that had been at their request—for him to test their security systems.

That was another reason Logan had hired him and Milek; they had brought in clients of their own. But Garek had made Logan keep that information from Candace. He'd wanted her to discover for herself the man he'd become—not have someone else tell her.

He had ruined any chance of that now. When he'd told her he was in too deep, he had made her think the worst of him again. But that was for the best—for her. For her safety…

He needed to keep her out of danger—because danger was all around him. As he unlocked and pushed open his apartment door, he heard the creak of floorboards moving beneath a person's weight. Whoever had broken into his apartment was still there.

He drew his weapon from his holster and stepped inside with his gun drawn and ready to fire.

Candace had found the evidence she'd needed to prove to herself and everyone else Garek Kozminski was still a thief. He hadn't stolen only her heart.

He must have stolen plenty of other things because he'd had the opportunity. She'd found tubes of plans— building plans, security plans—for museums and art galleries not just in River City or even America but all around the world.

She hadn't found what he might have stolen from those places. Those things had probably already been fenced. Or maybe he'd been hired to steal them for someone else. Was that what Chekov had really hired Garek to do?

Steal something?

She turned back to the plans—trying to figure out which place might be his next target. Most of the plans looked old, though; some dated from years ago. In addition to the dates, there were notes on them—pointing out the weaknesses in the security system. That must have been how he'd figured out where to break in. But then she noticed along with the weaknesses, there were recommendations on how to eliminate them.

And she remembered that strange comment Milek had made about his brother; everything wasn't always what it seemed. Garek Kozminski certainly wasn't.

"So which place do you think I'm hitting for Chekov?" a deep voice asked.

She shouldn't have been surprised he'd caught her. He

always moved so silently that, of course, she hadn't heard him come in. She turned to find him leaning against his bedroom doorjamb, his gun in his hand. He had heard her or maybe he'd seen the signs of her sloppy lock picking. But the barrel of his weapon was pointed down, at the hardwood floor, instead of at her.

"These plans are old," she said as she reached for them. The gun was still pointed at the floor, but her hands shook as she rolled up the papers. Maybe that was because of where she was, though.

In his bedroom…

It had just dawned on her that was where he'd caught her—after he'd told her to leave him alone. He probably thought she was stalking him.

And maybe she was.

"Doesn't mean I still couldn't use them," he said.

"After you recommended how they could improve their security systems, I doubt you could break in again."

He chuckled. "Oh, *I* could…" He chuckled again. "*You*, however, could not."

"I got in here," she said and waited for him to yell at her about it.

He shrugged. "I don't have anything I want to protect. A child could break in here." He snorted. "From the looks of the lock, I thought a child had."

She wasn't too proud to admit, "I don't have your skills for breaking and entering."

He sighed. "Fortunately for you, you weren't raised to be a thief."

And for the first time she realized how hard it must have been for him being born a Kozminski. He'd been expected to become a thief; he hadn't been given the choice to be what he'd wanted.

"No, I wasn't."

"What did your parents want you to be?" he asked.

She shrugged. "Whatever I wanted." They hadn't had any expectations for her.

"I don't really know anything about your family," he said.

Whereas everyone knew everything about his family. The Kozminskis were River City legend.

She shrugged. "Nothing much to tell. My dad is an army man. My mom a former beauty queen and housewife. She follows him to every base he gets assigned."

"So did you," he said. "That must have been hard for you—moving all the time."

She'd felt sorry for herself a time or two, but she shook her head now, disgusted with herself. She'd had no idea how hard a childhood could really be. Garek hadn't even had one.

"The moving wasn't that hard," she said. "It was my mom putting me in pageants that was hard."

She waited for him to laugh—like every other man she'd told that to had laughed at the ridiculous idea of her being in beauty contests. Garek must have been too pissed at her for breaking in—especially after he'd told her to leave him alone—to find any humor in her admission.

"I didn't see any trophies in your place," he said instead.

She laughed now. "That's because I never won."

"I find that hard to believe," he said. And finally he holstered his weapon and stepped away from the doorway.

Even though the gun had been put away, she was still shaking. Actually, she was shaking more because of the way he was looking at her—like he had looked at her that night, as if she was beautiful.

"I guess I haven't been the only one who has struggled to see the truth about the other," she said. While she'd thought he was a criminal, he thought she had been pretty enough to win a beauty contest.

"What do you think the truth is?" Garek asked.

She quoted his brother. "That everything isn't always what it seems."

"Why are you here?" He stepped even closer, so close she felt the heat of his body. "Why were you so desperate to get inside that you picked the lock?"

Heat rushed to her face. He must have thought she was stalking him. "I know you told me to leave you alone…"

He nodded and acknowledged, "I did say that…"

"And you said you'd leave me alone."

"I said that, too." He reached for her, his hands closing around her shoulders. "And I meant it…"

She swallowed, trying to force down her embarrassment. "So I should leave you alone…" She hadn't found what she'd thought she would find. But maybe she'd found what she had needed to find.

He shook his head. "I told you to leave me alone and said I would leave you alone," he reiterated. "But even as I was saying it, I knew it wasn't possible."

Her heart began to pound heavily and quickly in her chest. "Why not?"

"Because of this…" His hands moved from her shoulders to her face, which he held while he lowered his head and kissed her deeply. Passionately.

His lips moved over hers, his teeth nipping gently until she opened her mouth. Then he slid his tongue deep; it moved sensually over hers. He pulled back, panting for breath. "Because I want you…"

She wanted him, too. It was crazy. She still couldn't trust him. Even if he had been legit in the past, he was working for a mobster now and by his own admission was in deep. She needed to leave him alone like she'd promised she would.

But she couldn't leave. *She* was in too deep.

She wanted to know if she'd romanticized her memories of that night—if she was remembering it—and them—as more than they'd been. So she reached for him. Her hands cupping his jaw, she pulled his mouth down to hers. And she kissed him with all the passion burning inside her. She nipped at his lips and slipped her tongue inside his mouth.

He groaned. Then he was lifting her—as easily as he had that night in the alley—as easily as if she were one of those petite, girly girls she'd always secretly wished she'd been. With him, she felt like that; she felt feminine.

He laid her on the mattress, atop the plans she hadn't rolled up yet. Then he pulled off his coat and his holster and gun. He dropped them beside the bed. But he wasn't moving quickly enough for Candace.

She reached out and grabbed his belt, tugging it loose. But he caught her hand when her fingers touched the zipper tab. Had he changed his mind? Didn't he want her?

But then he turned his attention to undressing her. He removed her holster, then pulled her sweater up and over her head. A gasp of breath slipped through his lips, and he murmured, "Red satin…"

"It's Christmastime," she explained. And she liked red. She also liked silky things against her skin.

She liked his fingertips, too, as they glided along her

collarbone then over the swells of her breasts. He pushed the cups down to tease her nipples.

She shifted on the bed and moaned as tension built inside her body. She needed him. Now.

But he continued to tease her, with his lips and his tongue stroking over her nipples. He unsnapped, unzipped and pushed down her jeans. And again he murmured, "Red satin…"

She reached for the clasp on his pants again. This time he let her lower the zipper and release his pulsing erection. He groaned as her fingers skimmed over him.

He tugged off his shirt, revealing his muscular chest and washboard abs and bruises. She gasped and intended to ask about those bruises.

But when she opened her mouth, he leaned down and kissed her like he always kissed her—with such passion—that she couldn't think. She could only feel. She stroked her tongue along his. Her questions would keep for later; she needed him now.

He must have needed her, too. He kicked off his pants and joined her on top of those rustling plans. His body covered hers, like it had that night on the couch in her apartment. She loved the weight of him on top of her. But she really wanted him inside her.

She nipped at his shoulder and then the side of his neck. She felt his pulse leap beneath her lips. Then his mouth covered hers, and he kissed her like she wanted him to make love to her—his tongue thrusting inside her mouth. He kissed her deeply. And as he kissed her, he removed her bra and her panties. Her legs tangled with his, and she thrust up and pushed against his erection.

But he was in no hurry—not like she was. He took his time with her, with her mouth, and then he moved his lips down her body. He kissed her shoulders and then her breasts.

She writhed beneath him as the tension in her body drove her to madness. She wanted to drive him crazy, too. So she kissed him everywhere she could reach— his shoulder, his arm, his chest...

And she reached between their bodies, sliding her hand up and down his shaft. As if to reciprocate he slid his finger inside her, in and out, while his thumb teased her most sensitive spot. She screamed his name as she came apart.

Then he was inside her, filling her. She locked her legs around his waist and bucked up, knocking him to his side. They rolled across the plans until she was on top. And with the madness driving her, she rode him as he stroked her breasts. An orgasm rippled through her, overwhelming her with pleasure—with ecstasy. She screamed his name.

He grasped her hips, moving her faster as he thrust deeper. She came again. Then he joined her, his body tensing before filling hers.

She hadn't imagined that night, nor had her memories of it exaggerated what had happened. It had been as wild and wonderful as she remembered.

Maybe even more so...

He pulled her down on top of him, clasping her naked body against his as he stayed inside her. He clasped his arms around her, holding tightly, as if he didn't intend to let her get away again.

Or as if he intended to protect her. He could protect her from danger; he had saved her life twice. But could he protect himself from danger?

Her heart pounded as frantically as it had when they'd made love—as fear for his safety overwhelmed her.

Garek would need to protect himself because he was undoubtedly in danger. Viktor Chekov's right-hand man had been murdered just weeks ago. If Garek got any closer to the mobster, he might be next.

Nicholas Rus stared down at the body lying atop the steel table in the morgue. The guy's throat bore deep scratches. But those wounds hadn't killed him. The hole in his chest had done that.

The bullet had already been removed and rushed to the FBI lab. Nicholas had to know who'd killed him and with what weapon. He had to know if the man who'd attacked Candace Baker had anything to do with Viktor Chekov.

This was the man who'd grabbed Candace in the alley. Had he intended to kill her or only hurt her? And on whose orders?

His cell rang, startling Nick. He hadn't realized he'd have reception in the morgue. He clicked the talk button. "Agent Rus."

"Nicholas?"

"Chief Lynch." While Nick was on assignment in River City, the Chicago Bureau chief was still his boss. He'd had to approve the rush order for ballistics.

"I got the results."

The chief must have rushed them even more than Nicholas had thought possible.

"It's the same gun," Lynch continued, "the one that killed the man your witness says Chekov shot."

Nick didn't know if he should curse or celebrate. The gun was still in play—not disposed of as he'd feared.

But Chekov had used it to kill the man who'd tried to kill Candace. What did that mean?

Was he tying up loose ends? He had no looser ends than Garek and even his own daughter.

"This is big, Nicholas. How are you handling the investigation without more agents?" Lynch asked. "I'll send Dalton Reyes up to help."

Reyes was the Bureau's expert on organized crime. A former gang member, the guy could handle himself undercover. But there had been no time to bring him in.

"Chekov wouldn't have trusted some guy off the street," Nick explained, "no matter what background we established for Reyes."

"So you don't have an agent on the inside?"

"I have someone undercover on the inside," Nick admitted. But he wasn't an agent.

"How'd you get someone inside so quickly?"

"It's someone who used to work for Chekov, someone who once dated his daughter."

Lynch whistled. "Sounds like he might be Chekov's next victim."

Nicholas was already worried that might be the case.

"Let me know if you need Dalton," Lynch said. "I'll send him up to help."

Nick thanked his boss before hanging up. He appreciated the offer. But as he stared down at the man on the slab, he worried he'd already waited too long to accept help. And he might have cost Garek Kozminski his life.

Chapter 12

Cold penetrated Garek's coat and flesh, chilling him to the bone. Just a short while ago, he'd been warm. Hell, he'd been hot—driving deep inside Candace's body. He had made love to her again and again. Then he'd held her, tightly, so she wouldn't slip away from him like she had that first night.

He wouldn't lose her like he'd worried he had. But then he had wound up having to leave her. She hadn't awakened when his cell rang or when he loosened his hold on her and slipped from the bed.

"Why'd you summon me here?" Garek asked as he glanced around the morgue and shuddered. He'd rather have met him in an alley again. But nobody was likely to witness them together here.

And it had been a summons—not a request. He had been given no opportunity to refuse. But Rus had promised there was a police detail watching his place, watching Candace to make sure she stayed safe even after he'd left her. Without that promise, Garek would have refused to leave her—no matter how pissed Rus might have been.

"I need you to identify a body," the FBI agent replied. He pointed to the one lying on the morgue slab.

Garek stared at the body. The guy was big, his skin winter pale but for a profusion of tattoos. He shrugged. "I don't know." He looked like a lot of hired muscle.

"Could he be the guy you saw running out of the alley that night? Or the one who tried running you over?"

Garek peered more closely at the body. And he noticed the scratches. Milek had said Candace had left her mark on the guy. He cursed. Not that he was sad the guy was dead. But now that he was dead, he wouldn't be able to explain why he'd tried killing Candace.

Had it been personal, like Rus had thought? Someone she'd arrested when she'd been a cop. Or had someone hired him to hurt Candace?

"How'd he die?" he asked. In addition to the tattoos, there were bruises. There was also a hole in his chest, which could have been caused by a bullet or a knife. Due to the autopsy incisions, Garek couldn't tell which.

"Shot…"

Garek shivered. "I know it's too soon to tell but could it have been the same gun…"

"It was," Rus replied. "I rushed the ballistics."

Garek cursed.

"This is good news," Rus said, although he didn't sound all that thrilled either. "The gun is still out there. It killed Candace's attacker."

"But who is this guy?" Garek asked. "I don't recognize him."

"So you don't think he works for Chekov?"

Garek shrugged. "I don't know everyone who works for Chekov. He could have worked for him. But why would Chekov kill him?"

"You know if Viktor Chekov is unsatisfied with your work, you don't get a pink slip," Rus said. "You get a toe tag."

Garek suspected there was more to Tori's boyfriend's death than Viktor's dissatisfaction with Alexander Polinsky's work. He must have done something else to piss off his boss. Or someone else...

Garek must have pissed him off, too. But instead of going after him, Chekov had sent this goon after Candace. Then he'd killed him. Because the man had failed? Or because Viktor had personally decided to go after her?

"You have to be extra careful," Rus said. He narrowed his eyes and studied Garek as if trying to see inside his mind. "You can't afford any distractions."

Garek sighed; maybe the man had seen inside his mind. There was usually only one thing on it. "Like Candace?"

"She can't afford for you to be distracted either," Rus said.

No, she couldn't. Because if Viktor had decided to go after Candace, it would be hard to save her. Making love with her—while wonderful—had been a mistake. He needed to be totally focused now—for her sake as much as his. Or they would both wind up, like her attacker, in the morgue.

Candace had been summoned to the office, Logan's office. When her cell rang, she'd hurriedly answered it—afraid it might wake Garek. She need not have worried. He was already gone.

When had he left? And where had he gone?

He'd left no note. No explanation.

Had he done it out of vengeance? Getting her back for her leaving while he'd been sleeping that first night they'd spent together?

She hadn't thought there would be another night. Apparently there shouldn't have been. She'd just made a fool of herself again—falling for a man who had no respect for her.

But he had had desire. He'd made love to her greedily but also generously. He'd given her even more pleasure than he'd taken. So he cared about her—he had to.

Logan snapped his fingers. "What's the matter? Didn't you get any sleep last night?"

Sleep had been the problem. If she'd stayed awake, she would have known why Garek had left and where he'd gone. To Chekov?

What the hell did Chekov want Garek to do for him? Break into one of those museums or art galleries? Was he doing that now?

"I'm fine," she said.

"You didn't go to the ER like I told you to," he said.

Since HIPAA laws prevented him from looking at her medical records, Nikki must have given her up. Candace couldn't blame her, though; she knew how much the girl hated secrets and lies.

"I'm fine," she repeated.

"No more attempts on your life?"

She shook her head. Not her life. Just her heart…

For a year Garek had flirted with her and propositioned her. She didn't know if he'd begun to steal her heart then or if it had happened that first night she'd given in to her attraction to him.

She sighed.

"That disappoints you?" he asked.

She was disappointed in herself—because she'd let her attraction to Garek distract her. Someone had tried to kill her; she needed to find out who and why and how it was related to Garek and Viktor Chekov.

"It disappoints me that I haven't found out who attacked me."

He slid a photo across his desk. She picked it up and stared at it. The man's face had been covered with the mask when he'd attacked her, so she didn't recognize the meaty features. She recognized the scratches on his neck, though; she had done that. Fortunately, she'd let her nails grow the two weeks she'd been off work. She'd even treated herself to a manicure.

"That's him," she said. "Who is he and what happened to him?"

Was that where Garek had gone? To take care of this man?

"Donald Doornbos."

She shrugged. The name meant nothing to her. "Known associates?"

Logan chuckled. "You'd have to ask Agent Rus. He just sent this over to see if you could identify the man."

"He's my attacker," she said. "But I've never seen him before that night."

"You didn't arrest him when you were a cop?"

"Rus already knows I didn't." Or he would have called her down to River City PD.

Logan took the photo back from her. "Yeah…"

"So does he work for Viktor Chekov?"

"I don't know," Logan said. "Rus didn't say."

"What did he say?"

"Not much," Logan replied. And a muscle twitched along his jaw, indicating his irritation. He didn't like it any more than she did that he didn't know what was going on.

"Cause of death?"

"Gunshot wound."

"Who shot him?" Garek? Had it been in self-defense? Or revenge? This was probably the same man who'd tried to run them down in the alley.

"His body was found in a parking lot."

"Of Chekov's club?"

Logan shook his head. "No."

"He could have been killed there or at Chekov's estate and his body dumped elsewhere." Everyone assumed that was what had happened with Chekov's previous employee—Alexander Polinsky. Or at least that was what the officers she still knew on the force had told her.

"This is Rus's investigation," Logan said. "Not yours."

She opened her mouth to argue. But he held up his hand and continued, "You're a bodyguard now. Not a cop."

She'd been hearing this a lot lately. She liked protecting people and hadn't missed being a cop—until now.

"And I have an assignment for you."

"I thought you wanted to make sure I was cleared medically before you gave me an assignment?"

That muscle twitched again with irritation. This time she had no doubt it was with her. "You've been telling me that you're fine," he said, tossing her words back at her. "So you're fine to take an assignment."

"You're going to put me on Chekov's daughter's protection duty," she said. It was the only assignment she wanted, so she could find out what the hell was going on with Garek and Viktor Chekov.

"No," he replied. "You've only been off a couple of weeks, so you can't have forgotten I'm the boss. I give out the assignments."

She arched a brow in skepticism. "Really? Didn't Garek bring you Chekov as a client?"

Logan nodded. "He's brought in other clients, as well."

The museums and art galleries.

"Why didn't you tell me that before?" When she'd criticized his hiring the Kozminskis.

"Garek didn't want me to," Logan said.

He had wanted her to think the worst of him. Why? Just for his amusement?

"And the clients *Garek* brings Payne Protection want to work with *Garek*," Logan said. "I have an assignment for you. It's in Chicago—"

She shook her head. "No."

"You didn't even let me finish."

"You don't need to," she said. "This isn't a legit assignment. You just want me out of town." Probably at Garek's request.

He sighed and rubbed his forehead. Apparently his headache had returned. "You're making me regret hiring you back."

"Your wife asked me to come back," she reminded him.

"She shouldn't have," he said.

"So you don't want me working for you?"

"You're not working for me," he said. "I have a legit assignment—a female lawyer who has requested a female bodyguard for protection—in Chicago."

"Send Nikki," she suggested.

"No," he said. "I need one of my best bodyguards on this assignment."

"Nikki could be—if you'd give her a chance."

Beyond just irritated, he glared at her now. She waited for him to fire her. But he just shook his head.

"When someone was trying to kill you, did you leave the state to protect someone else?" she asked.

"They weren't trying to kill me," he said. "They were trying to kill Parker."

"You didn't know that at the time," she said.

He shrugged. "It doesn't matter now."

"No," she agreed. "Because you're no longer in danger."

"And the guy who was trying to kill you is dead," he said. "So you're free to go to Chicago."

"I'm not free to go anywhere until I know who he was working for," she said. But she stood up to leave. "And I have my suspicions."

"All you have are suspicions," Logan said.

She nodded. "Yes, until I get evidence."

"Stay away from Chekov," Logan warned her as she headed for the door. "And stay away from Garek, too."

She didn't think that was going to be a problem since she had no idea where he'd gone. So she just nodded again as she walked out of his office. She closed the door with a soft click, turned and nearly collided with Nikki.

Nikki threw her arms around her neck and hugged her. "Thank you!"

"For what?"

"For what you told him—I would be one of the best bodyguards he has if he gave me a chance."

Candace laughed. "You have his office bugged?"

Nikki pulled back and pressed a finger to her lips then whispered, "Of course."

"He has no idea how good you are," Candace said.

Nikki shrugged. "It doesn't matter. I'll work for Cooper as soon as he starts his franchise. Maybe you should, too."

She wouldn't be working for anyone unless she found out who'd hired that man to attack her—because someone must have hired him. And if they'd hired him, they had probably already hired someone else to complete the job. She couldn't worry about protecting anyone else right now; she had to worry about protecting herself.

Stacy touched the twitching muscle along her husband's jaw first with her fingertips and then with her lips. His hands caught her waist and pressed her against him. He lowered his head and kissed her lips. While her passion ignited, he hadn't distracted her from her concern.

"What's wrong?" she asked him.

He shook his head and glanced around the room at the rest of his family. They'd all gathered at Penny's to decorate her Christmas tree. Christmas was still a couple of weeks away, but the wedding planner liked to decorate early so she could enjoy her tree.

But Penny, being Penny, had fed them all first. Now she handed an ax to Nicholas Rus.

The FBI agent looked horrified. He had been uncomfortable all through dinner, too—as if he hadn't expected to be included in a family tradition. He didn't know how welcoming and loving Penny Payne was.

"Now it's time to cut down the tree," Penny told him. "The best ones are in back of the house."

Rus handed the ax to Cooper, the former marine. "I've never cut down a tree before."

"You can't swing an ax?" Parker teased him.

Parker was like Garek in that he always teased. With Parker, it was just a natural part of his personality. With her brother Garek, it was a coping mechanism—not for himself but for her and Milek. Since they'd been kids, he'd joked with them to make them feel better and worry less.

"Maybe he just doesn't want to," Nikki said as she pulled on her hat and headed toward the door. She took the ax from Cooper.

And Logan dropped his hands from Stacy and hurried after his sister. There was no way he would let Nikki swing the ax; he worried she might hurt herself—which was the same reason he wouldn't give her a protection assignment. He needed to let up or he risked losing her— like Stacy felt she had lost her brothers.

Cooper and Parker hurried out after Logan. Their wives—Tanya and Sharon—had chosen cleanup duty in the kitchen over trudging out in the snow. Like Stacy, they also wanted to stay inside the house with their babies who slept in the nursery Penny had decorated for her new grandbabies. Tanya and Cooper's son was just a month older than baby Penny. Parker and Sharon had two children; his two-year-old son who'd fallen asleep despite his protests he wasn't tired and their month-old daughter.

Penny touched Nicholas Rus's shoulder. "Go ahead," she urged. "Help them pick out a tree."

He looked as horrified as he had when she'd handed him the ax. "I don't want to intrude," he said. "It seems like Nikki is already upset."

"That's my husband's fault," Stacy said. "Not yours."

He turned to her with a skeptical look. Nikki had made her opinion of him clear.

Penny sighed. She knew it, too. She grabbed a coat from the hook by the door. "I'm going to make sure they pick one with full enough branches." She turned back to Rus. "You are welcome to join us."

He nodded, but he didn't move toward the door. She sighed again and headed out.

"She means it," Stacy said. "She welcomed me and my brothers into her family, too." Penny was warm and inviting and forgiving.

Her brightly decorated Victorian farmhouse was a reflection of her warmth. A fire burned in the hearth.

"Your brothers aren't here."

"No," she said and a pang struck her heart. Would they forgive her before Christmas? "And that's my fault."

He shook his head. "Don't blame yourself."

There was something in his tone—something that caught her attention. She studied his face, and she saw the guilt flicker in eyes that were the same brilliant blue of her husband's. "You know that Garek's involved with Viktor Chekov. You even know what it's about, don't you?" Another pang struck her heart. "Oh, God, Milek's involved, too."

She'd reached out to him to help Garek. Instead she'd put him in danger, too.

Rus didn't deny it. He refused to say anything at all. But she saw the worry on his face. And she knew she wasn't the only one concerned that she might lose her brothers. Forever.

Chapter 13

The door swung back and forth in a broken jamb. Someone hadn't just picked his lock this time. They'd broken down his door. His heart hammered with fear. Had Candace been inside when it had happened?

Rus had promised he would call Garek if the agents following Candace saw any threat. This was damn sure a threat. He drew his weapon from his holster. But this threat was meant for him.

Gun drawn, he stepped inside his apartment. Viktor Chekov sat in the middle of his couch, his feet propped up on the coffee table. At either end of the couch stood a man with a gun—the barrels pointed at Garek.

He could shoot one of them but not both. He couldn't win this gunfight. So he holstered his weapon. "If I'd known you were coming to visit, I would have left the door unlocked and some appetizers out."

Why the hell was Viktor visiting? Garek had made certain no one had followed him down to the River City morgue. If anyone caught him meeting with Special Agent Rus, he was a dead man for sure. That was why so few people could know about his assignment for Rus—because the more people who knew, the more likely it was Chekov might find out.

"We haven't been here long," Viktor said.

"Why are you here?" he asked. "Milek is with Tori right now." Garek had been with Rus for a while—pouring through Donald Doornbos's past to find a connection between him and Chekov. Garek had even stayed after Rus had left for dinner at Penny Payne's. He could have gone to dinner, too. He'd been invited.

But Candace had probably been invited, too. And he hadn't been ready to see her yet. Of course every time he closed his eyes he saw her, lying naked in his bed—her silky skin all flushed with passion, her lips wet and swollen from his kisses…

"Maybe I should have had your boss at Payne Protection assign your brother to protect my daughter," Viktor said. "It seems like he is the more focused one of the two of you. But then he has no distractions like you have."

Garek tensed. "Distractions?"

A snide grin twisted Viktor's face. "The woman bodyguard, the former cop."

Fear clutched Garek's heart.

Viktor knew about Candace. For how long?

"Maybe I should have her assigned for Tori's protection," Viktor said. "I find I may be down a bodyguard."

The dead guy had worked for him then.

"Somebody quit?" Garek asked.

Viktor cocked his head. "Quit? More likely he will be fired."

Oh, he was talking about him—which brought back Rus's warning. Viktor Chekov didn't give out pink slips; he gave out toe tags.

"I don't have any distractions," Garek claimed.

Chekov stood up and reached for Garek. He patted his face with just enough force it stung. "Don't lie to me."

"I wouldn't," Garek assured him.

"Then maybe you're lying to yourself," Chekov said. "I saw you chase after that woman."

Had he sent someone after her before Garek had followed her out?

"I didn't follow her right out," Garek protested. But someone else had. "But as you pointed out, I work with her. I wanted to make sure she made it safely to her vehicle." Which she hadn't…

Viktor laughed. "So now you're a gentleman?"

Maybe he would have been—had a woman like Penny Payne raised him. But his own mother hadn't been anything like Penny; she hadn't cared about her children at all. Even after her husband had tried to assault her daughter, she'd blamed Stacy and them; she'd even testified against them rather than admit she'd been married to a monster.

"And a woman like Candace Baker doesn't need anyone else to protect her," Viktor said with grudging respect.

And that vice of fear tightened around Garek's heart. Viktor had to be behind the attacks on her or how else would he know how well she could take care of herself?

Garek shrugged. "You're right. That's why she's not a distraction. She's nothing."

Viktor snorted.

"She's a former cop," Garek reminded him. "Do you really think a former cop would ever get involved with a Kozminski? Or a Kozminski with a former cop?"

Viktor laughed. "Your sister married a former cop."

"My sister never went to prison," he said. "She never committed a crime." He could not say the same—no matter how much he wished he could.

He wanted to be a man Candace could admire and respect. Maybe that was why he had accepted Rus's undercover assignment—because if he was successful, Candace would learn what he had done. His effort to impress her might cost them both their lives, though. He had to convince Chekov that Candace meant nothing to him.

He laughed now. "And do you seriously think I would ever go for a woman like her? She's tougher than I am. She's not my type at all."

"I thought every woman was your type," one of the other men remarked.

"Like Polinsky," the other man murmured.

Garek caught the comment and filed it away to consider later. It must have been why Chekov had killed him. Garek nodded at the first guy. "Exactly. Every woman is my type—never just one woman."

Viktor slapped him again—harder. "Then you better be careful around Tori. She seems to be getting attached to you again."

Garek didn't know how since she was still mourning another man—the lover her own father had murdered. But maybe Tori was acting interested in Garek so Viktor didn't fire him—or kill him.

But maybe her acting was why Chekov had gone after Candace. To eliminate his daughter's competition.

"*I* would never hurt Tori," he said. Not like Viktor had.

Chekov narrowed his dark eyes and nodded. "Good, Garek, then I won't fire you…" He patted his cheek with less sting this time. "Today…"

He headed toward the door, his lackeys rushing after him. "But there's always tomorrow…"

He needed to find that damn gun before Chekov used it again. On him…

Hearing the creak of the broken door, Candace released the breath she'd been holding. But it didn't ease the tightness in her chest—the pain in her heart. *She's nothing.*

Just another conquest.

She waited for the anger—for the pain—to rush over her. But she couldn't shake the fear; she trembled with it. When they'd broken in the door, she'd been in the bedroom—going through those plans again. So she'd drawn her weapon and she'd waited for them to come for her.

But they'd settled in the living room. And they'd waited for Garek. She hadn't known what they were going to do to him. Beat him—like she suspected they had before. Kill him…

She knew Chekov wasn't above that. Everyone suspected he'd killed his own right-hand man a couple of weeks ago. So why would Garek seek out an assignment working for such a madman?

She stepped from the bedroom and asked, "Why?"

He whirled toward her, his eyes wide and his handsome face pale with shock. "You were here?"

She nodded.

"They didn't see you?"

"They didn't look."

He released a shaky breath. "That's good. That's good…"

"Nothing's good about this," she said. Gesturing toward the door, she continued, "Look what they've done to your place. Why would you want to work for someone like that? Someone that dangerous?"

He clenched his jaw and shook his head. "I don't want to. I have to…"

There it was again—another cryptic comment. "What's really going on?" she asked.

"Nothing that concerns you," he replied.

She uttered a bitter laugh. "I'm nothing. I know that…" She'd suspected it herself but she'd hoped she was wrong—about him, about them…

She had hoped they could have a future. But with the way Chekov was treating Garek, she worried he wouldn't have a future with *anyone*.

"Candace…" He murmured her name, his voice gruff with emotion. It was in his eyes, too—the silver going dark gray with regret and frustration and something else…

Something she was probably just imagining.

He reached for her, dragging her up against his body. His was shaking slightly. He'd probably thought Chekov was going to kill him. But then he murmured, "They might have killed you if they'd known you were here…"

He cared. It was in his voice—in his eyes—in the desperate way he clutched her against him.

Candace's breath shuddered out, and she wrapped

her arms around him, clinging to him. "You need to get away from Chekov," she said. "You need to quit."

"You don't quit Chekov," he said.

"You did before."

"I went to jail," he reminded her.

She shuddered as she remembered why he'd gone to jail. Murder. But she accepted now there was more to that story, too. The man he'd killed had been a threat to his sister. He'd done it to protect Stacy. She wondered who he was protecting now.

"You could go to jail again," she warned him, "if you don't get away from him."

His lips curved into a slight smile. "I'd be lucky if I just went to jail."

She shivered again. "Garek, please, get away from him!"

"Like you did me?" he asked. "Like you ran away that first night we spent together?"

She couldn't deny she'd run. "You took off this morning," she reminded him. "You didn't wake me. You left me no note, no explanation."

"Is that why you came back?" he asked. "For an explanation?"

It wasn't exactly why she'd come back but she nodded.

"You want to know where I was this morning?" he asked. "The morgue."

"You identified the man who tried to kill me," she said. "Did he work for Chekov?"

He shrugged. "I don't know. All I know is you need to stay away from me. You need to leave River City again. And this time you need to make sure nobody can track you down—not even Nikki."

She doubted anyone could hide from Nikki. But she shook her head. "I'm not running."

"Then you're a fool," he said. "You need to stay away from me. I'm just going to hurt you." He touched her face then, his fingertips sliding along her jaw. His thumb brushed across her bottom lip. He stared hungrily at her mouth, as if he was dying for a taste of it. But he didn't lower his head. "And I don't want you to get hurt…"

"It's too late for that," she said. The things he'd said, the way he'd pushed her away—that had hurt her. But what hurt her more was he was still keeping things from her—things he would want her to know if he ever intended to let her get close to him—as close as she had let him get to her. She'd let him close enough to steal her heart.

"I'm sorry," he murmured.

"Me, too," she said. "I'm sorry you're a coward."

He stepped back as if she'd struck him. "What?"

"You're a coward," she accused him. "You're the one who's running."

He laughed now. "How's that?"

"You're running from me," she said. "You're pushing me away."

"For your own good!"

"Really?" she challenged him. "My own good? I can take care of myself. I don't need you to protect me. I've been protecting myself for thirty years."

"Really," he shot the word back at her. "You could have been killed—twice."

She laughed. "Twice? You think those are the only times I've ever been in danger? That's nothing. Those weren't even close calls compared to what I've been through. I've almost been *blown up* in Afghanistan and here. I've been shot. Stabbed. Hit over the head."

He flinched as if he could feel the pain she'd felt.

"You're using danger as an excuse to push me away," she said. "To stop me from getting any closer to you!" She stabbed him in the chest with the tip of her finger. "You pursued me for a year. You chased me and wore me down but now that you have me—you're scared."

His throat moved as he swallowed hard. But he didn't deny what she was saying.

"What are you scared of?" she asked. "Are you scared I'm going to hurt you?"

He laughed again, but it sounded forced and nervous. "I have never been scared of getting hurt."

He probably believed that, but she doubted him and raised a brow in skepticism.

"The only thing I'm scared of," he said, "is you're going to get hurt."

She sighed. "And I already told you it's too late…" And maybe it was. She'd spent too many years wishing Logan would love her. She wasn't going to waste any more time just wishing for a man's love—even Garek's. She nodded. "Yeah, it's too late…" She headed for the door.

He reached out again, but she jerked away before he could touch her. "Candace, Chekov could have men out there—waiting to see who leaves here. They could follow you."

She chuckled. "Like I can't lose a tail…"

"Candace…"

"You wanted me to leave," she reminded him. "I'm leaving. And this time I will stay away." She didn't want to wish or even to fight for a man's love anymore; she wanted it given freely to her.

As she walked out Garek's broken door, she accepted they had no chance for a life together. Chekov would probably kill Garek before he ever got a chance to overcome his fear of letting her close. And because he wouldn't let her close, she wouldn't be there to protect him—to protect what they could have had, had he given them a chance.

Nick stared at the Christmas tree glowing brightly in Mrs. Payne's living room. Lights of every size had been strung around it, and ornaments covered it. Most of them handmade and with a story.

He wasn't part of that story, of this family. But she kept trying to pull him into it. Shouldn't she hate him like her kids hated him? He was living proof her dead husband had cheated on her.

But instead of pushing him away, she pulled him closer. Even now she squeezed his hand as she passed him a mug of hot chocolate. "Thank you for staying," she said.

He wasn't sure why she'd asked him to stay as everyone else had been leaving. Maybe she thought he was mad. She had tricked him into dinner. He'd thought it was just one of her usual offers for a home-cooked dinner. He hadn't realized she'd dragged him into a family tradition.

He probably wouldn't have refused her request even if he'd known. He was unable to refuse her anything. He wasn't the one who'd betrayed her, but he was the only one still alive to carry the burden of guilt for that betrayal.

"Thank you for dinner," he said.

She touched his face. He wasn't used to maternal affection. He wasn't used to maternal. "You barely ate," she said.

He had been uncomfortable over more than just his younger half sister's glares. Stacy Kozminski-Payne's obvious concern for her brothers had bothered him and increased his usual burden of guilt.

"I'm sorry I ambushed you with the family dinner," Penny said.

He chuckled. "I am glad you're on the right side of the law. You'd be dangerous if you weren't."

She murmured, "Speaking of dangerous…"

He tensed. This woman had some kind of psychic sixth sense. She always knew what was going on with her family—with every member, biological or whom she had emotionally adopted like she had the Kozminskis, like she was trying with him.

"What is going on with Garek Kozminski?" she asked.

"Why do you think I would know?" he wondered. It was supposed to be an undercover operation.

She smiled. "Because you're like me, Nicholas."

He could have pointed out that wasn't possible. He had none of her DNA or her nurturing. They were nothing alike. But he didn't argue with her.

"You know what's going on with everyone," she said. "You know before *they* know."

He laughed. "You might be psychic," he said. "I'm just good at my job."

She nodded. "That's what Chief Lynch said about you."

She had met his Bureau boss at the weddings of two

of his agent friends. He hadn't realized they'd exchanged more than pleasantries, though.

"He said it's all you have," she added. "That it's all you care about."

He shrugged. "I enjoy my work."

"You need more in your life."

A face—a *beautiful* face—flashed through his mind, but he blinked the image away.

"Work is all I need," he assured her and himself.

She sighed. "You know you need more. You're so close to getting it, Nicholas. You're so close to becoming part of a real family."

He hated the pang that hit his chest and reminded him how that was all he'd ever wanted. He forced a laugh. "Nikki will never accept me."

"She will," Penny said. "Your brothers already have. But the Kozminskis are family, too."

They had once been enemies of the Paynes—at least of Logan and Parker. But now they all acted like brothers. Maybe there was hope for him and Nikki to overcome their differences someday.

"And if you've put Garek and Milek in danger," she continued, "and something happens to them…"

She was just fishing. That was all. But he couldn't lie to her, so he said nothing.

"This is where you're supposed to assure me nothing will happen to them," she said, her warm brown eyes full of concern.

But he couldn't lie to her, so he said nothing.

Chapter 14

Fury gripped Garek, clutching his stomach. He reached out and tore the broken door from the bent hinges. It dropped onto the floor. He didn't care there was no door. There was nothing in that apartment he cared about—now Candace had left.

"Damn her," he said. "Damn her…"

She was right. Even though he wasn't the one who'd left that night, even though he hadn't gone anywhere, he was running, too. He was running from her and using her safety as an excuse to do it.

Hell, she was Candace Baker. She was stronger, smarter and braver than he was. There was nothing she hadn't handled or couldn't handle. Even Viktor Chekov…

Disgusted with himself—with his cowardice as she'd called it—he kicked the door. But he got no satisfaction. The tight knot in his gut didn't ease. He had to find her—had to be with her. Had to admit she was right.

He was scared. And not just for her. He was scared *of* her. Because she could hurt him far worse than Viktor Chekov could. As he started out the door, his cell phone rang. That cell phone—the one only Nick Rus called.

He grabbed it from his pocket. "Did you find another body you want me to identify?" He hoped like hell not.

Rus sighed. "No. I just got a call Candace shook the tail I had on her."

Garek chuckled. "Of course she did."

"My guy said he wasn't the only one watching her," Rus added.

Garek cursed now. "Chekov." It was how he knew so much about her. Hell, he'd probably even known she'd been in the apartment when he'd had his guys knock down the door. "Did she shake him, too?"

Rus drew in an audible breath now, as if bracing himself for an admission. "My guy doesn't know."

Garek kicked the damn door again. "I'll find her." He had intended to look for her anyway. But now there was even more urgency. He clicked off the cell and dialed her number.

Or he'd thought he'd dialed it. It didn't ring or go to voice mail. Had he punched in the right number? He didn't have it programmed in the phone Agent Rus had given him. But he'd memorized it long ago. He used to call her often—mostly just to tease her.

And because he loved the sound of her voice in his ear. Even when it was sharp with irritation, it sounded sexy to him. Everything about her was sexy to him— even her stubbornness. He punched in the number again. But again it didn't ring. It didn't even go to voice mail. What the hell did that mean?

He punched in another number.

And a woman answered immediately. "Hello?"

"Niks, I need you to run a trace on Candace's phone."

"What's going on with you two?" she asked.

Not enough—because he'd been stubborn. Because he'd been scared. He should have told her everything. He shouldn't have kept any secrets from her.

"She's pissed at me," he admitted. Was that why she'd shut off her phone?

"Tell me something I don't know," Nikki said with a laugh.

He couldn't—not until he told Candace first—how he felt and what he was keeping from her. "Tell me where she is."

Through the phone, he heard keys clicking. Then a curse. "Sorry, Garek, her phone's dead. No way to tap into her GPS and get a location on her."

"Damn her," he said again.

"You think she deliberately disabled it?" Nikki asked, her voice a little lighter with hope.

And Garek cursed himself now. He shouldn't have automatically assumed she'd done it. But it was better than the alternative—that someone had abducted her and destroyed her phone so she couldn't be found.

"I'll find her," Garek said.

"She's not easy to find if she doesn't want to be," Nikki warned him.

But Garek was worried now she hadn't chosen to hide—maybe someone was hiding her instead. Chekov?

If he'd hurt her, Rus wouldn't need the gun or Tori's testimony anymore. There wouldn't be any trial. Garek would take care of him. But first he had to take care of Candace—had to make sure she was okay...

* * *

Because Candace hadn't been certain who was following her—Rus's men or Viktor Chekov's—she had made certain to lose her tail. She wouldn't have risked anyone following her here; she wouldn't have risked this woman's safety for any reason.

She walked up the steps of Mrs. Payne's wrap-around porch and right into the arms that the woman held open for her, like she held open the front door. Candace wouldn't have risked Mrs. Payne's safety, but she'd needed her. She'd needed this.

Mrs. Payne ushered her inside the warmth of her house, closing the door behind her. Candace glanced uneasily out the window into the darkness. She had lost the tails, hadn't she? There was no one out there.

"Sorry to bother you so late," she said with a flash of guilt as she noticed the clock.

"It's not late," Penny said. "And you are always welcome. You were welcome earlier for dinner."

Candace noticed the tree glowing brightly in the front room. Mrs. Payne was a wedding planner who owned a wedding chapel with a reception hall in its basement. Probably because she did it so often, she was an awesome decorator.

"The tree is beautiful," she said. "But it always is."

Candace had always been too busy—too focused—to worry about decorating. But now she felt a longing for a tree of her own—for someone to help her decorate it. For someone to cuddle with in front of the tree.

And she imagined Garek as that someone. But the image quickly faded—replaced by the picture Logan had shown her from the morgue. But in her mind, the man in the photo was Garek—not the stranger who had attacked her.

She shivered.

"Let me get you some hot chocolate," Mrs. Payne said.

"No, please don't go to any trouble," Candace said. "I shouldn't have come here." And risked someone following her.

Penny patted her hand. "I'm glad you came. I can see you need to talk."

Candace shook her head, but then frustration overwhelmed her and the words spilled out. "I already talked too much," she said. "What I needed was for *him* to listen. But he didn't."

Penny smiled. "Garek?"

Candace nodded.

"Men don't always hear us right away," Penny said. "But eventually the words get through to them."

Tears stung Candace's eyes. But she furiously blinked them away. She wasn't sure she wanted Mrs. Payne to give her hope. Then the disappointment would only hurt more. "Garek is more stubborn than most men."

Penny laughed. "Garek? Stubborn?" Then her smile faded and she tilted her head as she considered it. "He acts so laid-back and happy-go-lucky I hadn't realized how stubborn he actually is."

"He is stubborn," Candace insisted.

"He is," Penny agreed. "He hung in there a year—trying to get you to see him for the man he is. He kept trying to get you to give him a chance."

"I was just a challenge to him," Candace said. "Because now that I see him, he's scared."

Penny laughed. "Of course he is. Who wants to be completely vulnerable to someone else?"

Candace shivered again. She didn't want that either. But she was vulnerable with Garek. He'd always seen in her what no other man had: beauty, desirability.

"Was I too hard on him?"

"Always," Penny said. "You were determined to think the worst of him."

"That was my way of running," Candace admitted.

"So you're both runners," Penny said with a smile. "He chased you first, so now it's your turn to chase him."

Candace shook her head. "I don't want to chase a guy ever again. I don't want to force someone to love me."

"You can't force someone to love you," Penny said.

"I know that." Candace sighed. "I know that…" Or she would have been Penny's daughter-in-law instead of Stacy Kozminski.

"The right person will love you," Penny said. "But he may be too stubborn to admit it."

"Damn him," Candace murmured.

"You're stubborn, too," Penny reminded her.

She was. If only she'd given him a chance earlier— before he'd gotten involved with Chekov again.

"You were determined to think the worst of him," Penny continued. "And you're still thinking the worst of him."

"I'm not wrong about his being stubborn." But she could have been wrong about Chekov. There could be another reason he was working for Chekov…

Realization dawned. He'd known about her reporting the assault in the alley. He'd been called down to the morgue to identify the attacker. Who'd called him both times? It had to have been Special Agent Rus. Was he working for Rus?

Mrs. Payne touched the end of her nose. "I think you might have it this time."

Of course Mrs. Payne would know. Nothing escaped her attention. And she had sources everywhere.

"Is he—"

Mrs. Payne pressed a finger over her lips now. "Just trust your heart, Candace. It won't lie to you."

She hugged the petite woman. "Thank you!" She always made Candace feel better. No matter how many times she'd made a fool of herself.

She would probably be making a fool of herself again when she ran back to Garek after telling him that she was really going to leave him alone this time. But she needed to know if she was right—if he was working for Rus.

With another hug, she hurried back to her car. Snow was falling more heavily now—enough that it had blanketed her car. She quickly brushed it off and slid behind the wheel. Her cell lay in pieces on the passenger's seat. She'd taken it apart as a precaution. Chekov was powerful; he might have bugged her phone—especially if he had any suspicion Garek might have been trying to entrap him.

That was why he'd roughed him up, why he'd broken into his apartment to threaten him. If she and Mrs. Payne had figured out Garek was working for the FBI, Chekov had probably figured it out, too—which put Garek's life in extreme danger.

She shouldn't have left him earlier—no matter how hard he'd been pushing her away. She tried to accelerate, but her wheels skidded in the snow. She eased off the gas and grasped the wheel tightly as she turned out of the driveway and onto the street.

She sped up on the straight stretches of road. But they were snow covered and slick. So, for the curves, she needed to slow down. But headlights suddenly appeared behind her, burning brightly and quickly coming closer.

"Slow down," she murmured. The guy was going to lose control more than she momentarily had.

But he couldn't hear her. Or apparently see her, since he continued to bear down on her. Then she realized he did see her, and he intended to plow right into her vehicle.

She accelerated again, trying to speed up and get some distance between them. But her tires spun before gaining traction. The other vehicle didn't slow; instead it smashed into her rear bumper.

Her car flew forward, propelled by the other vehicle and the snow. It spun, then rolled. Lights and darkness flashed as her car somersaulted into the ditch. Like those flashes of light, stars danced around her vision. She blinked to clear it and reached for her weapon.

Because she knew this was no accident. She had been purposely forced off the road. Whoever was attacking her this time would not dare to fail—because with Viktor Chekov, failure meant death.

Penny flinched with each shot fired as it echoed throughout the river valley she called home—where she'd raised her children. She hadn't raised Candace, but she'd known her long enough that she felt like one of hers.

Had she lost her?

Candace had left just moments ago. She would not have been far away yet—especially with the snow falling so hard. So she was definitely within range of those gunshots—even if the sound of them was carrying on the cold night air. Before the gunshots, Penny had heard what had sounded like a crash—tires squealing, metal crunching…

That sound had carried, too.

But just like she instinctively knew those shots were being fired at Candace, she knew the crash had involved her, too. Due to the late hour and the snowstorm, there wouldn't have been many other cars on the road to crash right around the time Candace had left.

It wasn't a coincidence. The accident and the gunshots involved her.

And if Candace was hurt—or worse—Penny knew Garek would never forgive himself. And he would never get over losing her.

Chapter 15

Garek slid down the snowy embankment as he rushed toward the car that had gone off the road and into the deep ditch. It was Candace's car. If not for Mrs. Payne's call, he might not have found her. And he wouldn't have found the car if the lights hadn't been left on, burning holes in the snow in front of its smashed bumper.

Snow kept falling while a gusty wind blew the flakes that had already fallen around the ground—covering the road and the tracks of the vehicle as it had gone off the road. But her car hadn't gone off alone: parts of two vehicles had lain in the snow above the bank. Bits of black plastic and chrome and glass. And bits of Candace's blue car.

Penny had been right about hearing a crash and about it being Candace's vehicle. But when he hunched over to peer inside the wrecked car, he found it empty, but for the pieces of her phone strewn about the passenger side. It looked as if it had been run over by a car, too.

No wonder Nikki hadn't been able to track down its GPS signal.

But Candace wasn't inside the vehicle. She was gone.

Where the hell had she gone? Had *they*—whoever had crashed into her—taken her?

He shook his head, refusing to believe it. They couldn't have just taken Candace. Not *his* Candace. Not without one hell of a fight. She would have left behind more than a broken phone. She would have broken someone's body, too.

"Candace!" he called out to her.

Of course she might have been too mad still to answer him. No. If she was mad at him, she would yell or fight him. She wouldn't stay quiet.

She had only been silent when Chekov and his men had broken into his apartment. That must have been who had run her off the road. Chekov must not have believed him when Garek had claimed she meant nothing to him.

Fortunately she hadn't believed him either. She'd known he'd been lying to Chekov. But he hadn't told her what she actually meant to him: everything.

Was that why Chekov kept going after her? Did he know what Garek was up to—that he was working for Special Agent Rus? Then why not just fire him?

Of course Chekov didn't fire unsatisfactory employees. He terminated them—permanently. The man in the morgue must have worked for him.

Candace wasn't in the morgue, though. No rescue crews or police had arrived on the scene. Garek had beaten them all there.

The slick roads hadn't slowed him down. After Penny's

call—and the fear in her voice—nothing would have kept Garek from getting to Candace.

But she wasn't here. Where was she? He had grabbed a flashlight from his vehicle, but he didn't need it.

Now that the snow wasn't falling as hard as it had earlier, the moon was full and bright; its light illuminated the night and gleamed and glittered on the snow. Then he realized it wasn't the snow glittering. It was glass on the snow—glass from the driver's side window. Had Candace smashed it out or had someone else?

Then he noticed there was more than glass in the snow. There were bright crimson drops of blood. She was hurt. She was out there somewhere—injured or worse.

Mrs. Payne had warned him the crash wasn't all she'd heard. There had been gunshots, too.

Was the blood because someone had been cut on the broken glass of the vehicle? Injured in the accident? Or was the blood from a gunshot wound?

"Candace!" he yelled her name. But he wasn't certain she could hear him. He wasn't certain she could hear anything anymore. "Candace!"

Why had he been such a fool—such a coward like she'd called him? If he hadn't pushed her away, they would have been together. They could have protected each other.

Instead she had gone off alone. And while Candace was tough and smart, she was probably outnumbered. Because the wind wasn't as brisk in the ditch, it hadn't obliterated the tracks down here like it had on the road above. So he could see footprints in the snow. There was more than one set—more than two.

There was more than one person after her now. But

she wasn't alone anymore. And he wanted them to know that—wanted them to know help had arrived.

He didn't care if that put him at risk, too. He would rather they came after him than her. He would gladly give up his life for hers.

"Candace!" he yelled again. His voice cracked while panic clutched his heart, cracking it, too. If something had happened to her...

He wouldn't—he *couldn't*—consider it. She had to be okay. He had to find her. If he had a guardian angel—like he'd thought when the car hadn't struck them in the alley—then he needed that angel's help now to find the woman he loved.

"I love her," he murmured to himself. And maybe to that angel. He needed all the help he could get to find her. And fast.

He wasn't running from her anymore. He was running to her.

Milek's gut tightened with the fear that cracked his brother's voice. "I can't find her. She's bleeding. She's h-hurt!"

"We'll find her," he promised. "I'm on my way."

"Hurry!" Garek urged before clicking off his cell.

Milek had never heard his brother sound like that. Garek had always seemed so strong. But maybe he'd just acted that way because he'd been the oldest, and he'd wanted to be the one on whom he and Stacy could depend.

They hadn't had anyone else to depend on. Their mother had had little to do with their upbringing; she'd cared only about money and men.

And their father's first love had been stealing. It had meant more to him than his children. Eventually it had taken him from them completely—leaving them alone with only each other to turn to.

And both he and Stacy had turned to Garek. They had always depended on Garek. Now he needed to depend on them.

Milek punched another number into his phone. Despite the late hour, his call was answered immediately.

"Yes?" Stacy asked. And despite the time, she sounded wide-awake.

"He needs us," Milek said. "All of us. Candace has been run off the road."

Stacy gasped. "Is she all right?"

"He doesn't know. He found the wreckage of her car, but he can't find her," Milek said. "He needs everyone's help to find her."

Milek was already walking out of his apartment. He sucked in a breath at the cold. If she was out there, they didn't have a moment to lose to find her. If she wasn't already hurt—like Garek obviously feared—then she was still at risk of freezing to death.

"Of course," Stacy said. "I'll let Logan know."

"Garek needs *you*, too," Milek admitted. In case they didn't find her...

Garek would need his family. All of his family. Milek knew that—he knew the loss Garek would feel—because he lived with that loss, with that gaping hole where his heart had once been.

He began to pray they found Candace alive, so his brother didn't have to live in the hell of regrets where Milek lived.

Candace's teeth chattered uncontrollably, snapping her jaw together. Afraid the noise might reveal her location, she tried to clench her jaw. But it was numb, her face chafed from the wind and the cold despite her having wrapped her scarf around her face. She had dressed for the elements—or so she'd thought—in her heavy coat, gloves and boots.

She had lost the feeling in her feet a while ago, though. But she trudged on through the snow, leading whoever was pursuing her farther and farther away from Mrs. Payne's home. She had been close enough she could have run back to her—could have used her phone to call for help. But help wouldn't have arrived before the men would have found her. She would have led whoever was after her right back to Mrs. Payne.

And she knew someone was following her. At first she had managed to run—to stay ahead of them. But she had slowed down as she'd grown colder—the chill penetrating deeply into her bones.

She had thought they had slowed down, too. Maybe she'd hit at least one of them with all the shots she had fired. She'd been lucky they hadn't hit her when they'd returned fire.

So many shots had been fired—driving into the snow near her, whistling past her head and shoulders as she'd crouched beside her vehicle. When the gunfire had ceased for a moment—probably while they'd reloaded—she had turned and begun to run.

There had been at least two of them, and maybe another behind the wheel in the big black truck that had driven her off the road. Maybe that was who was coming after her now—because he moved faster than the other men. Those men had been big—like the guy in the alley. They had lumbered down the bank—their footsteps slow and heavy.

This man moved differently. She could hear his foot-steps—his quick footsteps—crunching in the snow as he rushed forward. He could probably see her easily since the moonlight reflected off the snow, making the night as bright as day.

She couldn't outrun someone moving that fast. She was too cold. Too exhausted—both physically and emo-tionally. Because even while she ran, all she could think of was Garek. Was he okay?

Had Chekov already gone after him?

Was he dead—before she'd had a chance to talk to him? Before she'd had a chance to tell him that she'd been wrong about him? And she'd been wrong to resist him for a year. If only she'd given him a chance earlier...

Now they might not have a chance at all. But Candace was a fighter. She wouldn't easily give up.

So she hurried toward cover—toward the shadows of a stand of pine trees, their boughs heavy with snow. She ducked under those branches, knocking snow from them. It rained down onto her head, sliding beneath her scarf and down the back of her neck.

She gasped at the shock of it and shivered again. That gasp carried on the cold.

Those footsteps paused for a moment. He must have heard her. He knew he was close.

And now since the wind had stopped blowing, he could easily follow her tracks. He would come for her.

She glanced down at the glint of the gun she clutched in one of her gloved hands. Her fingers were so numb she hadn't realized she still held her weapon. Unless she could find the strength to swing it at her pursuer's head, it was useless.

She had emptied the magazine earlier—as the men

had come down the embankment toward her, their guns drawn. And she hadn't had time to grab another magazine from her purse—which had been wedged somewhere under the passenger's seat. If she'd been able to grab that, she would have had her pepper spray, TASER and knife to use as weapons, too.

Now she had nothing but her wits and physical strength. And paralyzed with cold, she wasn't sure how she could fight. But she wouldn't go down without one.

The sound of the crunching snow grew softer but only because the footsteps had slowed. But the sound grew closer as the person neared the stand of pines. He had found her.

So she drew in a breath and shifted her grasp on her weapon. She clutched it in both hands and prepared to swing it like a hammer.

The element of surprise was her only defense. If she could hit him hard enough to knock him out, or at least daze him long enough so she could get his weapon from him...

It was her only chance of survival.

Chapter 16

His heart pounded as quickly and heavily as when he'd been running—as when he'd been anxiously searching for her. And it had nothing to do with the fact that she had almost killed him. Or would have, if she had any strength left...

If the men had found her before he had...

He shuddered at the thought of what they would have done to her—how they might have hurt her. It wouldn't have just been a job to them to get rid of Candace. It would have been vengeance—because he was pretty sure she'd hit at least one of them with a bullet. That was why their tracks had eventually turned back toward the road—why their vehicle hadn't been parked there.

At least one of them had obviously needed medical attention. He worried Candace needed medical attention, too. For hypothermia for certain. Maybe for other injuries, as well. She could have been shot, too, or hurt in the crash.

"I'm lucky your gun was empty," Garek said as he carried Candace back toward the road. He held her carefully—hoping not to exacerbate any injuries she might have. But he needed to get her out of the cold—back to warmth.

Her lips, blue in her pale face, barely moved as she murmured, "I wouldn't have shot *you*..."

She'd swung her empty gun at him, though. Fortunately her blow had struck his shoulder and glanced off—instead of hitting his head. If she had knocked him out in the cold, they both might have died out there—wherever the hell they were. She'd walked—or run—more than a mile from the crash site.

He focused on their tracks, but the road—and help—seemed too far away. "Where are you hurt?" he asked. "There's blood on the snow."

She shook her head, and her hair—cold and wet with snow—brushed against his face. "It isn't mine."

"But I used it to track you down."

"I must've hit one of them," she said.

He had already figured as much. Candace was an excellent shot. She wouldn't have emptied her gun and not hit at least one of them. The men had to have left to seek medical attention. Or else they wouldn't have stopped until they'd found her.

He could call Agent Rus to send agents or officers to the local emergency rooms. They would be able to track down these guys—if they weren't already dead. Or if they had really left...

He heard the crunch of snow—of footsteps carrying

on the cold. Candace must have heard it, too, because she tensed in his arms. They were no longer alone.

And from the noise, it sounded as if there was more than one man. More than two.

Maybe the men had left for help but not medical help. Maybe they'd gone to get backup. They'd obviously needed it against Candace.

Her voice a hoarse whisper, she asked, "Do you have bullets in your gun?"

He nodded. But before he could reach for his weapon, she'd drawn it from his holster. And as a shadow stepped into their path, she pointed the gun—at his brother.

Milek held up his hands. "Don't shoot!"

Her breath shuddered out against Garek's throat. "I couldn't have pulled the trigger," she murmured, as she slumped in Garek's arms.

She wasn't unconscious; Candace was no fainter. But she was struggling for strength.

"How much farther is the road?" Garek asked his brother.

Milek sighed. "It's a ways yet. Logan and Parker are right behind me."

But Milek would have rushed ahead. He didn't care about getting shot—probably wouldn't have minded even if Candace had been able to pull the trigger. He'd lost what had mattered most to him.

Until now—until Garek had worried he'd lost Candace—he hadn't understood the depths of his brother's grief and despair. But Candace wasn't out of the woods yet—figuratively or literally. He rushed forward and nearly stumbled and slipped in the snow.

Milek reached for her and offered, "Let me help."

But Garek's arms instinctively tightened around her. "No. I have her." And now he never intended to let her go.

"Is she okay?" Logan asked as he and his twin joined them. "We saw the blood."

"We called 911," Parker said. "There's an ambulance on its way."

Candace shook her head. "I'm fine…"

But her skin was as pale as the snow except for her lips. They were nearly as blue as her eyes. Her lids drooped over her eyes, though, as she fought for consciousness. If he hadn't found her, she might have just lain down in the snow and fallen asleep.

It was often what happened when people died of hypothermia. They just went to sleep and never woke up. He tightened his arms around her, trying to warm her. And he tilted his head, listening for the telltale sound of sirens. With as cold as it was, the sharp noise would carry. They would hear the ambulance long before it neared. But he heard nothing yet.

Still he hurried toward the road, with his brother and brothers-in-law helping him through the snow. No one tried taking Candace from him. They must have known he wasn't letting her go without a fight.

Not again…

Never again…

The ambulance doors swung shut, closing on Candace and Garek, before the emergency vehicle raced away. Candace hadn't gone without a fight; she had insisted she didn't need medical attention. But Garek had insisted she get checked out. And he'd refused to leave her side.

A sigh slipped through Stacy's lips. She was torn. Had she done the right thing in tracking down Candace for her brother? She glanced down at the wreckage of the female bodyguard's car and shuddered. Or had she put the woman—her brother obviously loved—in danger?

He had barely acknowledged her presence—when he'd come up the bank with Candace clutched so tightly in his arms. The look on his face—the worry and the love—had struck her heart with a painful pang.

"I'll bring his car to the hospital," Milek murmured as he tried to slip past her.

Stacy reached out and clutched his arm. "Thank you…"

He shrugged off her hand and her gratitude. "I did it for Garek."

He was making it clear he didn't need her. But he needed her more than Garek did. Garek had found Candace; he'd saved her.

Milek had never been given the chance to save the woman he loved.

"I should have told you," she admitted. "I shouldn't have kept Amber's secret." She'd grown up with the woman. Amber had been more than a friend. She'd been a sister to Stacy—a lifeline to sanity in her crazy Kozminski world. She missed her, too.

He nodded in silent agreement.

She wished he would yell at her. Scream. Throw things. But Milek never lost his temper. He just withdrew—completely. He'd even withdrawn from Garek until she'd asked him to help. Now, seeing the bruises on his face, she realized she shouldn't have done that either. Instead of helping her family, she'd put them in danger.

As Milek walked away, she shivered—not at the coldness outside but the coldness that was all he ever offered her. Then strong arms wrapped around her, holding her close.

"You should have stayed at the house with Mom and baby Penny," Logan said.

"I thought Garek might need me," she said.

Logan sighed. "He found Candace. She's tough. She'll be all right."

This time. But until whoever was after her was caught, there would be a next time.

"I really screwed up," she said. "I shouldn't have had Nikki find her."

"Did you see them?" Logan asked. "See how they were together?"

She sighed. "I could hear them arguing even after they closed the ambulance doors."

Logan chuckled. "Who does that remind you of?"

She tilted her head back to stare up at the man she loved more than she had ever thought possible to love anyone. And she smiled.

"I didn't see it," he said with a head shake of disgust. "But you were right about them." His gaze left hers as he glanced down at the man examining the car wreckage.

"Special Agent Nicholas Rus investigating an accident scene?" she asked skeptically.

"And you were right that there's more to this assignment of Garek's…"

She had been right about Candace's and Garek's feelings for each other. But she hadn't been right about everything. She'd misjudged her brother. Milek wasn't the only one to whom she owed an apology.

But an apology would never be enough for Milek—not with all he'd lost. Hopefully Garek would forgive her interference—if he had the chance.

"He's in danger, too," she said.

Logan nodded. "We'll protect them," he promised. "Nothing will happen to them."

She wanted to believe her husband. She knew he always worked hard to keep his promises. But some things were beyond even his control.

"Where did you bring me?" Candace asked.

She should have been grateful he hadn't made her stay in the hospital. The emergency room doctor had wanted to admit her and keep her overnight. But she hadn't wanted to risk the safety of the other patients—in case those men dared to track her down there.

There was no way they could have followed Garek from the hospital. He'd driven like a maniac—but with such skill and control she hadn't worried. She also didn't question he had lost whoever might have been trying to tail them. Chekov's men or Nicholas Rus's.

She did question where they were, though, and not just because she wasn't certain to which area of the city he'd taken her. It wasn't as remote as Penny Payne's home. But it was suburban. The house sat off the road on a big lot. Pine boughs and lights had been strung from a low picket fence in front of the home. The first light of day glinted off the sparkling windows of the traditional brick home, making it look as if it was winking at her—like Garek had winked at her the past year when he'd mercilessly flirted with her.

"This doesn't look like a safe house," she mused as he pulled his SUV into the attached garage and quickly lowered the door behind them. She appreciated his precaution, but she doubted anyone would have looked for them here.

"It's not."

Before he could walk around to open her door, she pushed it open. They'd warmed her at the hospital with some special blankets and IVs. Her strength had returned, as well. But she shut the door softly and followed him to where he punched in a code on the keyless lock for the house.

He probably could have cracked the lock easily enough, but he seemed to know the code. He held open the door to the house for her.

She walked into a mudroom area and kicked off her boots. But she kept walking, fascinated with the home. While it was a completely different style, something about it reminded her of Penny Payne's house with its bright colors and rich trim. Maybe because it felt like a home...

There was even a Christmas tree standing naked in the front window, waiting for someone to decorate it. Bags of new decorations lay on the floor beneath it. Someone wouldn't have willingly offered this place as even a temporary safe house. They wouldn't want it damaged in case they were tracked down here.

"Who owns this home?" she asked.

"Me."

The admission shocked her more than anything else she'd learned about Garek Kozminski. She shook her head in disbelief. "But you have your apartment."

He shrugged. "I bought the house right before..."

"You took the assignment working for Viktor." He obviously hadn't had plans to go back to work for the mobster.

"I'm not working for Viktor."

He'd said it before. But she'd thought then it was just

semantics—because he actually worked for Payne Protection.

"You're not working for Logan either," she said, because it was obvious their boss had had no clue what was really going on with Garek.

He shook his head. "I'm working for the FBI."

She was right. Or rather Penny Payne had been right. If Candace hadn't talked to the matriarch, she might not have figured it out. And if she hadn't been attacked again, would he have told her?

She'd been attacked twice before, and he hadn't told her what was really going on. Since he'd told her now, he hadn't kept his secret before because Agent Rus had sworn him to silence, or he wouldn't have just revealed the truth.

"Why didn't you tell me?" she asked.

"It's an undercover assignment."

Milek's comment about things not always being what they seemed suddenly resonated with her. "Your brother knows."

"I needed his help," Garek said.

Anger coursed through her and she slammed her hands into his chest. "What about me?"

He hadn't turned to her for help. Had he thought she wasn't capable of keeping a secret?

She had worked undercover with the River City Police Department. Sure, most of those assignments had been as a prostitute, but she knew how to maintain a cover.

He could have confided in her—if he'd wanted. But he hadn't wanted her to know the truth. He'd wanted her to think the worst of him.

He hadn't just been running from her; he'd wanted

her to run from him, too. He hadn't wanted to give them a chance.

Pain joined her anger. "I want to go home," she said.

He shook his head. "It's not safe."

It wasn't safe for her with him, either, because he kept hurting her worse than even the men who'd driven her off the road. "I'm not staying with you!"

He reached for her, trying to pull her into his arms. And she felt the panic she'd felt when her car had tumbled over the embankment. So she shoved him again.

Garek stumbled back, but her fury staggered him more than her physically shoving at him. "I thought you would be happy."

"Happy you didn't trust me enough to tell me the truth?"

"I trust you," he said. Candace was probably the most trustworthy person he'd ever met. It was one of the things he had always found most attractive about her. "I didn't tell you because I didn't want to put you in danger—which I obviously did."

She shoved him again.

But he refused to budge this time; instead he wrapped his arms around her and held her tightly against him. "You've been in danger ever since you came back to River City—because of me."

"I'm in danger every time I take an assignment with Payne Protection," she said. "I've been in danger with every job I've ever had. I've survived war. And being a cop and a bodyguard. You weren't worried about putting me in danger. You preferred my thinking the worst of you. You didn't want me getting too close to you."

He was close to her now, so close his body reacted,

tensing as desire rushed through him. The heat of that desire chased the chill away. He had never wanted anyone the way he wanted—the way he *needed*—Candace Baker. And it had scared the crap out of him.

"That's what this has been about," Candace said, "you running from me—from what we might have if either of us was brave enough to give it a chance."

He leaned down and brushed his lips across hers. "It doesn't feel like either of us is running now."

Her breath caught, and she stared at him, her blue eyes dilating with desire. She wanted him, too—as desperately as he wanted her.

But he forced himself to release her and step back.

She cursed. "I thought you weren't running anymore."

"I'm not," he said. "That's why I'm going to tell you everything."

"There's more?" she asked, and she wrapped her arms around herself as if cold. Or scared...

He sighed. "I guess I liked people thinking the worst of me..."

"So you could keep them from getting too close to you," she surmised.

He shrugged, but his shoulders were tense. And he realized why. "Anybody who got close to me let me down—my dad, my uncle, my mom..."

"Your mom," she repeated. She must have heard the bitterness in his voice. "She testified against you in the death of her husband."

He nodded. "Yeah, she was trying to put all her children away." He wanted to throw something or break something. But he contained his anger. Now. He hadn't that night. "Her creep of a husband attacks and nearly rapes her daughter, and she blames her. She blames Stacy."

"And you and Milek," she said. "You went to prison for manslaughter."

He curved his lips into a slight smile. "You've liked calling me a killer."

"It's not true." She didn't ask a question; it was as if she already knew.

And she did know him—better than anyone else ever had. He wanted her to know the rest of it. But she finished the story for him, as if she'd been there. "You took the blame for your brother and sister."

"Stacy was unconscious," he said. "She didn't do anything. Neither did I…" Frustration and regret ate at him now. "Son of a bitch got the jump on me—knocked me out cold. When I woke up, he was already dead."

"Milek did it?"

He nodded. "It's not like he lied about it. He told everyone he'd done it."

"But no one believed him," she said.

"The judge sure didn't," he said. "But then he wanted *me* to turn on Chekov. I could have gotten out of jail time if I'd worn a wire and tricked Chekov into implicating himself in one of his many crimes."

She gasped. "You were a kid. He wanted you to put your life at risk?"

"I would have," Garek admitted. "If it had been just me, but Chekov would have gone after Milek and Stacy, too. And they had been even younger than me. I couldn't leave them unprotected."

"So you went to jail for something you hadn't done. You took the blame for Milek."

"He went to juvenile detention," he said. "And he had

done nothing wrong. He saved Stacy and me from that bastard." He should have been the one who'd done it; he should have protected his siblings.

"Poor Milek," she said with a sigh.

She seemed to understand what his brother had gone through—the guilt he had felt all these years. Did she understand why Garek had done what he had?

He couldn't read her feelings for him. For the first time in his life, he'd told someone the truth—the whole truth—about himself. Was it too much? Was he too much?

Or not enough?

Milek stared at the worn-out newspaper clipping. He didn't need to look at the words; he knew what it said by heart. Or heartbreak…

He stared instead at the picture of Amber and their son. The picture accompanied their obituaries. That was the article he'd clipped; the words he knew by rote.

They had been dead for nearly a year now. Everyone thought that was how he'd finally learned of his son's existence. They all thought he hadn't known—Amber had kept that secret from him. Instead she'd kept a secret for him—even from her best friend.

A man like him couldn't be a father. He had lost control and killed a man. While that had been fifteen years ago, he hadn't changed. That capacity was still in him; the anger and rage could erupt at any time.

He hadn't deserved Amber or their son. But now he could never earn the right to love them. He had lost them forever.

The door rattled, so he shoved the picture back in his

pocket just before Nicholas Rus stepped back into his office at River City Police Department.

"Did you get any sleep at all last night?" Rus asked him as he dropped into the chair behind his desk.

Milek shook his head. "No. But neither did you."

"Garek lost the tail I had on him."

Milek laughed. "Of course he did." He was the only one who'd followed his brother without his knowing. "He'll keep Candace safe."

"They'll keep each other safe," Rus said.

Milek wasn't as convinced as the FBI agent. "Pull Garek out and put me in instead."

Rus shook his head. "That would be too dangerous."

Milek shrugged. He didn't care how dangerous it was. He had nothing to lose.

Garek had everything to lose—and he nearly had. Again and again.

If Candace hadn't survived tonight, Milek wasn't sure his brother would have either. For certain he would have gone after Chekov and it wouldn't have been to put him behind bars. It would have been to put him in the grave.

"Are you mad at me again?" Garek asked, his deep voice tentative.

Candace shook her head as tears choked her throat. She blinked furiously. But a tear fell, sliding down her cheek. She turned away, more embarrassed by her weakness than any humiliation she had ever endured.

But Garek's arms closed around her and he turned her toward him. His thumb brushed away the tear and dried the trail. "What's wrong?" he asked. "What did I do now?"

She shook her head. "It's not what you did. It's what I did."

His brow furrowed. "You didn't do anything wrong."

"I misjudged you," she said. "And I wouldn't let it go. I kept bringing up your past. And I had it all wrong." She had called him a thief and a killer.

"I didn't correct you," Garek said. "I didn't let anyone else correct you either. I wanted you to think the worst."

Pain clutched her heart. "You wanted to keep me away."

His arms slid around her. "I don't want to keep you away any longer."

She understood why he had though—how he had worried she would disappoint him as everyone else in his life had. His father had used him. His mother had betrayed him. Nobody but his siblings had loved him.

Until now…

She opened her mouth to declare her feelings, but his lips covered hers. He kissed her deeply, desperately.

And her desire ignited. She clutched at his shoulders and the nape of his neck, holding his head down. And she kissed him back. Her lips nibbled at his, and she slid her tongue into his mouth.

He groaned. But then he took over—tilting his head to deepen the kiss even more. He thrust his tongue in and out of her mouth.

She gasped as passion flooded her. Just his kiss had brought her pleasure. But it wasn't enough. The tension began to wind up inside her body again.

His hands were there—stroking her body. He must have unbuttoned buttons and unsnapped snaps because her clothes fell away. His followed, dropping next to those bags of decorations onto the floor.

Then he pulled her down with him—onto the plush rug in the center of the hardwood floor.

"There's a bed upstairs," he murmured.

"Later," she murmured back—between kisses. She couldn't wait for a bed. She had to have him now.

He pulled her down on top of him, arched his hips and thrust inside her. She clutched at his shoulders, then his chest as she moved on him. The tension wound more tightly inside her, threatening to snap her in two.

His hands stroked over her—from her hips, up her sides to her breasts. He teased her nipples with his thumbs, winding that pressure more tightly inside her. She whimpered and moaned at the delicious tension.

But he kept thrusting, driving her up and out of her mind. Then the tension broke as pleasure overwhelmed her. She screamed his name.

Then he cried out hers as he filled her.

She collapsed onto his chest, panting for breath. Once she could speak, she would tell him—she would profess her love. But if she told him that she loved him…

Would he let her help him with Chekov? Or would he be determined to protect her again?

He lay back, his heart racing beneath her breasts. And he struggled for breath, too. But he stroked circles on her back. Finally when he could speak again, he said, "We have a job to do."

"You'll let me help you with Chekov?" She hadn't even had to ask.

His hand trembled slightly against her back. "I was talking about the tree. We have a tree to decorate."

She had wanted to decorate a tree like Mrs. Payne's. She'd wanted a house that was a home—like Mrs.

Payne's. But this place wouldn't be home if they didn't live long enough to live there together.

Not that he wanted to live with her. He had been honest with her. He'd let her get close to him. But he hadn't professed his feelings either.

He rolled her off him. Then he pulled on his pants and handed her his shirt. "If you don't put something on…"

They would make love again. Her body hummed with pleasure, but it—and she—was greedy for more. He picked up one of the bags and handed it to her.

"We'll never get this tree decorated."

Shirtless, he strung the lights; she'd never seen any sexier man than he was. She paid less attention to where she was hanging the bulbs than to the way his muscles bulged in his arms and his back. When she rose on tip-toe to reach the higher branches, he ran his fingertips along her bare thigh. She wanted to do more than decorate the tree.

But before she made love with him again—and she wanted—she needed—to make love to him, she wanted to talk about something else.

"Let me help you with Chekov," she said.

His fingers skimmed down and then off her thigh. She tensed, waiting for his objection.

All he said was, "It's not your fight. It has nothing to do with you."

It had everything to do with her because she loved him and that made his fight hers. But more than that…

"Chekov made it my fight when he kept trying to kill me," she said.

He sighed. "That's why you shouldn't be involved."

"It's too late. I am involved."

He stared at her, his silvery eyes dark gray with turbulent emotions. He shook his head. But she didn't think he was rejecting her offer.

She thought he was giving in…

But then metal creaked as the back door opened on squeaky hinges. He pressed a finger to his lips and handed over his gun to her while he shoved a magazine in hers. Now frustration and regret flashed in his eyes.

But there was no way anyone could have followed him—not the way he'd driven here. So whoever had found them must have known where they were some other way. Maybe they'd searched property records and discovered he'd recently bought this house.

How many men were coming through that door? Two had shot at her while one had stayed in the truck on the road. So there might be three of them. They could be outnumbered.

Garek held her gaze for a moment, as if he was trying to tell her something. Then he gave the signal—a quick nod of his head.

Even if they were outnumbered, they wouldn't go out without a fight. She just wished she had told him she loved him…because now she might never have the chance.

Chapter 17

Nicholas Rus flinched at the sound of guns cocking, the barrels too near his face for him to react. He didn't dare to move even enough to draw his own weapon. But he hadn't thought he would need to draw his weapon here.

"You two sure are trigger-happy," he said. Not that they'd fired. Yet. He wasn't sure they wouldn't, even after having identified him as their intruder.

"We have reason to be a little edgy," Garek sarcastically pointed out as he pulled his gun away from Nick's head.

Nick released the breath that had caught in his lungs when he'd heard the gun cock. "Yeah, you have reason. Are you both all right?" he asked. "You didn't stick around at the crash site to give your report."

"Candace had been out in the cold for hours. We needed to get her to the hospital to make sure she didn't have frostbite or hypothermia," Garek said.

"You didn't stay in the hospital," Nick said. Because he had gone by there to see them—to make sure they were all right.

"It would have been too dangerous for other patients and staff," Candace said, "if Chekov's men tracked me down there."

It would have been, had he not had agents posted in the hospital, too. "You don't know Chekov had anything to do with you getting run off the road."

"And shot at," she said. Candace hadn't uncocked the gun she held; it wasn't pointed at his face anymore. But it was close—close enough for her to shoot him quickly if she wanted.

"You don't know that was Chekov's men," he repeated. "We haven't linked the other man to Chekov yet."

"Yet," she said. "But you will. And you'll link these men, too."

"That's why you should have stuck around the hospital," he said. "To give me an incident report and their descriptions. You're the only one who saw the men."

She uttered a ragged sigh of frustration. "I'll need to think about it—to try to remember more details. It all happened so quickly."

"She's exhausted," Garek said. "That's why I brought her home. So she'd be safe and warm."

Nick took in their state of undress, but he just raised a brow and refrained from comment. He wasn't sure how far he could trust Garek Kozminski—especially if he made any disrespectful comments in front of the woman the man obviously loved.

But Candace was the one still holding the gun.

"You are safe here," Nick assured her. "Nobody knows where you are. You don't need the gun."

She glared at him, but despite her obvious anger with him, she finally uncocked the gun.

"Why are you mad at me?" he wondered.

"How dare you…" she murmured. "How dare you drag him back into that life!"

Nick groaned. "You told her! God, man, don't you know anything about going undercover? You're not supposed to tell anyone but your handler anything."

"Some handler you are," Candace said. "You're going to get him killed."

"No," Nick said. "You are."

Candace flinched.

And he instantly regretted his remark. He hadn't meant to hurt her. But he knew that a woman could distract a man—take his mind off his job and put him in danger. He knew because a woman kept distracting him.

What had happened between them had been a mistake, though. And it wouldn't happen again. She wasn't even in River City, so she wouldn't tempt him again.

It was clear Candace mattered to Garek, though.

"You're out of line," Garek told him, his silver eyes metal sharp with anger.

But Rus ignored him to explain, "He's so worried about your safety he's not watching out for himself. He's distracted, and he's going to wind up dead."

Garek closed the door behind Agent Rus and headed upstairs to Candace. Maybe she'd just been cold—like she'd claimed when she'd gone up to find the bedroom. But he'd been surprised she hadn't stayed for his meeting with the FBI agent—she hadn't insisted on planning her part of the undercover operation.

"Are you all right?" he asked.

He had expected—and maybe hoped—to find her in the antique four-poster bed he'd bought with the house and hadn't yet slept in himself.

But she had grabbed her clothes from the living room floor before going upstairs, and now she was fully dressed. She didn't answer him; she didn't even look at him. Instead she stared out the window, probably watching Rus drive away.

"Maybe you should have stayed in the hospital like the doctor wanted."

"I'm fine," she said but then shook her head. "No, I'm not."

"Then let me take you back to the hospital." He shouldn't have agreed to her leaving against doctor's orders. She had been in a vehicle crash and then out in the snow and cold much too long.

"Physically I'm fine," she assured him.

"Then Rus did upset you." He sighed with frustration that he hadn't hit the special agent.

"He's right," she said, her voice soft with regret and worry. "I am going to get you killed."

Here was his out. He could use her fear for his safety to send her away. But it wouldn't matter. He would still be distracted because he would be missing her. He would be worried that someone might have followed wherever she'd gone.

"No." He shook his head now. "From now on, we work together."

Her eyes brightened with surprise and hope. "You're not going to listen to Agent Rus?"

He sighed. "I probably shouldn't have listened to him in the first place. I shouldn't have let him talk me into taking this assignment."

"But you did," she said. "You wanted to do this."

He grinned. She knew him well now. She knew he wouldn't have done something he hadn't wanted to do. "I felt like I needed to," he admitted.

"You regretted not taking Chekov down all those years ago—when the judge offered you that deal."

He sighed. "I was a scared kid back then."

And when it came to Candace, he was a scared man. For the past year he had deliberately misled her about his character in order to keep her from getting too close. Now he worried she wouldn't stay close to him since she knew him better than anyone else ever had—even his family. He'd always acted strong and fearless for them. Only Candace knew his fears and weaknesses.

She was his biggest weakness.

"You were just a kid," she said with sympathy instead of condemnation, "and you were all alone."

"I had Stacy and Milek."

"They were younger than you, and probably even more scared."

Remembering how scared they'd been brought back a rush of emotion. He couldn't speak, could only nod.

She reached out then, wrapping her arms around him—holding him like he'd never been held. And another kind of emotion rushed over him. He wanted to express his feelings, but he didn't want to distract her either—not when they both needed to be focused to take down Chekov.

"We end this now," he said.

It was past time for Viktor Chekov's reign of terror in River City to be done.

Candace nodded. "The sooner the better. What do we need to do?"

"We have to find that damn gun—" he'd looked everywhere for it, though "—before he disposes of it."

"Or uses it to kill again."

Candace had faced down some dangerous men over the course of her career. But she had never been as uneasy as she was taking this meeting with Viktor Chekov. She had to stay true to the character she'd already shown him, though—or the character he had probably witnessed, if not in person, then on security footage. So she'd bullied her way past his usual sidekicks and into his back office at the club.

He should have been furious with her. Instead he'd looked up from his desk and laughed. "I've been expecting you, Ms. Baker. You're quite determined."

He had no idea how determined. She needed this man behind bars, so she could tell Garek how she felt about him—how much she loved him.

She shrugged off the compliment and acknowledged, "I am determined—when I'm right."

He stood and walked around the front of his massive desk. The office was big, too, and dimly lit.

So Candace couldn't determine his age. He could have gone prematurely gray, and that was why his hair was so thoroughly silver now. His face had few wrinkles—just lines of ruthlessness, which were reflected in his dark eyes. He reached out and grabbed her shoulder.

She tensed, but she didn't react. "And I'm right about

who is the better bodyguard for your daughter. I would be a much better bodyguard than Garek Kozminski."

"I cannot figure out what it is between you and Garek," he said, and those dark eyes narrowed as he studied her face. "Is it love or hate?"

For a long while she hadn't known either. So she just shrugged.

And he laughed again. "I feel the same way about that damn boy."

Garek hadn't been a boy for a long time—if ever. He'd had too much responsibility—too much disappointment in his life and too much tragedy. This man had been part of all of that.

"Sit," he told her. But he didn't give her time to comply; he pushed her down into one of the chairs in front of his desk while he sat on the edge of the desk nearest her.

She knew exactly what she felt for *him*. Revulsion. Mistrust. Anger. She wouldn't acknowledge fear. She had survived her deployment and her assignments—undercover and protection—because she hadn't admitted to feeling any fear.

"Then you must agree I'm the better person to protect your daughter," she said.

He arched a gray brow. "Why is that?"

"You can't trust Garek Kozminski," she said, "especially not around any female."

A glint twinkled in the older man's dark eyes. "Garek has always been a heartbreaker. Did he break your heart? Is that why you're trying to steal his job?"

"Revenge?" she asked. "You think that's what this is?" She didn't care what he thought if it would make him trust her enough to hire her, too.

He chuckled. "Hell hath no fury like a woman scorned…"

She uttered a heavy sigh. "I have felt scorned…"

But she'd been wrong. Garek had only been lying to protect her. He hadn't wanted to hurt her any more than he'd wanted to risk her hurting him.

"But this isn't about Garek Kozminski," she said. "He only got hired because his sister married our boss." She had thought that a year ago.

But she hadn't known then how many clients Garek had brought to the agency. He hadn't had to join Payne Protection; he'd had an active security business of his own. But he would do anything for family—for his brother and sister and the Payne family, which had become his. He was the most loyal and generous man she had ever known.

"He has no business being a bodyguard," she said. Knowing what a lie it was, she could barely utter the next line. "He has no experience protecting people." Except he had been doing it pretty much his whole life.

"I have a lot of experience," she continued. "I could show you my résumé." She had brought it along in a folder, but one of his men had taken it from her before letting her inside the club.

The business wasn't open yet, so it was only her and Viktor and his men. It could have been a suicide mission. Garek was with Tori at the Chekov estate. Hopefully he would find the safe and the gun while she occupied Chekov.

Garek wasn't certain how much he dared to look with Tori along, though. He didn't completely trust the young woman; neither did Candace. So even if he found the safe, he was going to wait for another time to crack it—

for an opportunity to be alone in the house. He already had an idea of what night would present the best opportunity—the night Viktor Chekov hosted his company Christmas party at the club.

But that plan would only work if Garek had someone else to protect Tori in his place. Viktor had already beaten him up and threatened him for letting Milek take too many of his shifts. So someone else had to take over his protection duty. That was why Candace had made her move to replace him.

The older man chuckled. "I am quite aware of your résumé, Ms. Baker," he said. "Ex-soldier, ex-cop."

"That's why I should be protecting your daughter," she said, "not Garek."

Chekov nodded as if in agreement. But then he moved quickly, pulling something from behind his back. Light glinted off the metal of his gun as he pressed the barrel against her temple.

She drew in a breath and held it, afraid to move because he might cock the gun.

If he hadn't already...

With eyes dark with hatred and maybe madness, he ruthlessly told her, "I have no use for cops—ex or otherwise."

Chapter 18

"Daddy!" Tori shrieked as she rushed into the room ahead of Garek.

She had stopped him from drawing his gun—from shooting Viktor dead. But he held his hand close to his holster, ready to draw and shoot. He wouldn't be fast enough, though. With the gun pressed against her head, Candace would be dead before Garek could put a bullet in Viktor's brain.

"Don't hurt her," Tori implored her father.

"Why not?" he asked. "I thought you'd want me to get rid of your competition."

Tori stiffened—all concern gone. She snorted derisively. "She's no competition for me."

Garek caught Candace's flinch. She was such a strong, beautiful woman, but she had a vulnerability, an insecurity...

He wanted to tell her that he loved her. But it would

seal her death warrant for certain. He hadn't liked this part of the plan—the part where she forced a meeting with Viktor alone while he picked up Tori at her father's house. He'd intended to search it for the safe, but the place had been crawling with guards and other staff. Ostensibly there had been so many people there getting ready for the holidays—decorating the house and grounds.

But the Christmas party was being held at the club the following evening. And maybe it was the club Garek should have searched first for the gun.

Had it been here all along—in Viktor's office—and now in his hand? Was the weapon pointed at Candace's head the one that had already taken the lives of two men?

"He's just testing me," Candace spoke to Tori carefully and casually, acting as though she had taken no offense at what the spoiled girl had said.

She shouldn't have taken any offense; she was the woman Garek wanted—the one he loved. She didn't know, though. He hadn't told her; now he wished he had.

Candace continued, "He's seeing if I'm strong enough to protect you..." She caught Viktor's wrist and snapped the gun from his hand. Then she checked the cartridge. "It's not even loaded."

She exchanged a glance with Garek. A significant glance. It wasn't the gun. And now that it was away from her head and he could focus on the weapon; it was the wrong caliber.

So she handed it back to Chekov.

Garek tensed, waiting for Viktor's short temper to ignite—waiting for him to strike out at her as he had at him so many times. But the masochistic mobster surprised him as he leaned his head back and barked out the loudest laugh Garek had ever heard him utter.

"You need to teach her that move," Viktor said with a dismissive gesture at his daughter. "So I don't have to hire guards to protect her. She needs to know how to protect herself."

Tori sucked in an audible breath. She was the one who was offended now.

"I can teach her all the self-defense maneuvers I know," Candace offered.

Viktor nodded as he walked back around his desk and dropped into his chair. "You're right," he acknowledged.

Had the older man just been testing her? Garek wondered. Or was he simply trying to salvage his ego now and he'd really intended to scare her away?

He could have told Viktor that Candace didn't scare easily. At least she wasn't afraid of physical threats, just emotional ones. It was another thing they had in common.

"She does need a female bodyguard." Viktor pointed at Candace. "You have the job."

Garek tensed, waiting for his pink slip. Would it be a bullet? Fortunately the gun wasn't loaded.

Viktor turned his finger toward Garek. But then he pulled his thumb back as if cocking a gun. "You—I have other uses for you…"

Candace shot him a glance of concern. Was Viktor going to coerce him into a crime? Or kill him?

"She's in," Special Agent Rus said as he snapped off his cell phone. He and Milek were sitting in a Bureau SUV, in an alley, near the club.

But they wouldn't have been effective as Candace's

backup. They wouldn't have made it inside the club before Viktor hurt her—or worse.

Rus sighed. "But Garek doesn't sound very happy about it."

Milek nodded; he hadn't had to hear his brother to know he wouldn't have been thrilled. He knew Garek well. Or at least he'd always thought he'd known him well. But he had never realized Garek could fall so hard for someone like he had fallen for Candace.

Of course Garek hadn't admitted it—probably not even to himself, let alone to her. But his brother needed to share his feelings before it was too late. Before he didn't get the chance…

"I still think you should have sent me in," Milek persisted. "I could have gotten closer to Tori than Garek had and certainly closer than Candace will." While Tori had once loved Garek, she had been flirting with Milek when he'd filled in for his brother as her bodyguard. "I could have made sure she follows through with testifying against her father."

A muscle twitched along Rus's jaw. Her recanting her eyewitness story of Viktor murdering his right-hand man was obviously a concern for Rus and rightfully so. Garek was convinced the young woman would never testify against her father.

Rus shook his head. "She wouldn't have fallen for you. Everybody knows about you and Amber."

"Amber's gone." Murdered along with their son. She had died thinking Milek hadn't cared about her or about the child they'd created together. He should have explained why he'd stayed away—for her and for their son. They had deserved a better man than he was. "She's dead, and there's nothing I can do about that."

If only he'd known she was in danger…

If only he'd been talking to her…

But he'd forced himself to stay away from her—from them. He'd considered himself the threat to her safety and her happiness.

Rus sighed and pushed a hand through his hair. That hand shook slightly, and he wouldn't quite meet Milek's gaze. He was clearly uncomfortable.

Then Milek recognized the FBI agent's emotion because it was one he'd been struggling with for years: guilt. Why was Nicholas Rus guilt stricken, though?

Suspicion niggled within Milek and he mused, "You know something…"

"I know a lot," Rus vaguely admitted. Then he quoted Milek to himself, "I know everything's not always what it seems…"

Milek's heart lifted for a moment, but he refused to hope. It just wasn't possible…

But then he hadn't thought it possible his big brother would actually fall in love. Now that he had, hopefully he and Candace would survive this assignment.

"He's playing with us," Candace said as both anger and fear coursed through her. She had never met anyone as diabolical as Viktor Chekov. "He must know we're looking for that murder weapon. That's why he pulled the gun on me."

"He pulled the gun because he's a sick bastard," Garek said. As he drove, he gripped the steering wheel so tightly his knuckles had turned white. He was obviously every bit as angry as she was—maybe more.

"But why else would he have sent those men after

me?" she asked. "He must somehow know your real assignment is for the FBI."

Garek shrugged. "I don't know what he knows or if he's just a sadist. He murdered the man his daughter loved."

Candace gasped. She'd known Alexander Polinsky had worked for Chekov, but she hadn't realized he had also been involved with Tori.

"I feel bad," she said. "I thought she was just a spoiled bitch. I hadn't realized she was hurting."

"Oh, she's definitely a spoiled bitch," Garek said. "But she is pretty devastated—devastated enough to go to the FBI and report what she'd witnessed."

"She saw her father kill the man she loved?" Candace's heart ached for the other woman's loss. "He knows she could have gone to the police or be worried she might. She really could be in danger."

"That's why I've been watching her, too," Garek said. "Or having Milek watch her when I—"

"Have been rescuing me," she said. Now guilt flashed through her. Maybe Agent Rus was right and she would be the one who'd wind up getting him killed. "I should have stayed out of it."

Bitterness deepened his voice when he said, "You would have if Stacy hadn't tracked you down and talked you into coming back."

She didn't want him blaming his sister for the danger Candace had willingly put herself in. Even when she'd considered the Kozminskis dangerous criminals, she had envied their family's closeness and loyalty. They had been like the Paynes in that respect. But now they were estranged, and she didn't want to be responsible for any part of that.

She chuckled. "You think Stacy could have talked me into something I didn't want to do?"

"How did she?" he asked, and he spared a glance from the road and the rearview mirror for her. His silver eyes held curiosity and something else. Hope?

Did he want her to admit her feelings?

She hadn't yet admitted to her feelings—even to herself—when she'd come back. She'd had other motives.

"I took what she'd told me about you going to work for Chekov as an opportunity to prove I was right about you," she said. "She handed me the means to prove you were the criminal I'd been saying you were."

He chuckled now. "So you wanted to say I told you so to Logan and whoever else had defended me to you?"

She sighed. "I didn't have to prove to other people I was right about you. I had to prove it to me," she explained. "So I had an excuse for running from you…"

He took one hand from the wheel and reached across the console. His palm skimmed over her thigh. Her skin heated and tingled from even the brief touch over her jeans. "I don't blame you for running. In my own way, I was doing the same thing."

Frustration clenched her heart over the year they had wasted—a year they could have been together—without someone trying to kill them. "I should have trusted you."

"Why?" he asked with a laugh. "I gave you no reason to trust me. I wanted you to believe the worst of me."

"I was wrong to not look into you further, to not find out what kind of man you really are…" An amazing man. A loving brother. A fearless protector.

He squeezed her leg, making her tingle inside, before releasing her. He drew the SUV to the curb outside her apartment building and shifted it into Park.

"You didn't need to bring me home," she said. "I could have driven myself."

"You're not staying here," he informed her. And that was probably why he had refused to let her drive herself. "You're picking up whatever clothes you need for that party tomorrow night…"

Every year Viktor Chekov threw a Christmas party for all his employees and associates at the club. Candace had been ordered to attend as Tori's bodyguard, but he'd wanted her to dress like a guest—not a bodyguard.

He had looked at her then as if imagining what she looked like beneath her clothes. She had barely resisted the urge to shudder in revulsion. Not that she actually thought the man found her attractive; he had probably only done it for Garek's reaction, which he'd carefully guarded.

But she'd seen the flash of annoyance on his handsome face. And something else…

Jealousy?

He reached across the console and squeezed her leg again. "After you get what you need here, we're going back to my house."

Not his apartment.

His house.

She wanted it to be theirs—to be their *home* someday. But first they had to survive this assignment. Then they would be able to find out if they could survive each other. His fingers trailed around her thigh, between her legs.

Her breath caught as desire overwhelmed her. She wasn't sure she could wait until they got back to his house.

"We could stay here tonight," she offered—because she wanted him now.

He chuckled but reached for the door. Cold air blasted her as he opened it. Then she opened her door and stepped into the snow that the wintry wind whipped around them. The icy flakes stung her face and trapped her breath in her lungs.

He wrapped his arm around her for warmth and possibly protection as they hurried toward her lobby. "Maybe we should stay here," he murmured, his breath coming out in white clouds. "It's miserable out…"

The lobby was only marginally warmer. She reached for the button of the elevator, but he shook his head and led her toward the stairway. She had been a bodyguard longer than he had, but he was better at the job—better at protecting people. Stairwells were easier to escape than elevators—in case someone was after them.

"Why would he have hired me if he is the one trying to kill me?" she wondered aloud.

Garek glanced at her. "You were totally convinced Viktor was behind the attempts. What's changed? Has Rus gotten to you with his paroled felon theory?"

"If Chekov really wanted me dead, he could have killed me today," she said, "in his office."

Garek shuddered. "Maybe he knew Rus and Milek were close." That was the only reason he'd stopped protesting her going alone to meet his former boss and current client. "They would have come in had you'd been in there any longer."

He had come to her rescue instead. And he continued to protect her, placing his body between hers and every door that opened onto the stairwell. When they reached her floor, he stepped out in front of her, his weapon drawn.

She could have been offended he was trying to take

care of her—as if she didn't know how to take care of herself. Instead she felt something she had never felt before—cared for. His protectiveness and concern touched her heart almost as deeply as his honesty had. She was the one who always took care of and protected others. He was the only person in her life who wanted to protect and take care of her.

As they neared her door, he gasped. And she drew her own weapon. But there was no one else in the hallway. "What is it?" she asked.

He gestured toward her door. And she saw it had been treated like his apartment door had been. It hung from a broken jamb. He pointed for her to step back. But she was no longer touched or flattered. She was pissed. So she followed him through the broken door.

And she gasped now—at the chaos inside. Her apartment had been totally tossed—furniture overturned. Even her dishes had been knocked out of the open cupboards and lay in shards on the floor. Her gun drawn, she headed down the hall to her bedroom. Her clothes lay in a pile on the floor—the fabrics torn into pieces.

Garek shook his head in disbelief. "This is crazy," he murmured, "even for Viktor."

"It must be a warning," she said. Maybe that was what everything else had been—just a warning to not go after him, to not try to find evidence for his conviction. It was probably the only reason she wasn't dead. He hadn't wanted to kill her—either when he sent the men after her or put that gun against her head himself. "He's warning you to not betray him."

Garek shook his head again—not totally convinced. "We should call Rus."

"And what will he do?" she asked. "It's not as if we don't already know who's responsible."

"This isn't like Viktor, though," Garek said.

She turned toward him. "Really? I was there when he had his guys break into your apartment this same way—smashing the door down."

"But they didn't touch anything inside," he reminded her. "They didn't even search the place."

Which was fortunate for her since they would have found her hiding in the bedroom. Unless they'd already known she was there…

"Maybe he sent the men I shot the other night," she said. Because this *assault* on her apartment was definitely personal and vengeful.

Garek shuddered. "You're right. There's no reason to call Rus right now. Let's get out of here."

She glanced around at the chaos that had once been her home. Growing up as a military brat, she had never gotten attached to any place before, and she wasn't attached to this apartment either. But her things…

She sighed.

"There's nothing to salvage here," Garek said. "You're going to need all new stuff."

She had never gotten attached to things either. Every move had been a purge for her family. Out with the old. In with the new. She didn't have keepsakes like Penny Payne's Christmas tree of sentimental ornaments.

She wanted that, though.

"Yeah," she agreed. "There's nothing here for me." But him…

He caught her hand and led her back out of the apartment, back down the stairwell to the lobby. Before they stepped onto the street, he squeezed her hand and regretfully murmured, "I'm sorry…"

"Why?" she asked. "You didn't do it."

"It was because of me, though."

"Maybe not," she said. "Maybe Agent Rus has been right after all."

And even Garek had thought that level of destruction out of character for Viktor Chekov.

"Maybe this has nothing to do with you and everything to do with me," she said.

But he stared at her doubtfully. "I would consider it a possibility if not for how the door was broken down."

It was too weird a coincidence. It must have been Chekov—playing with them some more.

"Let's go…" she said and wanted to add *home*.

But she held the word inside just like she had held in the other words when they'd made love. She was more scared of expressing her feelings than she was of whatever game Chekov was playing with them.

But then they stepped onto the street and gunfire erupted. And as Garek went down, she wished she'd said all the words. She wished she had told him how much she loved him. But all she could do now was scream.

Chapter 19

"The bullet in your leg matches the one that killed Donald Doornbos and Alexander Polinsky," Nicholas said. It was the only good thing that had come of the shooting outside Candace's apartment building. They knew the gun was still in play.

So maybe Nicholas's special assignment could be salvaged yet. Maybe Viktor Chekov could finally be arrested and actually convicted. If he could trust the man Nick had enlisted to carry out the assignment didn't kill the mobster first...

Garek shook with fury, or maybe it was standing on his injured leg that had him wobbly. He glanced down at his bandaged thigh. "The bullet's not in my leg anymore."

"You shouldn't be checking yourself out yet, though," Nicholas said. While he was lying low so nobody spotted the two of them together, he'd heard the doctor warning Garek to take it easy while he'd lingered in the hall outside the private room. He had waited until the doctor had left to slip inside and close the door.

Not that Garek's cover hadn't already been blown. Why else would someone have tried to kill him or Candace? And it had been more than once. If not for that bullet matching the gun's ballistics, he would have cancelled Garek's assignment and pulled him out.

"We have to end this now," Garek said. "Eventually Chekov's common sense will overtake his arrogance and he'll get rid of that weapon."

Nicholas was surprised the notorious mobster hadn't. But then everything about this assignment had surprised him.

"I didn't think it would go like this," he admitted. With an eyewitness willing to testify, he had thought he would have a slam dunk open murder case for a grand jury and then a jury—once he recovered the murder weapon. And he'd thought a man like Garek Kozminski—a former thief and former associate of Chekov's—would easily recover that murder weapon. "I didn't think you'd get hurt."

Garek snorted. "I'm not hurt."

"You took a bullet in your leg," Nick reminded him. But maybe he shouldn't have. He didn't want Garek backing out of the assignment now—not when they were so close. But Chekov was close, too. "Three gunmen ambushed you and Candace when you left her building. You could have both been killed."

"We're not the ones in the morgue," Garek said.

Two of the gunmen were while the third had gotten away; he must have been the one who'd had the gun.

The weapons recovered at the scene had been tested and hadn't matched—like the bullet from Garek's leg had.

"We'll find the other guy," Nick vowed.

They had to in order to recover the weapon—unless he'd brought it back to Chekov already. Hopefully he had because Nick needed that gun discovered in Chekov's possession.

"We've already identified the dead men," he told Garek, "and we'll track down their known associates."

"Was Donald Doornbos one of them?" Garek asked.

Nick nodded.

"Any connection to Chekov?"

Nick sighed. "Who in River City doesn't have a connection to Chekov?"

"Thanks to your assignment—nobody anymore," Garek said. "Payne Protection has him as a client."

Regret had Nick flinching. Penny was right. The family would never forgive him if something happened to one of them. Fortunately nobody knew about the shooting last night outside Candace's apartment. At least he didn't think they knew because he had received no outraged phone calls.

And Garek was alone at the hospital.

"Where's Candace?" he asked. The two had seemed to be inseparable until now.

In order to protect whatever was left of Garek's cover, Nicholas hadn't gone to the scene last night, but he'd been told she hadn't been hurt. Garek had probably taken the bullet meant for her. Or maybe the bullet had been meant for him. Maybe Chekov was already aware Garek was really working for the Bureau.

Should he call off the investigation?

Garek glanced at his watch and sighed. "Candace is Christmas shopping with Tori Chekov."

"Alone?"

"Milek is nearby," Garek said.

It was an FBI investigation; there should have been some agents on protection duty. But Nicholas could understand Garek not trusting any of them—because it certainly appeared Viktor Chekov was somehow aware of the investigation.

Why else had he gone after the man trying to take him down? Actually what Chekov had done was even more diabolical, he'd gone after the person who mattered most to Garek Kozminski: Candace.

"Should we call this off?" he asked.

Garek tensed, then laughed. "Why would you ask that *now*?"

"Because it's gotten dangerous as hell," Nick replied. "And it's clear your cover was probably compromised."

Garek shrugged. "It may have been. Or it may be Chekov is just a sick bastard. We still have a chance of putting him behind bars. We need to take that chance."

"You're the one taking chances," Nick said, "with your lives." And he was afraid the risk might be too great—Garek and Candace might not live till Christmas.

Candace hadn't wanted to leave him—wounded and alone at the hospital. But she was also so mad Garek had been shot she didn't want the man responsible to get away with it. He had already killed and hurt enough people.

Even his own daughter...

"Garek told you," Tori said as she pushed hangers back on a rack of dresses.

"What?"

"You know about Alexander," she said. "I can see the sympathy on your face."

She hadn't realized she was showing any sympathy. Worry, anger, exhaustion…those were all the things she was feeling now. It hadn't helped that Tori had dragged her through every store in the entire mall either. At least the woman had let Candace teach her some self-defense maneuvers before the shopping trip.

"Don't pity me," Tori said defensively.

After last night—after Garek had taken a bullet right in front of her—probably for her—Candace could sympathize even more with what Tori had gone through when her lover had been shot in front of her.

Fortunately for Candace, she hadn't lost him. Garek had managed to get back up, and he had returned fire with her. And before she'd left the hospital, the doctor had assured her that he would be fine. The bullet had done no real damage to his leg.

"I don't pity you," Candace assured her. "I'm sorry…"

"Sorry he told you?" Tori asked. "Now you can't hate me?"

"I don't hate you," Candace said.

"You didn't like me, though."

She didn't like her any more now. She just understood her better. And she also respected how quickly the woman had caught on to the self-defense maneuvers. Tori Chekov was smarter and stronger than Candace had initially thought.

"If I were you, I wouldn't like me either," Tori said. "What woman would actually like the old girlfriend of the man she loves?"

Candace didn't deny her feelings for Garek but she

didn't admit to them either. She needed to declare her love directly to Garek before she confessed it to anyone else.

Tori took one of the dresses from the rack and held it against Candace. "This is it," she said. "And blue is Garek's favorite color."

Candace didn't know Garek's favorite anything. While she had learned a lot about him recently, Tori Chekov had known him longer. And she was making it clear to Candace.

She shook her head. "I'm not shopping for me."

Tori Chekov was supposed to be Christmas shopping, but all she had done was shop for herself. Until now—until she'd taken this sudden and unsettling interest in Candace's wardrobe.

"You need a dress for the Christmas party," Tori said.

Candace cocked her head. "How do you know I don't have one?"

She would have worn the red one she'd worn to the club that night—and to last year's Payne Protection Agency's Christmas party—but it lay in tatters on her bedroom floor.

Tori shrugged. "You don't seem like a cocktail dress kind of person."

"I was wearing one the first night I came to the club," Candace reminded her.

"But you can't wear that anymore." Tori bit her lip to stop herself as her face flushed with color.

"You know about my apartment," Candace said. "You know it was broken into and my things destroyed."

Tori grimaced. "I'm sorry…"

"Did you hear your father order someone to do that?" she asked. "You could testify to it, too."

"Too?" Tori asked. Anger flashed in her dark eyes. "Garek did tell you everything…"

And Candace agreed with his conviction that Tori wasn't likely to testify against her father—even after he had killed the man she loved. They needed to find that gun. They needed to see their plan through.

She took the deep blue velvet dress from Tori. "It is a pretty color."

"It'll look beautiful on you," Tori said as she grabbed a gold dress and held it up against herself.

"And you'll look beautiful in anything," Candace said—because Tori Chekov was one of those women who probably would have looked stunning even in army fatigues.

But she couldn't hate her. All she could do was promise her, "We'll make sure there's justice for Alexander."

Tears filled Tori's dark eyes, and she nodded. "Thank you…"

Last night she had been tempted to call off the assignment—to let Chekov scare them off. But then she'd gotten angry and determined to put him away for the rest of his life. She was even more determined now to follow through on the assignment. She just hoped no more lives were lost—especially not hers or Garek's.

Wincing against the twinge of pain in his leg, Garek hobbled across his living room. He leaned over and plugged in the extension cord for the lights, setting the tree to twinkling and glowing. Then he took a present from his pocket and slid it under the tree.

Candace wasn't the only one who had gone Christmas shopping. He had made a stop on his way home—at his sister's store. He only hoped he had a chance to give the gift to Candace—that they survived the assignment.

Stacy had apologized for involving Candace and for doubting him. His gut tightened even now as he remembered her tears and her concern when she'd seen his leg. He'd been concerned, too—that she knew the truth. That everyone knew about his *undercover* assignment. If Chekov didn't already know, he was bound to find out soon. Garek hoped it was after he found the murder weapon, though.

Boards creaked overhead, and he reached for his weapon. Who had found his house? He had been so careful to make sure no one had followed them last time they'd come here or had followed him tonight.

But Rus knew about it. Someone else could have found out however the FBI agent had. Or maybe even from the FBI agent. Had Garek been a fool to trust him?

Biologically Nicholas Rus was a Payne, but Penny hadn't raised him. So he didn't necessarily possess the integrity and honor of the other Paynes. Maybe he could be bought; maybe Chekov had paid him off.

Grasping his gun, Garek headed to the stairs. Each step was an exercise in torture, making him flinch as pain shot through the wound in his leg. Maybe he had already overdone it—as the doctor had warned him. Maybe he should have stayed another night. But he hadn't had that luxury. With the Christmas party tonight at the club, he'd never have a better time to search Chekov's home.

If only the weapon had been returned to Chekov…

If only Garek could find it…

But to find it, he had to escape whoever had broken

into his home. But he hadn't noticed the lock had been picked. There had been no telltale gouges.

Whoever had broken in was good. Finally upstairs, he moved toward where he'd heard the noise—in the master bedroom. And he found his intruder standing before the antique oval mirror, which was one of the antiques he'd bought with the house—like the four-poster bed.

His intruder wasn't just good. She was beautiful. His breath escaped in a gasp of awe.

She whirled toward him. Then she rushed over to him, throwing her arms around his neck. "Are you all right?" Candace asked.

He nodded. "Yeah…" But since he had promised to be honest with her from now on, he admitted, "My leg hurts like hell, though."

"How did you make it up the stairs?"

"Painfully," he murmured. "I didn't know you were coming here."

"I made sure I wasn't followed," she assured him. "And I remembered the code for the door."

He nodded. "That's why there were no marks on it."

She smiled. "You'll have to teach me how to pick a lock better."

He wouldn't deny her the knowledge; the skill had proven useful even after he had quit his family business. He just hoped he had time to teach her. "You're already dressed for the party."

The dress was a deep blue that matched her eyes, and in a warm velvet that hugged her curves and even covered her arms. But then she turned again and showed him where the fabric dipped low in the back, showing off the sexy ridge of her long spine. He couldn't help himself, or maybe had to help himself, so he leaned forward and brushed his lips across the bare skin of her back.

She shivered.

"Maybe you should find another dress," he suggested.

"You don't like this one?" she asked, and disappointment lowered her voice.

"I like this dress too much," he said. "And so will every other man in the club."

He wouldn't be there, though. He would be at Chekov's estate—breaking in and then finding the damn safe—if Chekov or his men didn't catch him first.

And if they caught him, he wanted to make sure he didn't have this regret—that he hadn't taken the dress off her. So he pushed the sleeves and the dress from her shoulders until it dropped to the floor.

She wore only a thin strip of lace beneath it. Not even a bra. He groaned as his body hardened and began to pulse, demanding release. Demanding her...

He quickly dropped his coat and shirt onto the floor next to hers. But to take off his pants, he had to sit on the bed—had to wriggle to get them off.

"Garek," she murmured, joining him on the bed. But she reached out and skimmed her fingers along the edge of his bloodstained bandage. "We can't do this. You're hurt."

He was hurting; his body aching with tension, with wanting her. Just her fingers on his thigh had his heart pounding faster and harder.

He pushed her back onto the bed and said, "I'd have to be dead to not want you."

Her eyes widened with fear. She was afraid he might wind up dead. Tonight.

He didn't want her afraid. He wanted her—wanted

her wild with desire for him, like he was for her. So he touched her, running his fingers and his lips over every silky inch of her skin.

She moaned and writhed as he kissed her breasts and then moved his mouth lower, to make love to her body. She screamed his name as pleasure claimed her. But then she pushed him back. And she took over, making love to him with her mouth and then her body.

She carefully lowered herself onto him—moving slowly as if to not jar his leg. He was beyond feeling pain—he could only feel her heat and her passion. Out of his mind with need, he thrust up and grasped her hips. She met his frantic rhythm and screamed again as another orgasm shuddered through her. Then finally the tension broke inside his body, and he came—filling her.

She moved to separate their bodies, but he clutched at her hips, holding her. Joined as they were, he felt as if he were part of her, and she was part of him. He didn't want to lose their closeness. He didn't want to lose her. He stroked his fingers down her naked back, over the sexy ridge of her spine.

She shivered and murmured his name, "Garek…"

There was regret in her voice; she had to leave. They both knew it. But he still held her, reluctant to separate. What if this was the last time they were together? Should he tell her what he felt for her?

Should he give her the present he'd put under the tree?

But then she might be distracted. And he would never forgive himself if he was the reason something happened to her. Even if she wasn't distracted—and something happened—he would still be the one to blame. Despite Stacy's guilt over tracking her down, he was the one who'd gotten her mixed up in his dangerous assignment—in his dangerous past. Not that she hadn't faced her share of danger on her own. She was strong. He had to trust she could take care of herself—as she always had. But he wanted to take care of her, too.

"I'm going to be late," she said. "We shouldn't have done this…"

"Then maybe it's a good thing I got shot," he said.

Her lips curved into a smile. "What do you think this was? Sympathy sex?"

"Wasn't it?" he asked. "I feel very sympathized with…"

She laughed—like he had wanted her to. And finally he released her. She sprang up from him and from the bed. Grabbing her dress up from the floor, she headed toward the bathroom but left the door open.

Like him, she must have been reluctant to be apart from him. To leave him…

He needed to get up, too. But he moved slowly, as pain shot through his leg. He flinched, but he had no regrets.

"While you're at the club with Tori and Viktor, I'll search the house," he said.

She was already aware of the plan. They had *all* gone through it before she had confronted Chekov and stolen his job the other morning.

But he needed to repeat it, needed to remind himself it would all be over soon. "I'll find the safe tonight for certain."

She stepped out of the bathroom, fully dressed again. She looked so beautiful but there was also sadness in her blue eyes now. A fear—not for herself, of course. Her fear was for him.

"You're hurt," she said again. "Milek could search the house instead."

He shook his head. "He's not as good as I am," he

said it with no arrogance. It was just a statement of fact. When they were learning the family *business*, he had made certain he was better than his younger brother, so their father had taken him on jobs instead of Milek. And that was why Viktor had wanted him—instead of his brother—after their father had gone to prison.

"You didn't get better because you were competitive," she said. "You got better because you were protective."

She had gotten close to him—closer than he had even feared she would. It was as if she could see into his mind, his soul, his heart…

"Milek might be able to find the safe," Garek continued, "but he wouldn't be able to crack it. *I* have to do this. I am the best man for the job."

She nodded. "It's going to end tonight…" She didn't say the rest of it. But he was close to her, also—so much so he could read her mind, too.

One way or another it would end. Tonight was the night they might both die.

She kissed him—skimming her lips over his. Then she headed for the door, her heels clipping across the hardwood. But at the bedroom doorway, she paused and whispered, "I love you…"

Or maybe he'd only seen into her heart and imagined or wished she'd said the words. Before he could say anything back, she was gone.

And with his leg, he wouldn't be able to make it down the stairs before she left. He could only hope she had seen into his heart, and she knew he loved her, too.

And he hoped they both lived to say the words to each other again.

Chapter 20

Milek stared through the windshield at the snow falling on the hood of his SUV. Each flake melted the minute it hit the warm metal and slid off like teardrops.

"Where do you need me?" he asked, speaking into the microphone with which Special Agent Rus had wired him. Tonight everyone was wired but Candace.

Chekov may have hired the ex-cop to protect his daughter. But he wouldn't have trusted her enough to confess to her. And he would have searched her for a wire anyway. He had when she'd picked up his daughter to go shopping earlier.

Milek, through his binoculars, had watched the exchange in the driveway. With the way Chekov's hands had lingered, it was good Garek hadn't witnessed the pat down. Not that the gangster wasn't already fully aware of how Garek felt about the female bodyguard. No one could miss his feelings; he wore them all over his face. Even the ever-oblivious Tori had noticed right away the first night Candace had shown up at the club.

"I need you out near the estate," Rus replied. "In case Garek needs you to help him. His leg is still a mess. He shouldn't be out there alone."

"He shouldn't be out there at all," Milek said. But he couldn't argue his brother was the better safecracker.

"Garek can get past the security system," Rus said. "He can get past the skeleton crew of human security Chekov left out there, too. But he can't get out of there in a hurry if he needs to—not with that leg. That's where you'll be best. You know the estate."

"*Garek* wanted me at the club," Milek reminded the FBI agent.

Rus might have been the one in charge of the investigation, but during their meeting the other morning, Garek had made it clear he was in charge of this plan. And it was clear why.

Milek said, "He's more concerned about Candace's safety than his own."

"I brought in a team from Chicago," Rus said. "Guys I know I can trust."

Uneasiness lifted goose bumps on Milek's skin. "You have guys here you can't trust?"

"I don't know," Rus admitted. "I don't understand why anyone's going after Candace."

"To get to Garek."

"But why would anyone want to get to Garek?" Rus asked. "Unless they knew what he was really doing working for Chekov. And how would they know?"

Milek sucked in a breath. "You think someone betrayed the investigation?"

"I don't," Rus said. "I thought I had a team in place I could trust—that I'd gotten rid of most of the corruption in the department."

"But you never know who you can really trust…" After that day—that horrible day—when he'd killed a man, Milek had been unable to even trust himself.

Rus's sigh rattled the cell phone. "I'm sorry," he said. "About the other night…"

"Are you sorry about what you said?" Milek asked.

He hadn't really said anything, though. His cryptic comment about everything not always being what it appeared to be could have been alluding to anything. It was something Milek said all the time himself.

It was like this assignment Garek had agreed to take. Stacy and Candace had thought he had gone back to his old life. But that hadn't been case at all. Garek had been trying to correct the mistakes of his old life—trying to take down a man he could have taken down fifteen years ago and would have if he hadn't been protecting him and Stacy.

And maybe there was something else that really wasn't what it appeared to be regarding this assignment. Maybe Viktor Chekov was not the only danger in this case.

After a long pause, Rus sighed again. "I don't know if I should have said something now. Or a year ago…"

Now Milek had no doubt about what Special Agent Rus was alluding to. But he couldn't consider all the implications of the man's admission. Not now. He had to give all his attention to tonight—for Garek's and Candace's sake—for their lives.

And Milek had just drawn another conclusion about this case equally unsettling—they had been focused on the wrong person this entire time. There was another threat out there, and they had to determine who before it was too late.

Red and green strobe lights flashed across the crowded dance floor. The whole club vibrated with the beat of the bass. Candace's head lightened as she twirled away and then back into her dance partner's arms.

Viktor Chekov had to be younger than he looked, or he moved very well for an older man. He held her closely against him as he continued to move them around the dance floor.

She was supposed to be working this shift of protection duty for Tori, but Chekov was monopolizing her time, at least her dance card. That worked with the plan, though, so Candace could make sure Chekov didn't leave the party early to head home. Garek was there, searching the estate for that weapon. Hopefully he'd already found it and left because she wasn't certain how much longer she could keep up—or put up—with Chekov on the dance floor.

Fortunately—or unfortunately—she'd had his full attention since she had walked into the club.

"I can't get over how beautiful you look," he murmured again, his mouth close to her ear. His hand trailed down her bare back.

She barely resisted the urge to shudder with revulsion. She had an even stronger urge to grab his hand and break it. Garek was the only one she wanted touching her. Hopefully he was touching the safe now, cracking it open and finding the damn gun.

But even then would it be enough? If Tori backed out of testifying against her father, would they have enough to convict him? Or would he remain as unscathed as he always had?

"Tori picked out the dress for me," she said.

"That's right," he said. "The two of you went *shopping* today." His voice held patronization and disparagement—as if he thought all women just liked to shop.

She leaned back and stared up into his face to gauge his reaction as she said, "Well, I had no choice. After my apartment was ransacked, I will have to buy all new clothes, not just this dress."

His dark eyes widened with shock. "What happened to your apartment?" he asked, as if he hadn't heard her correctly.

Why was he so surprised if he'd ordered the destruction? Maybe he hadn't thought his guys would carry the threat so far, though.

"The door was broken down," she said. "Kind of like Garek's had been."

The gangster's dark eyes narrowed. "There was a break-in at Garek's," he acknowledged. "But that's the only break-in I am aware of."

He had just admitted the truth about Garek's; of course he might have known she'd been there—hiding in the bedroom when his men had broken down the door. But still, he'd told the truth. So why would he lie about her place? He had no reason to lie to her. But if Viktor hadn't known about the break-in, how had Tori known?

She'd claimed she'd heard it from him.

Viktor spun her again but instead of reeling her back into his arms, he led her off the floor—to that roped-off table where Tori sat with some of his other men. Milek must have been with Garek.

But Special Agent Rus had assured she would have

other backup in the club. She hadn't met them, though, so she wasn't sure who they were—or if they were really even there. And she had no way of signaling for help; she wasn't wired with a microphone.

It would have been too dangerous. With as close as she'd been dancing with Chekov, he would have noticed if she'd been wearing a wire. Maybe that was why he'd been so handsy—because he didn't seem interested now. He held out the chair next to his daughter for Candace. But he didn't take one at the table himself.

"Enjoy the rest of your evening," Viktor said. He gestured at his men who stood and hurried to his side.

"Where—where are you going?" Candace asked.

He tilted his head, and his dark eyes flashed a warning at her imprudence. "You are protecting Tori," he reminded her. "No one else…"

She wanted to protect Garek. And if Chekov caught him at the estate, he would need protection—especially if Chekov was bringing all those guys with him.

"Of course," Candace quickly agreed with him. "I just thought this was your party…"

"It is," he said. "And I've put in an appearance. Now it's time for me to leave."

Before she could say anything else—come up with any other excuse to stall him—he walked away—in the middle of his entourage. Would Rus's backup even realize he was leaving? Would they warn Garek in time?

She reached for her purse and the cell phone she'd left inside. But it was no longer hanging over the back of her chair. Where had it gone?

"Daddy stayed longer than he usually does at this party," Tori informed her. "Probably because he was busy dancing with *you*…"

Dancing in the hot and crowded club had made Candace thirsty—so thirsty she picked up her water from the table and took a quick gulp.

"He couldn't take his eyes off you," Tori continued. "I can't imagine Garek would have been too thrilled with the way you two were behaving."

It sounded as if Tori was the one who wasn't too thrilled. Candace turned toward the other woman. "We were just talking…"

And she remembered what Viktor had said. "…about the break-in at my apartment."

Tori tensed. "What about the break-in?"

"He didn't know anything about it."

"Of course he wouldn't admit to it," she said with a disparaging snort. "He knows you're an ex-cop. He probably knows you and Garek are working together to get evidence against him."

How did she know? How did Tori know everything?

Candace narrowed her eyes and tried to focus on the woman. But it was as if the strobe lights had started flashing faster—blinding her. She could see only red and green—no images. And her head began to pound.

She had been drugged.

And there was only one person who could have done it and only one reason why: Tori; she was the one who wanted Candace dead. And now that she'd been drugged, Candace had no way of protecting herself.

Viktor's safe wasn't in his den. Of course that would have been too obvious. The safe was in his master suite—in the floor of the walk-in closet. It was more than a safe, really. It was a vault. And like a vault, it hadn't been easy to open. Garek could have used dynamite. Or backup.

But he'd had to sneak in—slowly, thanks to his wounded leg—and alone. He'd bypassed the security system with no problem. Hell, he knew the code. Even if Tori hadn't told him, he'd watched Viktor enter it enough times to figure it out. Her birthday...

How could a man who seemed to love his daughter as much as Viktor loved Tori have killed the man she loved right in front of her? It made no sense. But could a man like Viktor—a man as ruthless and violent—really love anyone—even his own daughter?

Agent Rus would have to convince the woman that her father didn't love her, if he had any hope of getting her to testify against him. Garek doubted she would. No matter how much he had hurt her, she wouldn't betray her father.

Any more than Garek thought Viktor would have betrayed her...

What had Alexander Polinsky done? He'd heard the man was a player. Maybe Viktor had found out the guy had cheated on Tori. But then why would she have been upset about his killing him?

Garek shook his head and returned his attention to the vault. He didn't have much time. Chekov never stayed long at his own parties. It was why he held them at the club instead of the estate—so he could go home whenever he wanted.

There were guards outside, though. And Milek. He'd heard his voice earlier. But since he'd stepped inside that closet, he hadn't heard any of the voices through his earpiece. Either things were awfully quiet outside. Or the closet was soundproof and signal proof.

That probably meant they couldn't hear Garek either—if he needed to call for help. Despite the warmth of the house, Garek shivered.

This was not good.

Maybe he needed to step out of the closet and make contact—at least let them know where he was inside the massive house. But then the lock clicked and the door popped open. The vault was deep and filled nearly to the top. Heavy plastic bags displayed contents of money and drugs. And there were guns…

Long guns. Automatic rifles. Handguns. He needed to call in the others to help him catalogue the contents. As far as he could see there were no tapes. Viktor was probably too smart to have his office wired, to risk recording his meetings and have those recordings fall into the wrong hands. Into hands like Garek's.

"Hey, can anyone hear me?" he asked.

Not even static emanated from his earpiece, nor the echo of his own voice. He doubted anyone could hear him.

He leaned into the vault and drew out a couple of the handguns. They were the same caliber of the bullet that had been pulled from his leg. But somehow he knew they weren't the weapon for which he searched.

There were a lot of guns in that vault, but he suspected not one of them was the murder weapon he needed for evidence. But would Viktor have the weapon if he wasn't the murderer?

Oh, the man was a killer. He'd killed before, and he would kill again if he wasn't stopped. But had he killed Alexander Polinsky?

Maybe someone had heard him, because he heard a

door open—the only door he would be able to hear in the soundproof room—the door to the closet itself.

"Milek?" he called out hopefully.

"Your brother won't be able to help you anymore," Viktor said.

His deadly tone chilled Garek's blood. Had he found Milek outside? Had he killed him?

He shouldn't have gotten his brother involved. But like always, Milek had given him no choice. He still followed him around like he had when they were kids.

But his brother wasn't his only concern. Viktor had been with Candace. What had he done to her?

Garek looked up from the vault to confront the killer. And he stared directly into the barrel of a gun. If he'd ever actually had a guardian angel, the celestial being must have deserted him, or he would have had some warning that Chekov was coming.

Now it was too late. Whatever had been done to his brother and the woman he loved—Garek was about to suffer the same ill fate.

Chapter 21

"What do you mean—you lost contact with both of them?" Nicholas demanded to know.

His heart began to hammer in his chest. His whole investigation was falling apart. And if that fell apart, so would his chance of ever really being part of the Payne family. They would never forgive him if Garek or Candace were harmed. Hell, he'd never forgive himself. Those people had come to mean a lot to him, too.

"What about Milek Kozminski?" he asked.

"We found his SUV running, the door open and blood on the seat and on the snow beside it."

"Oh, God…" It didn't look good for Milek either.

"Yeah," Agent Dalton Reyes said. "You should have brought me in from the beginning, instead of using bodyguards to carry out an investigation like this. Organized crime is my specialty."

"It was theirs, too," Nick said, "before they became bodyguards. They worked for Chekov years ago."

Dalton breathed a sigh of respect. He had once been a gang member himself. He understood the education and skill gained through a life lived even momentarily on the wrong side of the law.

"I'm surprised they've lived this long," Reyes said. "You don't leave an organization like Chekov's alive."

Just like you didn't leave a gang and live. Dalton knew the danger well.

"We have to find them," Nicholas said.

"You want us to go inside the estate?" Reyes asked. "We don't have a warrant."

"Milek's blood is your warrant," Nick said. "He's in imminent danger. You have cause to go in."

"But whatever we find inside could be inadmissible in court," the other agent pointed out. He knew what it took to make a case.

Nicholas cursed his opinion of a warrant. A conviction didn't matter as much to him as saving lives— especially *these* lives.

"We have to find them," he repeated and added, "Alive."

"That may not be an option," Reyes warned him.

There was no other option. If they hadn't survived this investigation, Nicholas would never forgive himself and neither would the Paynes. He would have no reason to stay in River City. It didn't matter that his career would be over; he would lose much more than that.

He could only hope the Kozminskis and Candace had not already lost everything as well—including their lives.

Pain throbbed dully in Candace's head—not as if she had taken a blow to her skull but as if she had a hangover. She dragged her lids open and peered around. No lights flashed—red and green—like they had at the club. In fact it was black—wherever she was. She tried to reach out, to test her boundaries, but her arms couldn't move. Hard plastic bit into her wrists so sharply it nearly broke the skin. She stilled her movements and assessed her situation.

She had obviously been drugged. The water…

She had also been tied up, apparently with zip ties. They were harder to break than handcuffs. She might have been able to pick the lock on the handcuffs. But she needed a knife to cut the plastic and free herself.

She'd had a knife—in her purse. But that was already lost at the club. She didn't feel the gun she'd had holstered to her thigh either. It was gone. She was completely defenseless. And she hated the feeling.

Hell, she didn't even know where she was. Then a light flashed, blinding her. She squinted against it until her eyes adjusted to the sudden brightness of the fluorescent lights hanging down from the open rafters above her. She was lying on a cold concrete floor in a basement—probably of the club. And a woman stood over her.

Tori still wore the gold dress they had picked out on their shopping trip. She looked beautiful—or she would have—had jealousy and madness not twisted her face into a grotesque mask of hatred.

"Daddy thought you would teach me how to protect myself?" She laughed. "You can't even protect *yourself*."

Candace had no defense for that comment. The woman spoke the truth, so there was no point in arguing with her. There was probably no point in yelling either. If Tori had thought anyone could hear her, she would have gagged her. She had just tied her up instead.

"He has no idea I don't need any protection," Tori said. "I take care of myself."

But a man stood behind her—a heavily muscled man who looked vaguely familiar to Candace. He wasn't one of Chekov's men whom she'd met earlier. But this man had either run her off the road, or taken shots at her and Garek outside her apartment. Or both...

He was no doubt the person who'd carried her down the stairs, too. While Tori was stronger than Candace had initially thought, she wasn't strong enough to have carried her.

The woman bitterly continued, "I also take care of anyone who messes with me."

Yet it was probably this man who had tied her up—after carrying her. The zip ties had been pulled tightly—too tightly for Candace to easily free herself.

"*I* didn't mess with you," she told the crazy woman. She had done nothing to her but momentarily feel sorry for her.

Tori snorted. "You showed up here at the club—distracting Garek."

"You wanted his attention?"

Tori sighed. "A lifetime ago Garek was all I wanted."

She had loved him then. Stacy was lucky Candace hadn't acted like this when Logan had fallen for the female Kozminski instead of her. She'd been bitter, but she hadn't gone all *Fatal Attraction* like this.

"But I loved what Garek had more than who he was," Tori continued.

Candace tensed with confusion. "I don't understand..."

"He had Daddy's respect," she said. "My father adores Garek."

Remembering his bruises and the way Viktor had broken into his apartment, Candace had concerns about how Chekov showed his affection. No wonder Tori was so messed up.

"You're jealous of Garek?"

"I wanted Daddy to see him for the man he is," she said. "Weak…"

Candace laughed now. She had thought the wrong things about Garek most of the time she'd known him, but even she had never considered him weak. "Garek Kozminski?" she asked. "How is he weak?"

Tori pointed to her—with the barrel of the gun she grasped so tightly. Even if Candace could work her zip ties loose, she wasn't certain she could get that gun from the smaller woman without taking a bullet.

"You're his weakness," Tori said with disgust. "The minute you showed up, he lost all focus."

"On you…" This was all about jealousy. But Candace wasn't certain of whom the woman was jealous: her or Garek. Maybe both?

"So you were behind the attempts on my life?" Candace asked.

Tori just shrugged. But the man standing behind her looked at the female Chekov; clearly she was his boss. Not her father…

She had ordered him to go after Candace—like she had probably ordered that first man to follow her from the club. They'd all thought the spoiled Chekov princess had just been texting friends on her phone. They should have realized the woman had no friends. She must have been texting her own team of goons.

"Daddy noticed how easily Garek got distracted," she said and a brief, smug smile crossed her face. "He realized Garek wasn't as great and wonderful as he'd thought."

"Garek saved my life every time," Candace reminded her. And she hoped he would once again. But he was already hurt and completely across town. Would he figure out in time who was really responsible—would he know where to find her? "I think he's pretty great and wonderful."

Tori snorted. And as if she'd read Candace's mind, she said, "He won't save you this time. He won't even be able to save himself."

Candace held in a gasp as fear stabbed her heart. The woman was too smug; she knew something—something Candace wouldn't like to learn. "What's happened to Garek?"

Tori glanced at her watch as if she'd had everything timed. Of course she had been playing them all for weeks—even Special Agent Rus. "By now Daddy has caught Garek breaking into his safe."

Garek had been wearing a wire; that was the plan. He should have had a warning when Chekov returned to his estate. But then he'd been wounded. He wouldn't have been able to move fast enough to escape getting caught.

Tori clicked her tongue against her teeth in a *tsk*ing noise. "All that trouble and he didn't find what he was looking for."

Of course she would have known what Garek was looking for; Tori had put everything in motion when she'd gone to FBI agent Rus. Had that been on purpose, too? Had she known he would enlist Garek to help find the weapon? She may have even suggested it to him.

Tori wiggled the gun she held on Candace. "Because I have it. I had it all along. Garek gave his life for something he was never going to find."

Fear and panic clutched Candace's heart. If Chekov had caught him, would he kill Garek? The man was ruthless; of course he would. But she refused to give in to panic and despair. She had doubted Garek before. She wouldn't doubt him again. She would trust if anyone could survive—Garek could.

"What the hell's going on?" Chekov asked. "You had your brother out front—as a lookout—"

"What did you do to him?" Garek demanded to know. Milek couldn't be dead; he had already lost too much to lose his life, as well.

Chekov laughed. "Always so protective of your younger siblings—that protectiveness is what landed you in prison."

Garek played on it—reminding Chekov of his loyalty. "I landed in prison because I wouldn't give you up."

"You landed in prison because you killed a man," Chekov said. Clearly he believed Garek's mother's twisted testimony. "You did it to protect your siblings. And you didn't turn on me to protect them."

He hadn't done as good a job protecting Milek now. Or Candace…

"I need to know what happened to my brother," he persisted. "I need to know if he needs medical help."

Viktor chuckled. "I doubt it. From what I've seen he's as hardheaded as you are."

So he'd been hit over the head…

Depending on how hard he'd been struck, he could have survived. Garek drew in a breath and held on to hope, like he held on to the gun he'd taken from the vault.

"What the hell are you doing—breaking into my vault?" Viktor asked.

All his life Garek had handled stress with humor, so he strove for levity now. "Once a thief, always a thief…"

"Problem with you, Garek, is you weren't really a thief," Viktor said with great disappointment.

"I'm a Kozminski," Garek reminded him. And by virtue of his very heritage, he'd had no choice.

"Oh, you have the skills, obviously," Viktor said as he gestured at the open vault. "But you never had the heart of a true thief. You never really *wanted* to steal."

Garek couldn't deny that. "I was a disappointment to my father."

"He had to force you to do what he loved," Viktor said. "And after he went to jail, I had to force you to continue what he loved." Chekov gestured at the open vault again. "Is that what this is about? Revenge?"

"Maybe," Garek admitted. It was probably part of the reason why he had agreed to the assignment Rus had offered him—to get back at Viktor for his coercion and threats—for terrorizing him as a kid. The other part was just the man eluding justice for too long.

"You can't shoot me with the gun," Chekov said. "It's not loaded. None of them are." He cocked the one he held, though. "But this one…"

"You're going to shoot me like you shot Alexander Polinsky?" Garek asked.

Viktor tensed then repeated, "Like I shot Alexander?" He laughed but with sadness rather than humor. "Alexander was like a son to me. I would not have hurt him."

Garek could not doubt the sincerity and pain in Viktor's voice. He had obviously cared about the murdered man. Not that he still couldn't have killed him. Rumor had it he'd killed his own brother years ago—in order to get ahead in their *family*.

"Why would you accuse me of such a horrible thing?" Viktor asked, and he was clearly appalled.

Garek shook his head and hastened to clarify, "*I* didn't accuse you of anything."

"Who did?" Viktor demanded to know.

He would not give up Tori, so he just shrugged. "People are always saying things about you. Horrible things."

"But to say I killed a man I loved and respected?" Anger burned in Viktor's dark eyes. "Why would anyone say that?"

Why indeed? Garek could think of several reasons, but the main one was to deflect guilt. His stomach lurched as he briefly considered the implications of the realization. It couldn't be...

"Why would anyone have killed Alexander?" Garek asked.

Viktor shook his head. "I don't know. I figured it was about me—someone was trying to hurt me."

Garek had suspected the same reason for why someone had gone after Candace—to get to him. He'd suspected that person had been Viktor. Now he wondered.

"That's why I hired you—or Payne Protection—to protect Tori," Chekov continued. "I figured someone was after me and would use everyone close to me to get to me."

"So no one had any reason to want to kill Alexander Polinsky?"

"There was no reason," Viktor maintained, "no reason for him to die."

And now Garek had no doubts—not even a niggling one. Viktor Chekov had not killed his right-hand man. Fear clenched his heart as he realized who had. He hadn't wanted to consider it, but it was the only thing—*she* was the only person who made sense.

"Where's Candace?" he asked.

The man stared at him—as if he'd lost his mind. "Candace?"

"The female bodyguard you hired to protect Tori," he reminded him.

"She's protecting Tori," Viktor said—his voice full of condescension and then confusion.

She was protecting Tori. But who was protecting her?

Had she realized yet who the real killer was? Because Garek had just figured it out, and he hoped it wasn't too late to stop Tori Chekov from killing again. From killing the woman he loved...

Chapter 22

Logan pressed a quick kiss to her lips before he hurried out of their home. He wasn't going alone into the danger; he never did. He would meet his brothers. Parker and Cooper would back him up.

Would they be too late to save the others, though?

Stacy shivered.

"Close the door," Milek told her. But he didn't leave with the others. Instead of waiting for her to do it, he pulled it shut himself—with him inside with her. "It's freezing out there."

But it wasn't the cold that had chilled her. It was why he had come to their home—what he had told them.

She had expected him to leave with the others—even though he was hurt. Blood had crusted in his hair, turning the light blond strands dark and rusty colored. She lifted her hand to reach out to him but then she pulled it back—certain he would reject her, he would leave if she tried to get too close. He was like an injured animal—too hurt and mistrustful to let anyone close enough to help him.

"I can have Penny watch the baby," she said, "and I can bring you to the hospital." But she was already certain he wouldn't accept her help. "Or Penny can take you..."

"One of the FBI agents checked me out at Chekov's... once they found me."

Before Milek had shown up, Logan had taken a call from his half brother. From his end of the conversation and the worry in his voice, she'd thought she had lost her immediate family. That both her brothers had died. Then the doorbell had rung, and Logan had opened it to a pale and wounded Milek.

According to what Nicholas Rus had told Logan, some FBI agents had found Milek in the snow quite a distance from his vehicle—as if he'd been crawling toward the gates of the estate—determined to help his older brother. But he'd given up on Garek and had come to her.

And he hadn't left yet.

"Do you think he's dead?" she asked. Not that Stacy expected him to tell her the truth. She had kept the truth from him for years. He didn't owe her any honesty; he didn't owe her anything.

He shook his head and grimaced, the movement no doubt causing him pain. "I'm not as worried about Garek as I am Candace."

"She disappeared?"

He nodded and grimaced again. "Right under the noses of Rus's backup agents." His voice was gruff with disgust and frustration. "They never even saw her leave the party."

"Then she'll be close to the club," Stacy said. "They'll find her." They had to find her.

But Milek said nothing now. He offered no false assurances—because they would be false. When he finally spoke again, it was with brutal honesty. "I think they'll find her too late."

Too late to save her…

She shivered again—with concern and dread and regret. Just that afternoon Garek had come to see her at the jewelry store she owned, and he had bought one of her favorite pieces—something he had long admired. She'd wanted to just give it to him, but he had insisted on buying it. He hadn't confirmed anything, but she had guessed why he'd wanted it.

"I shouldn't have dragged her into this," she said. "I shouldn't have talked to her about Garek." Especially since she had been wrong. "I shouldn't have doubted him…" She had told Garek all that, and he'd acted as though he'd forgiven her—but it had been before tonight.

Before Candace had gone missing…

"I doubted him, too," Milek admitted, and now his grimace was of guilt instead of pain. "I wondered if he'd gone back to that life."

He had, but not for the reasons she had thought. He'd gone back to bring a man to justice. She had apologized to him earlier, but it wasn't enough. It would never be enough if Candace didn't survive—like Milek obviously feared.

Pain squeezed her heart, and she murmured, "He's going to hate me." She glanced at Milek. "Like you hate me…"

She turned away to spare him her tears. But strong arms wrapped around her. Logan was gone; it was Milek, holding her. Offering comfort…

"I don't hate you," he assured her. "I could never hate you. And neither could Garek."

But Stacy hated herself—for interfering in their lives, for costing Milek his happiness and maybe costing Garek his. Candace had to survive. At least one of her brothers needed to be able to spend the rest of his life with the love of his life.

Blood trickled over Candace's skin, trailing down to drip onto the floor behind her. The plastic cut deep into her wrists, but she ignored the pain and continued to work at freeing herself.

It was her only chance to escape. But she couldn't just free herself. She had to distract Tori, so the woman would lower the weapon she'd trained on her—because one twitch of her finger and she would blow a hole through Candace.

She already had a hole in her heart—an aching fear Garek had been hurt. How would Chekov react if he'd caught Garek in his safe?

Would he kill him?

Tori thought so and appeared to relish the horrible thought.

"Did you ever really love him?" Candace asked.

"Alexander?" Tori tilted her head as if considering the question. Then she emitted a lustful sigh. "He was so handsome and sexy. Maybe even more so than Garek."

Candace snorted now.

And Tori laughed. "You really love him." She pursed her lips with mock pity and added, "*Loved* him…"

Pain stabbed Candace's heart, and she gasped. Then she shook her head. "I refuse to believe he's dead." And that was why she fought with the zip ties, and finally the plastic gave a little. She could almost free herself. "Your father has a soft spot for Garek…"

Probably the only soft spot Viktor Chekov had—beyond his daughter.

"He won't kill him," Candace said, but she was assuring herself.

Tori shrugged. "It doesn't matter either way. You're not going to be together—because you will be dead." Her finger moved near the trigger, and she pointed the gun toward Candace's heart.

"Why kill me?" Candace asked. "What do I have to do with anything?"

Tori sighed but it was ragged with frustration. "You're smart. You must know why."

Candace shrugged, which helped her work the zip tie over her palms. A little farther was all she needed to free herself.

"You're jealous of Garek's feelings for me?" she asked. "You want me out of your way?"

Tori laughed. "Oh, please… I want Garek out of my way. I thought using you to distract him would get Daddy to fire him, at least…"

"I don't understand," Candace said. "Why did you go to Special Agent Rus? Why did you claim your father killed a man you killed?"

Tori uttered a patronizing chuckle. "I thought it was obvious. I want my father out of the way."

Candace had seen her love for him. "It's not obvious at all. If you wanted that, you would have tried to kill him instead of me."

"I don't want him dead," she said. "I just want him in prison."

"Are you afraid of him? Has he hurt you?"

"He's been holding me back," Tori said, "assuming because I'm a girl all I can do is play on my phone and shop." She snorted. "I wanted to be his right-hand man. But he chose Alexander over me."

"That's why you killed him." She was almost free.

Tori nodded. "Of course. He was in my way."

"Garek wasn't in your way."

"I didn't think he would be," Tori said. "I thought he'd changed. That he would help me bring Daddy down. But nothing was happening—except him and Daddy getting closer. And my father was still running everything."

Realization dawned. "And you want to…"

Tori smiled. "I will. If Daddy went to prison, I would be his go-between—or so everyone would think. I would be the one visiting him and carrying out his orders…"

"You think he would trust you—after you testified against him?"

"I won't need to testify now," Tori said. "I will only need to plant this weapon on Daddy. It will have killed so many people by then—including you. It will be easy to convict him. He'll never get out of prison."

"Garek won't believe it," Candace said.

Tori smirked. "If he survives Daddy…"

"You said yourself that your father has a soft spot for Garek," she said. "He won't hurt him. And Garek will figure out what you've done—you're responsible for all the killings."

Tori smiled and acknowledged, "If you hadn't distracted him like you have, he probably would have already figured out the truth."

She was right. Candace knew Garek would have—had he not been worried about her. He knew all these people and he would have put together the pieces of Tori Chekov's twisted jigsaw puzzle of deception and greed. But she'd gotten in his way.

"And after you die, he's going to be too distraught to figure out anything." Tori sighed. "And he's going to need me to console him."

He would be upset. And he would blame himself.

She raised the gun. "Don't worry, Candace, I'll take care of him for you."

Outrage coursed through Candace. She didn't want this woman touching Garek, trying to get close to him. She wanted this woman nowhere near him. So she ignored the pain as she forced the zip tie over her palms and down her fingers. But before she could move, shots rang out—reverberating off the walls of the basement.

She tensed, waiting for the pain as bullets tore through her.

Garek's heart hammered frantically inside his chest. The big man, who had been standing beside Tori like a trained ape, dropped his gun as he fell to the floor. But Tori held hers as she stood over Candace's prone body. Ignoring the pain in his leg, he hurried down the steps.

"And this is why my father shouldn't be in charge anymore," Tori murmured. "I can't believe, after catching you in his vault, he would let you live." She made the annoying *tsk*ing sound. "He's gotten too soft. Too soft to lead the *family* any longer."

"All this..." Garek gestured around at the basement, hoping to distract her—to draw her attention and her gun barrel—away from Candace.

He couldn't tell if she had been hit, if she was lying there bleeding. He wouldn't let himself look at her for fear he would bring Tori's focus back to her.

"You've done all this," he continued, "because you want to take over the *family*?"

"It's my birthright," Tori said bitterly. "Not yours. Not Alexander's."

"That's why you killed him?"

"Daddy was grooming him to take over," she said. "Alexander is not family. I am Daddy's only *real* family." Her mother had died during childbirth, so it had always been just her and her father. But Viktor had always called the men who worked for him *family*.

Garek nodded in agreement. "That's true. You are."

She swung her gun barrel toward him now. "You're not family either," she said. "But Daddy always treated you like you were."

"He used me to steal for him," Garek said. "That's not how you treat family."

"He let you work for him," Tori said with bitter resentment.

"He let me go to prison for him," he said. "That's the risk, when you do what we do. I had no choice, Tori—not with the way I was raised. I had to steal. That's all your father knows, too. But he wanted a better life for you. He didn't want you to have to do what he and I have done."

She shook her head, and now there wasn't just greed and resentment in her dark eyes—there was madness. "He didn't think I could handle it. He thinks I'm some weak female." She swung her gun back toward Candace.

He should have shot her when he'd had the chance—when she had been pointing that gun at him. He wouldn't have cared if she'd shot him. He didn't want her shooting Candace. Again?

The woman he loved lay unmoving on the concrete floor. And there was blood—behind her. Had she been shot in the back? How else would Tori have gotten the jump on her, though?

Or had he done it? Had one of the bullets he'd fired at Tori's cohort ricocheted off the concrete walls and struck the woman he loved?

Fear and panic threatened to overwhelm him, but he fought those feelings back. He had to focus.

"He didn't think *she* was a weak female, though," Tori said. "He respected her. He should see her now." She snorted disparagingly. Then she turned back to Garek, peering at him over her shoulder while her gun remained trained on Candace. "You should have seen him earlier—he was all over her on the dance floor."

She wanted him to react—to act like a jealous fool. All he could manage was a gasp, but that wasn't over what she'd said. It was over Candace's sudden movement.

She leaped up from the floor and grabbed for the gun. Her hands locked around the barrel, but Tori's finger was too close to the trigger. She fired.

Again and again. The sound and shots reverberated off the walls.

The agents above had to hear the gunfire. But Garek had convinced them to stay away. He'd promised he could handle Tori.

And he'd thought he could. But he had never known the woman at all. Not like he knew Candace…

She was strong. But not strong enough to fight off

an armed Tori. He jumped into the fray, wrapping his arms around Tori from behind—lifting her off her feet.

The gun clicked as the cartridge emptied. And Tori dropped it to the floor. Her body shook as sobs racked her.

"Are you okay?" he asked Candace—all his concern and fear for her.

She panted for breath but nodded. "I'm fine. I didn't get hit."

He wanted to reach for her, wanted to pull her into his arms and make sure she was really all right.

The same longing was in Candace's brilliant blue eyes. "And you?" she asked. "Chekov didn't hurt you?"

Garek shook his head. "No. He even told me where she had probably taken you."

If Chekov hadn't revealed the club had a basement, Garek doubted they would have found her—at least not in time. After Candace's murder, Tori would have had her goon dump the body somewhere it would have been found without a search warrant having to be obtained. And she would have wanted Candace's body to be found. She would have wanted Garek to suffer. And she would have wanted to implicate her father as the killer—like she'd been framing him all along.

Tori's body stilled as the tears abruptly stopped. "Daddy knows?"

"Yeah," Garek said. "He knows."

"Where is he?" she asked, and her voice cracked with madness.

How had Garek never noticed it? He'd always thought she was spoiled and unhappy. He hadn't realized her problems were so much deeper than that. But he suspected her father had known.

"Isn't he proud of me?" she asked. "Doesn't he know now he was wrong about me—that he's always been wrong about me?"

Garek didn't know what to say—didn't know what she wanted to hear, or if she would hear him at all in her current state. But before he could think of any words, she moved—striking out at him with her elbow and her foot. She followed the maneuver Candace had perfected and apparently taught her. She stomped on his foot and jammed her elbow into his ribs and the back of her head into his chin.

He lost his grip—for just a moment. But before he or Candace could reach for her again, she had dropped onto the ground. She didn't pick up the gun she'd dropped; she picked up the gun her sidekick had dropped.

Garek couldn't remember if the gun was empty or not. Had the man fired all his shots at him when he'd come through the door at the top of the stairs?

Candace shook her head, as if silently answering his unspoken question. They were so connected she must have read his mind. And the fear on her face answered his question.

There were bullets left. They both dove for Tori and the gun just as she began to fire it.

Chapter 23

The hospital waiting room overflowed with people and voices. Paynes. FBI special agents. Kozminskis. It was loud and crowded; it was chaos.

And usually it would have made Nicholas Rus very uncomfortable. He wasn't used to chaos—to family. But he realized now he'd always had one. He'd had a family in the Bureau with the fellow agents who had become good friends. Now he had another family: the Paynes.

He had expected them to be furious with him—for what he'd done, for the lives he'd risked when he'd gotten Garek involved in his investigation of Viktor Chekov. But Penny had hugged him. Stacy Kozminski-Payne had hugged him, too, and murmured, "Thank you."

"For what?" he'd asked.

She hadn't replied. She'd only rejoined her brother Milek, who'd slid his arm around her.

Had Milek told her what Nicholas had had no business revealing? He cursed himself for his admission. But he had come to care about his family—about all of his family, which included the Kozminskis. And Milek's pain over his loss had affected Nicholas the most.

But Milek wasn't the only one who'd experienced loss. The room went suddenly and completely silent. And the crowd parted as a silver-haired man walked through it—heading straight for Nicholas.

He had seen surveillance photos of Viktor Chekov. He had even seen him through a lens himself when he'd personally staked out the man. But Chekov looked different in person. Less ruthless. More haggard.

He had aged in the past few hours.

"Special Agent Rus," the man said. It wasn't a question or even much of a greeting. He was just acknowledging he knew who Nick was. "You're the one in charge."

Again an acknowledgment. Not a question. Was this where he swore vengeance on Rus and his entire family?

Garek had warned him that would happen. Viktor Chekov was vengeful and ruthless. He wouldn't forgive a betrayal—any betrayal.

Nicholas spared a glance to his family. He had only begun to admit what they meant to him. Would he have to leave them now—before he'd even really gotten to know them—to be part of them?

For their safety, he would. He would do what was best for them rather than himself.

He nodded. "Yeah, I'm in charge. The whole operation—the assignment—was *my* idea. Not Garek Kozminski's. I forced him to take part in it."

Viktor laughed, but without humor. "What—did you

threaten his family? That's the only way to force Garek Kozminski to do anything."

"I talked him into it," Nicholas insisted. Maybe he could convince Chekov that Garek had done it to find out what Nick had known about the murder of Milek's ex-girlfriend and son. The gangster might buy that…

But Garek didn't know what he knew. Rus had only admitted vague things to Milek.

"You didn't talk him into saving my daughter's life," Viktor said. "He could have shot her like he shot the man working for her—the men. But he spared her life. And then when she tried to take her own, he stopped her."

The bullet had only grazed Tori's forehead instead of killing her—like she'd wanted. Garek had saved her life.

"I want you to spare her, too," Chekov urged him.

Stunned the man could even ask such a thing—or rather demand—Nicholas shook his head. Was he going to threaten or offer him a bribe here? In a crowded waiting room of witnesses? Maybe the daughter wasn't the only crazy one in the Chekov family.

"She killed a man," Nick said. "She admitted it. She also killed the guy she hired to go after Candace. And she ordered those hits on her."

Maybe Chekov would go after Candace, too. He turned his attention to her as she stepped into the waiting room. Her wrists were bandaged from where she'd torn them up getting untied. The woman was fearless. Viktor wouldn't be able to scare her out of testifying against his daughter.

Garek stepped into the room behind her, his hand on her waist. Maybe it was for his own support since he limped. But Nicholas suspected it was because he couldn't *not* touch the woman he loved.

Chekov tapped his shoulder, drawing Nick's attention back to him. "You can arrest and convict Tori," he agreed. "But she's not the person you really wanted."

Nicholas focused on the older man again. "What are you saying?"

"Hers is not the arrest and conviction that will make your career." He tapped his chest. "I'm the one you want."

Nick shook his head—not in denial, though, just amazement. "Yeah, I want you," he admitted, "but not like this. I won't let you take the fall for someone else's crimes."

"I'm not suggesting that," Chekov said. "Pick a crime—any crime you want me to confess to, and I'll do it."

"What?" His mind reeled with the offer. "I still can't let her off."

Chekov sighed and nodded in reluctant agreement. "Work a deal for her," he suggested. "As tough as she thinks she is, she wouldn't survive prison. It's not the place for her. She belongs in a psychiatric hospital."

"He's right," Candace chimed in.

Nick had seen them enter the room, but he hadn't heard her and Garek make their way through the crowd to join them. Even with a limp, the former thief moved silently. And Candace must have lost her shoes during her ordeal that night because she wore hospital slippers instead of heels.

"You would agree to that?" Nicholas asked the female bodyguard. "She tried to kill you—several times."

Candace sighed. "She's messed up. She needs help."

Garek looked less convinced, clenching his jaw as he stood closely by Candace's side.

Chekov must have recognized Garek's resistance because he beseeched him, "Let her get help."

No one had helped Garek years ago—when he had gone to jail. Nicholas would understand if he refused to help the man who had threatened him and his family.

But Garek sighed. "She needs to stay there," he said. "She's a danger to others and herself. This can't be some short stint in a country club."

"It won't be," Nicholas assured Garek while also warning Chekov. "She's going to serve a long sentence."

"As long as she gets help," Chekov said and nodded his agreement. "Can I see her?" he asked. "Before I go with you to your office? Can I say goodbye to her?"

Nick nodded. There were guards with the woman; she wouldn't escape with her father. But he believed it wasn't what Chekov wanted. He really wanted her to get help—to heal—so much so he would give up his own freedom for her.

"She was wrong," Candace murmured. "Her father really does love her."

Garek heartily slapped Nick's back. "You did the freaking impossible. You got Chekov to serve himself up on a silver platter."

"You did it," Nick said. He couldn't claim any of the credit. "If you hadn't saved her…"

Garek shrugged off his accolades.

"If you hadn't taken this assignment…" Unlike Chekov, Nick hadn't threatened him to do it; he had only asked and the man had readily agreed.

Garek shook his head now, refusing any credit. "It's all you, Rus. You wanted him. You got him. Enjoy your victory." Garek entwined his fingers with Candace and tugged her toward the door. "I'm going to enjoy mine."

"I'm a victory?" Candace asked. But she was smiling, her eyes shining with love for Garek.

"We're alive," Garek said. "That's a victory and a cause for celebration." But he stopped only to hug his family. He didn't stay to celebrate with them. Like a man on a mission, he led Candace through the crowd.

Another hand slapped Nicholas's back. "You did it," Milek said. "You must be thrilled."

But Nicholas felt no great thrill over what was the coup of his career. He felt only envy as he watched Garek and Candace leave the waiting room—hand in hand.

They were going home—to the house Garek had bought in the suburbs right before Nick had enlisted him in his investigation. He'd wondered then why a man everyone had considered a playboy had bought a traditional house like that; now he knew.

He had already fallen in love with Candace.

He had already begun to envision a future with her.

Milek probably couldn't imagine the future anymore. But then he turned to Nick, and the knowledge was in his silver eyes.

While Nicholas hadn't dared to say too much, he had apparently said enough. Milek finally knew the whole truth now.

Happiness warmed Candace. She felt none of the cold outside as they rushed—as fast as they could with Garek's limp—into the house. He must have left the lights on because the Christmas tree twinkled.

Overwhelmed with the beauty of it and her happiness, Candace stopped in front of the tree and sighed. "It's so…"

"What?" Garek asked, and his arms wrapped around her from behind, looping around her waist. He pulled her tightly back against his chest.

"Perfect."

"I didn't know you were so into Christmas," he mused.

Candace laughed. "Neither did I." She had always been such a no-nonsense girl. Not into frilly dresses or decorations or holidays. But she had changed. Love—real love—had changed her. "But now I have reason to celebrate…"

Or did she? She had professed her love, but he hadn't professed his. Had he even heard her, though? She had just whispered the words as she'd left.

She needed to gather her courage and repeat them.

"We don't have reason to celebrate yet," he said.

"We don't?" she asked, and she turned in his arms to face him. Desire ignited, heating her skin—making it tingle. She wanted him so much—loved him so much. "You heard Chekov—it's over. He won't go after us or any of our family."

Garek chuckled. "No, he's too appreciative she's alive. That was some kind of Christmas miracle."

"Yes…" She reached up to link her arms around Garek's neck. "Thanks to you…"

But he slipped away from her, as he dropped to his knees. A grimace of pain twisted his chiseled features.

"Are you okay?" she asked, as concern and alarm and guilt filled her. She had only been thinking about desire earlier—about how much she wanted him. She'd forgotten he'd been hurt.

"I'm fine," he said—despite the grimace. "I'm just looking for something…" He dropped even lower to the floor as he reached beneath the tree.

She knelt down beside him. "What are you looking for?" she asked. "Let me get it for you."

"No," he said. "I have it." And he pulled out a small,

brightly wrapped package. The silver metallic paper glittered under the lights of the tree.

"What is that?" she asked.

He held it out to her. "Open it and find out."

She shook her head. "It's not Christmas yet."

"It will be soon," he said.

She sighed as she realized he was right. They had been so busy—trying to stay alive—time had flown. "I know I went shopping with Tori the other day, but I didn't start my Christmas shopping yet."

He reached out and brushed his fingers across the bodice of her velvet dress. "You got this."

"It was for me—not you."

Desire glowed in his silver eyes. "Oh, no, it's definitely for me…"

She smiled. He was always so charming. She had doubted his charm before, but she had no doubts about him anymore. She had nothing but love.

"Open the present," he urged her.

Her fingers trembled against the bow. She couldn't remember a man ever giving her such a beautifully wrapped gift—and ever showing such anticipation and excitement over her opening it. But she wasn't used to being the receiver; she would rather be the giver—especially with Garek. She felt as if nobody had ever really appreciated him for the wonderful man he was.

"I can wait," she said. "I can wait to open it when you open your present."

She wasn't certain what to get him, though.

As if he'd read her mind, he warned her, "You can't buy me what I want for Christmas."

"I can't?"

"It's nothing you can wrap up and put under the tree either."

"What do you want?" she asked.

"For you to open that damn present," he impatiently replied.

She laughed. But she pulled the red bow loose and lifted off the top of the small box. There was another box inside that box—this one was velvet like her dress. She recognized the logo etched into the velvet. "This is from Stacy's store…"

She'd always thought it so ironic the daughter of a convicted jewel thief designed jewelry and owned her own store. But she had also secretly admired and coveted Stacy's beautiful pieces.

"You shouldn't have," she murmured.

He tensed, and the color drained from his face. "I shouldn't have? Why not?"

"Stacy's designs are beautiful…"

He smacked his own forehead. "But they're Stacy's and the two of you don't have the greatest relationship after…"

Logan. She had never felt about her boss the way she felt about Garek, though. But before she could correct him, he continued, "Of course you wouldn't want something she had designed."

She laughed. "Of course I would. She's brilliant and everything she makes is beautiful. I just meant you shouldn't have gone to the expense or the trouble."

He stared at her now, and his eyes widened in disbelief. "How can you not believe you're worth every expense and all the trouble in the world?"

She shivered at the look in his eyes—at the intensity of that look—and what she saw in the silvery depths.

He hadn't said the words, hadn't returned her feelings when she'd confessed to them, but the love was there. In his eyes. Nobody had ever looked at her like he was looking at her.

"You have gone to a lot of trouble over me," she admitted. "You pursued me for a year, and then you nearly got killed coming to my rescue again and again."

"And you were worth it," he said. "Worth every minute I chased you, worth every hit and bullet I took for you."

She laughed. But he didn't. He didn't even smile. He was actually being serious.

Her fingers shaking, she reached out and pulled the velvet box from the gift box. And she popped open the lid. She'd known she would be impressed by whatever was inside, but she had expected earrings. Or maybe a pendant. Perhaps a bracelet…

She hadn't expected a ring. A brilliant round diamond sparkled from inside a ring of sapphires—all set in a shiny platinum setting. Her breath caught at the beauty and the implication. "This…this is a ring…"

Maybe it wasn't what she thought it was—what she hoped it was.

"It's a ring," Garek said. He took it from the jewelry box and held it out to her. "You told me you loved me."

She swallowed as emotion choked her. But she nodded in acknowledgment of the feelings she'd professed.

"Did you say it because you thought we weren't going to make it?" he asked. "I didn't say it, because I knew we would. And I wanted the first time I told you I loved you to be like this…"

"What is this?" she asked. Confusion and hope overwhelmed her. It could have just been a ring…

But as she'd learned, nothing was ever as simple as it seemed with Garek Kozminski.

"It's a proposal," he replied.

He was already on his knees. But he took her hand and slid the ring onto her finger. Somehow it fit perfectly—as if he'd known her size. Or maybe Stacy had.

"I'm telling you I love you and I'm asking you to marry me. Will you marry me, Candace Baker? Will you be my partner in crime, my protector, my heroine, my soul mate?"

Her breath shuddered out at the shock. She had just noticed the love in his eyes when he looked at her; she hadn't realized he loved her this much.

"Are you sure?" she asked. Because no man had ever professed his love to her, let alone proposed.

Anger flashed in his eyes, darkening the silver.

"I'm not rejecting you," she assured him. "I just don't—"

"You don't know how beautiful you are," he said, and now the anger was in his voice. "You have no idea how amazing you are."

Tears stung her eyes—because she actually believed him. He said it with such sincerity and certainty and irritation. But then the anger and irritation was gone.

His fingers caressed her cheek. "You awe me," he said. "With your beauty and your strength and intelligence." Then his fingertips trailed from her face, down her neck to her breast. "And you have such heart—so much loyalty and devotion and love."

The tears spilled, falling from her eyes to follow the path his fingers had taken down her face and throat.

"You said you loved me—"

"I do love you," she said. "I love you so much. I love your heart—your loyalty and devotion to your family. You are the amazing one. The strong one."

"Then marry me," he said. "Say yes."

She couldn't say anything—as the tears choked her. She could only nod and throw her arms around his neck.

Over the past year Garek had seen Candace in many states: embarrassed, angry, hurt, angry—he'd seen angry a lot. But he had never seen her as emotional as she was now.

"I'm sorry," he said. "I didn't mean to upset you." Maybe he shouldn't have yelled at her, but it frustrated the hell out of him that she thought so little of herself—she was so unaware of her beauty.

She was even beautiful when she cried. But he hated seeing her like this—hated even more that he'd caused her tears.

He clutched her closely, pulling her trembling body into his arms. "I should have known I'd screw this up," he berated himself. "That I'd get it all wrong—because it means too much. You mean too much…"

She pulled back, and her hands cupped his face now. "Your proposal was perfect," she assured him. "You're perfect."

He laughed at her outrageous claim. He was as far from perfect as a man could be. But maybe he shouldn't draw it to her attention.

As if she'd read his mind, she smiled and amended, "You're perfect for me."

"We're perfect for each other." He leaned in and covered her mouth with his. She tasted as sweet and excit-

ing as she always tasted, her tongue darting between his
lips. He groaned but forced himself to pull back.

"So you will?" he asked. "You'll actually marry me?"

She giggled—a sound he had never heard her make.
And she nodded again.

But he caught her chin in his hand and held her gaze.
"I need the words…"

"Yes, I will marry you," she said. "I love you." She
glanced down at her hand. "And I love my ring."

"And I love that dress," he said—even as he tugged
it off her. "I want to make love to my fiancée."

Her breath escaped on a gasp. "You're my fiancé."

"Don't get used to it," he warned her.

She tensed for a moment—until he pushed her onto
the floor and lowered his mouth to her breast. Then she
melted into the floor with a shaky sigh of pleasure.

"Don't get used to being my fiancée," he said. "Because you're going to be my wife as soon as Penny Payne
can plan our wedding and make it happen." Penny didn't
have the connection in the courthouse that she'd once
had—the judge who'd waived the waiting period for
marriage licenses. But knowing her, she had other means
to get him and Candace married quickly.

Candace smiled. Then she reached for him. His
clothes fell as quickly as her dress had. Their naked
bodies entwined so completely he couldn't tell where
one of them ended and the other began. He could feel
her heart beating against his—just as fast and frantically—as he slid inside her.

She was hot and wet and ready for him. Her body
tightened around his, pulling him deeply inside her—
joining them completely, irrevocably. They made love
as one—came as one. And they lay, panting for breath,

beneath the tree, wrapped in each other's arms. He had never been so happy and couldn't imagine ever being happier than he was at this moment.

Epilogue

Candace saw it—finally—as she stared into the mirror of the bride's dressing room. She saw the beauty Garek saw when he looked at her—the way he always looked at her. Her breath caught in surprise and pleasure. Her skin was pale and flawless, her eyes such an enormous and brilliant blue.

"You are stunning," Stacy told her.

The woman stepped up behind her and adjusted her veil. It was just a short little veil coming out of the hat atop her shiny black hair. Her dress was short, too, but with long sleeves and a lot of antique lace. She couldn't believe how quickly Penny, Stacy and Nikki had helped her find the perfect dress. She couldn't believe how quickly they had put together the perfect wedding.

"Thank you," she said.

Stacy shrugged off her gratitude. "I'm just stating a fact."

Candace shook her head. "I'm thanking you for so much more than the compliment. I'm thanking you for being my matron of honor."

"Thank you for asking me," Stacy said, and there was still the hint of surprise in her voice she'd had when Candace had asked her. Their history wasn't pretty, but they'd overcome their differences. And Candace had replaced her resentment of the female Kozminski with appreciation and respect.

"I wouldn't be here if not for you," she said. "You found me—"

"Nikki found you," Stacy said.

Nikki was a bridesmaid—dressed in the same blue velvet gown that Stacy wore. Candace hadn't left her out. But her bond with Stacy was stronger.

"You're the one who convinced me to come home," she said. "To Garek." More than the house he had bought, *he* was home to her. "You knew he had real feelings for me, and you helped me realize it was possible he could actually care about me."

"He adores you," Stacy assured her.

But Candace didn't need the assurance. She knew how much he loved her. And as her father walked her down the aisle to her groom, she saw it—as she always did now—when he looked at her. She barely noticed how pretty the church looked—aglow with Christmas lights and fragrant pine boughs. She saw only her groom, standing tall and straight, in a black tuxedo. He was so handsome, so sexy. And so in love…with her, as she was him.

This was his real Christmas assignment—his Christmas day wedding to the woman he loved more than his life itself. He had been wrong—so wrong—the day he had proposed. He'd thought then it wasn't possible for him to be any happier than he had been at that moment.

But he was happier now. So happy. And so in love. He took Candace from her father. The man wore his military uniform and a smile of reluctant approval. Garek, with his checkered past, probably wasn't the man he would have wanted for a son-in-law. But there was no denying he made Candace happy. And he would spend the rest of their lives making her as happy as she had made him.

Garek held her hands in his. And he stared deeply into the eyes of the woman he loved. The love she felt for him reflected back as they repeated their vows.

He was so happy he felt a twinge of guilt when his brother handed him Candace's ring. It wasn't fair he should be so happy and Milek so miserable. But his brother had been acting differently lately—almost as if he had some hope again. Maybe he would recover from his loss.

"I now pronounce you man and wife," the minister proclaimed.

Garek knew what came next, so he didn't wait until he was given permission. He stole the first kiss from his bride—just like she had stolen his heart. It was hers now and so was he—for the rest of their lives.

* * * * *

MILLS & BOON®

INTRIGUE
Romantic Suspense

A SEDUCTIVE COMBINATION OF DANGER AND DESIRE

MILLS & BOON®

**If you enjoyed this story,
you'll love the the full *Revenge Collection!***

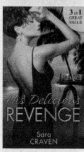

'The perfect Christmas read!' - Julia Williams

Jewellery designer Skylar loves living London, but when a surprise proposal goes wrong, she finds herself fleeing home to remote Puffin Island.

Burned by a terrible divorce, TV historian Alec is dazzled by Sky's beauty and so cynical that he assumes that's a bad thing! Luckily she's on the verge of getting engaged to someone else, so she won't be a constant source of temptation... but this Christmas, can Alec and Sky realise that they are what each other was looking for all along?

Order yours today at
www.millsandboon.co.uk

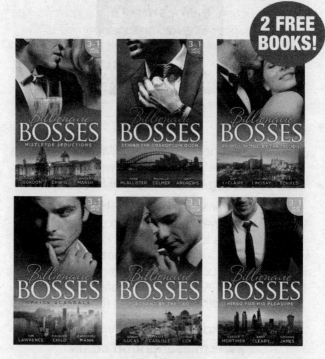